AF430363

THE BEST MAN

WINTER RENSHAW

THE BEST MAN

WINTER RENSHAW

© 2020

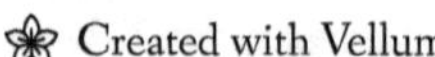 Created with Vellum

COPYRIGHT

COPYRIGHT 2020 WINTER RENSHAW
ALL RIGHTS RESERVED

COVER DESIGN: Louisa Maggio, LM Book Creations
EDITOR: Wendy Chan, The Passionate Proofreader
LINE/DEVELOPMENTAL EDITOR: Kelley Harvey
BETA READER: Ashley Cestra
PHOTOGRAPHER: Sandy Lang
MODEL: Felipe Martins

All rights reserved. No part of this book may be reproduced or transmitted in any form, including electronic or mechanical, without written permission from the publisher, except in the case of brief quotations embodied in critical articles or reviews.

This is a work of fiction. Names, characters, places, and incidents either are the product of the author's imagination or, if an actual place, are used fictitiously and any resemblance to actual persons, living or dead, business establishments, events, or locales is entirely coincidental. The publisher does not have any control and does not assume any responsibility for author or third-party websites or their content.

E-Books are not transferrable. They cannot be sold, given away, or shared. The unauthorized reproduction or distribution of this copyrighted work is a crime punishable by law. No part of this book may be scanned, uploaded to or downloaded from file sharing sites, or distributed in any other way via the Internet or any other means, electronic or print, without the publisher's permission. Criminal copyright infringement, including infringement without monetary gain, is investigated by the FBI and is punishable by up to 5 years in federal prison and a fine of $250,000.

This ebook is licensed for your personal enjoyment only. Thank you for respecting the author's work.

IMPORTANT!

If you did not obtain this book via Amazon or Kindle Unlimited, it has been stolen. Downloading this book without paying for it is *against the law,* and often times those files have been *corrupted with viruses and malware* that can damage your eReader or computer or steal your passwords and banking information. Always obtain my books via Amazon and Amazon only. Thank you for your support and for helping to combat piracy.

ALSO BY WINTER RENSHAW

THE NEVER SERIES

Never Kiss a Stranger

Never is a Promise

Never Say Never

Bitter Rivals

THE ARROGANT SERIES

Arrogant Bastard

Arrogant Master

Arrogant Playboy

THE RIXTON FALLS SERIES

Royal

Bachelor

Filthy

Priceless (an Amato Brothers crossover)

THE AMATO BROTHERS SERIES

Heartless

Reckless

Priceless

THE P.S. SERIES

P.S. I Hate You

P.S. I Miss You

P.S. I Dare You

THE MONTGOMERY BROTHERS DUET

Dark Paradise

Dark Promises

STANDALONES

Single Dad Next Door

Cold Hearted

The Perfect Illusion

Country Nights

Absinthe

The Rebound

Love and Other Lies

The Executive

Pricked

For Lila, Forever

The Marriage Pact

Hate the Game

The Cruelest Stranger

ALL BOOKS AVAILABLE HERE!

Free Content Available here!

I didn't know her name, but I heard her laugh, tasted her lips, felt her warm skin as I held her in my arms. Together we watched our young children playing in the sand, the warm ocean lapping at the shore behind them as the setting sun painted the sky. She was my soulmate and this was our life, our beautiful forever ...

Then I woke up—alone in a hospital room, connected to wires and machines.

There was no wife. No kids. Not a single soul waiting for me. That life I dreamt of—never existed.

The woman I loved, the woman I knew better than I knew myself—wasn't real.

Until she walked into my life six months later …

And it was both the best and worst day of my life because the woman of my dreams—was about to marry my best friend.

AUTHOR'S NOTE: This angsty forbidden romance contains zero cheating and no love triangle. But that's all I'm going to say.;-)

For the dreamers.
And for Mary Brannian.

"Maktub," she said. *"If I am really part of your dream, you'll come back one day."*
—Paolo Coelho, <u>The Alchemist</u>

PREFACE

Ancient Egyptians believed that dreams existed in a place between the living and the world on the other side. Early Romans, Grecians, and Mesopotamians regarded dream interpretation as an art form requiring advanced intellect and divine inspiration. Sigmund Freud is famous for theorizing that dreams are the result of suppressed or unfulfilled desires—particularly ones that are sexual or romantic in nature. Modern science suggests dreams are nothing more than electrical impulses in our brains, pulling random thoughts and images from our memories.

At the end of the day, all we truly know for sure is that dreams are a form of unconscious hallucinations. And while the content may be illusory, the emotions we feel in response to that content can, at times, be all too real.

1

Brie

NUMBERS DON'T LIE.

But men like the one beside me? With iridescent copper eyes, a jawline so sharp it could cut diamonds, and muscle-wrapped shoulders made for digging your fingers into as he pushes himself into the deepest parts of you?

They lie.

They lie all the time.

Especially in Hoboken hook-up bars like this one.

He told me his name, but already I've forgotten. Men like him don't tend to give real names, so there's no point in remembering. He also told me he's from Manhattan, and that once a month he rents a car for a weekend so he can get out of the city, breathe some fresh air, and hear himself think.

Sounds made up.

A story you tell someone to impress them, to make them think you're deep.

Different.

Special.

If I had to guess, he has a wife and a new baby in the 'burbs. Ridgewood or Franklin Lakes. Maybe his sex life isn't what it used to be. Maybe the family life wasn't what he expected. In my mind's eye I've imagined him packing a small suitcase, kissing his family goodbye, loading up in his luxury SUV and hauling ass to a little bar where nobody knows or marital status.

I steal a peek at his left hand.

It's too dim to spot a wedding band indentation.

"How long are you in town?" He leans in when he speaks to me, his voice smooth as velvet and sending a spray of goosebumps along my neck. The faintest hint of after-shave wafts from his warm skin. Faded with a hint of vetiver and mystique, I enjoy it. But I don't tell him that. If I flatter him, he'll think he's got a 'nibble' and he'll try to reel me in.

I don't want to be caught. I don't want to be reeled in.

I want to enjoy my glass of pinot, maybe take a walk around the block, and then head back to my hotel room, paint on a charcoal mud mask, and fall asleep with Seinfeld reruns flickering on my TV screen.

"Not much longer," I tell him, avoiding eye contact for a myriad of reasons, most of all being the fact that he's the most beautiful stranger (physically speaking) to ever have purchased me a drink and every time I allow myself to bask in that, I lose my train of thought. "A couple more days."

"Same." He sips his drink, something amber in a crystal tumbler. The kind of liquor you savor drop by pricey drop, the kind you don't rush to finish. "Where did you say you worked again?"

"Phoenix." I clear my throat. Nothing worse than a man who asks questions but doesn't take the time to listen.

"No, I remember that part," he proves me wrong. "I meant *where*? What company?"

"The Fletcher Firm." I lie for safety reasons.

I don't know this man from Adam—no need to give him Google ammo.

"Kind of young to be an actuary, aren't you?"

His next question catches me off-guard, and I nearly choke on my pinot. Most men—the ones laser focused on securing a piece of ass for the night—rarely remember what I do for a living once they've asked me. And the ones that do, have no idea what an actuary is or the education and tests that go into becoming one.

"I *am* young for an actuary, yes," I say. I turn my attention toward him without thinking twice. Big mistake. His hazel eyes glint, focused on me. My stomach tightens in response. "I fast-tracked." Taking a sip, I add, "I don't recommend it unless you're willing to sacrifice your social life—or any kind of life you may have—for the majority of your twenties."

So much of life passed me by. Semesters blurred into one another. Weekend invites were turned down in favor of studying for the next exam. In the end, I was racing to a finish line for no other reason than it felt like a safe choice in a world filled with so much uncertainty.

Go to college. Get a career. Everything else will fall into place ...

"You love it though, right?" he asks. "It was worth it?"

I nod. "I do love it."

Whether it was worth fast-tracking is another thing. If I could go back and do it differently, if I could slow down and spend more time with my sister before her unexpected passing, I'd do it in a heartbeat.

He covers my hand with his palm for half of a second before waving to the bartender. "Your drink is low."

"No, no. I'm good," I say, shaking my head at the bartender to cancel the order. "I'm going to head out soon."

The man checks his watch, a reflective silver piece with an oversized bezel and a simple, classic face before wrinkling his nose. "It's only nine-thirty ..."

For a second, I imagine his wife gifting him with that timepiece on their first anniversary. Or the day of his first big promotion. Or the day she told him she was pregnant.

Deep down, I know this is a story I'm telling to myself to make myself feel better for not taking a risk. At the end of the day we're always justifying everything, all of the time, in our own individual ways.

I turn away from him and stare at the purple remnants in the bottom of my chalice.

One sip and it's gone.

One sip and I'm out of here.

One sip and I'll never see the man with the gold-flecked irises again.

I must admit, I'm quite flattered by the fact that out of all the lovely and beautiful women in this bar tonight, this dashing Adonis approached *me*.

"I realize I'm in a singles bar on a Friday night," I say, "but I can assure you, you'd have better luck casting your line in another direction."

He half-laughs. "What?"

"You're fishing. You want sex." I blink. "Not judging you. Just saying, you're wasting valuable time and energy on me."

His brows meet. His gaze snaps to my left hand. "You're taken?"

I bite my lip, shake my head. "No."

"Then, what? You aren't into men?"

"I'm into men. I just don't sleep with people I don't know." I sit taller. "I don't do one night stands. Nothing personal."

"Fair enough. Dare I ask why?" He squints, and for a second, I think he might be genuinely interested in my answer because he doesn't take his attention off of me for one moment. I'm also impressed that he isn't shrinking away from the sting of rejection or denying that he was, in fact, only after one thing.

The world needs more people like him—at least, assuming he's every ounce the single, sex-prowling man he claims to be.

"A woman's odds of orgasming during a hook-up with a stranger is a paltry twenty-two percent and the average duration of said encounter is seven minutes. I can do better on my own.

Not to mention, over forty percent of men have had dozens of partners—and a third of those men have had over one hundred."

Once again ... numbers don't lie.

"Why'd you come here then?" he asks.

"Because drinking alone in my hotel room on my birthday would've been a new low for me." This time, I don't lie to this stranger. I have no reason to. Besides, stating anything other than this would be lying to myself.

I take full responsibility for not doing my research on this bar. I also take full responsibility for not walking out the door the instant I set foot in here and immediately overheard a couple of guys talking about how this was the "hottest hook up bar on Washington street."

This place is walking distance from my hotel—and by walking distance, I mean it's practically connected. Their walls are sandwiched together on a busy strip of downtown street, the New York City skyline in the distance and the faint stench of the Hudson River infused into every breath.

I stay in this neighborhood every time I travel here for work.

It's familiar. I know what to expect.

I toss back the final few milliliters of my pinot and place the goblet on my cardboard coaster before sliding it away.

"Happy birthday," he says.

I meet his gaze. My breath catches in my chest with the gusto of a silly school girl with a two-second crush. Heat blankets my body.

If I were an adventurous woman, his mouth would be on mine by now. My fingers would be deep in his sandy hair. We'd be going at it in the bathroom, his back against the door to keep unsuspecting patrons from barging in. Or maybe they would barge in, but we'd be going at it so hard we wouldn't notice or care. Maybe when it's over, we'd sprint to my hotel room for round two followed by breakfast in bed and round three in the morning. We'd go our own ways, sore and satisfied, and I'd file the entire encounter away in my memory.

But I'm not that girl.

And I'll never be.

I rise from the bar stool and collect my things. "Thank you for the drink. And for your honesty. It's refreshing."

He chews the inside of his lower lip, studying me. "So you're just going to go back to your hotel room now? Spend the rest of your birthday alone?"

I offer a surrendering shrug and lift my brows. "Yep."

"Where'd you get those numbers? Those statistics?" he asks.

"On one night stands?"

He nods.

"I don't know … some article I read a few years back. Why?"

"Because they're bullshit." His eyes glint. "I'm not in the forty-percent, I can tell you that. And I can promise you, I last a hell of a lot longer than seven minutes. And there's nothing I love more than making a woman come—whether it's on my cock, my fingers, or my tongue."

My throat constricts around the words attempting to come out, and I almost choke on them. Heat blankets my skin before settling between my thighs, and I'd love nothing more than an icy burst of February air right about now.

His words are a sharp and unexpected contrast against his reserved, gentlemanly exterior.

"It's too bad." He bites his lip, looks me up and down, and leans in. "Was really looking forward to tasting that heart-shaped mouth of yours tonight. Amongst other things …"

For a few endless seconds, I consider taking him back to my room. I contemplate throwing caution to the wind like confetti. I deliberate whether or not I would hate myself for it in the morning.

Lastly, I calculate the risk factors.

I cinch my hand around my purse strap and pull in a deep breath. "Good luck with … tonight. And thank you again for the wine."

I don't wait for him to respond, and as soon as my heels hit cement sidewalk outside, I release the breath I'd been harboring.

I'm several yards closer to my hotel's entrance when a man behind me yells, "Hey!"

Dozens of people litter the sidewalk. It could be anyone calling after anyone.

"Hey!" The voice is closer now, along with the soft trump of dress shoes scuffing concrete.

I steal a look from my periphery, and come to a complete stop when I realize it's the guy from the bar, and he's chasing after *me*. But before I have a chance to react or concoct some worst-case-scenario situation in my mind—he hands me my phone.

"You forgot this," he says. Our fingers brush in the exchange. Our moonlit gazes hold for what feels like forever.

Clearing my throat, I force out a quick, "Thank you."

He nods, and we both remain planted where we are, as if I'm waiting for him to speak or he's waiting for me to have a change or heart.

"I'm sorry ..." I point to my hotel—a rookie move given the fact that he's still just a nameless stranger looking to get a piece. "I'm going to head in ... alone."

"I know. You made it abundantly clear that you don't sleep with strangers." He laughs through his perfect, Greek God nose. "Next time we meet, we won't be strangers."

I smile, amused.

And then I head inside, opting not to share with him the statistical odds of the two of us ever running into one another again.

2

Cainan

ONE MONTH LATER ...

BEEP ... beep ... beep ... beep ...

I wake to a steady sound, slamming into an unfamiliar shell of a body, which as it turns out is mine. A dreamlike haze envelopes me, and when my surroundings come into focus, I'm met with white walls, white blankets, white machines connected to white wires leading to a strip of white tape on my wrist holding an IV in place.

I'm in a hospital.

I try to remember how I got here, but it's like trying to recall someone else's dream—an impossible task. And it only makes the throbbing inside my head intensify.

"My wife ..." My words are more air than sound, and it's painful to speak with a bone-dry mouth and burning throat.

"Mr. James?" A woman with hair the color of driven

snow leans over me. So much fucking white. "Don't move. Please."

She's a calm kind of rushed, hurried but not frenetic as she makes her way around the room, pressing buttons, paging for assistance and adjusting machine settings.

The room fades in and out, murky gray to pitch black, and then crystal clear before disappearing completely. The next time I open my eyes, I'm fenced by three more women and one white-coat-wearing man, all of them gazing down on me with squinted, skeptical expressions, as if they're witnessing a verifiable miracle in the making.

I'm certain *this* is nothing more than a bad dream—until my head pulsates with an iron-clad throb once again, accented by a searing poker-hot pain too real to be a delusion.

"Mr. James, I'm Dr. Shapiro. Four weeks ago, you were involved in a car accident." The doctor at the foot of the bed studies me. "You're at Hoboken University Medical Center, and you're in excellent hands."

They *all* study me.

I try to sit up, only for a nurse to place her hand on my shoulder. "Take it easy, Mr. James."

Another nurse hands me water. I take a sip. The clear, cold liquid that glides down my throat both soothes and stings. I swallow the razor-blade sensation and try to sit up again, but my arms shake in protest, muscles threatening to give out.

"Where's my wife?" Each word is excruciating, physically and otherwise.

She should be here.

Why isn't she here?

"Your *wife*?" The nurse with the water cup repeats my question as she exchanges glances with the dark-haired nurse on the opposite side of my bed. "Mr. James ... you don't have a wife."

I try to respond, which only causes me to cough. I'm handed the water once more, and when I get the coughing under control, I ask for my wife once more.

"Has anyone called her?" I hand the cup back. If I've been out of it for weeks, I imagine she's beside herself. And our kids. I can't begin to imagine what they've been going through. "Does she know I'm awake? Have my children seen me like this?"

"Sir ..." The nurse with the dark hair frowns.

"My *wife*," I say, harder this time.

"Mr. James." Dr. Shapiro comes closer, and a nurse steps out of the way. "You suffered extensive injuries in your accident ..."

The man rambles on, but I only catch fragments of what he's saying. Shattered pelvis. Spleen removal. Internal bleeding. Brain swelling. Medically-induced coma.

"It's not uncommon to be confused or disoriented upon awaking," he says.

But she was *just* here ...

She was *just* with me ...

Only we weren't in this room, we were at the beach—the little strip of sand beyond our summer home. She was in my arms as we lay warm under a hot sun, watching our children run from the rolling waves that rolled over the coastline, leaving tiny footprints up and down the shore.

A boy and a girl.

My wife smelled of sunscreen, and she wore an oversized straw hat with a black ribbon and thick-framed cat-eye sunglasses with red rims that matched her red sarong. I can picture it clearer than anything in this damn room.

I can hear her laugh, bubbly and contagious.

If I close my eyes, I can see her heart-shaped smile—the one that takes up half her face and can turn the worst of days completely upside down.

"We're going to let you rest, Mr. James, and then we'll order a few tests." The doctor digs in a deep pocket of his jacket, and then he sneaks a glance at his phone. "I'll be here for the next eight hours, if you have any additional questions. The nurses will ensure you're comfortable in the meantime. We'll discuss your treatment plan as soon as you're feeling up to it."

He tells the nurse with the dark hair to order a CT scan, mumbles something else I can't discern, and then he's gone. A moment later, the room clears save for myself and the third nurse—the one who's done nothing but stare at me with despondent eyes this entire time.

"There must be a mistake. Someone needs to call my wife *immediately*." I try to sit up, but an electric intensity unlike anything I've ever experienced shoots up my arm and settles along my back and shoulders.

The thought of her not knowing where I am sends a squeeze to my chest. What if she thinks I left her? What if she thinks I disappeared? What if she has no idea what happened? And what was I doing in Hoboken when our life is in Manhattan?

"What's her name?" Her question comes soft and low, almost like she's trying to ensure no one hears her. "Your wife?"

I open my mouth to speak ... only nothing comes out.

I can picture her as vivid as still blue waters on a windless day—but it's the strangest thing because her name escapes me.

Nothing but blank after infuriating blank.

"I ... I can't remember." I lean back, staring into the reflective void of a black TV screen on the opposite wall.

The nurse's gaze grows sadder, if that's possible. "It's okay. You've been through quite an ordeal."

She doesn't believe me.

"Would you like me to call your sister?" she asks.

My sister ... *Claire*.

If I can remember my sister's name, why can't I remember my own wife's?

"Yes," I say. "Call Claire. *Immediately*."

She'll be able to sort this out, I'm sure of it.

"Would you like me to adjust your bed?" The nurse straightens the covers over my legs. "I'm Miranda, by the way. I've been assigned to you since you arrived. I can tell you just about anything you need to know."

"Just ... call my sister."

"Of course, Mr. James. Can I grab you anything while I make that call?"

I lift my hand—the one without the IV—to my forehead. "Head's pounding like a goddamned jackhammer. Got anything for that?"

"Absolutely. Be right back ..."

Miranda hurries out the door, and I'm alone.

If I close my eyes, the room spins, but I can picture my wife with impeccable lucidity—the square line of her jaw, her heart-shaped lips that flip up in the corners, the candy-apple green of her eyes.

My heart aches, though it isn't a physical pain, it's deeper.

More profound.

Like the drowning of a human soul.

I remind myself that the doctor said it's normal to be

disoriented, and I promise myself everything will come back to me once I get my bearings.

The clock on the wall reads eight minutes past seven. The sky beyond the windows is half-lit. I haven't the slightest clue if it's AM or PM. I couldn't tell you what day it is or what month it is for that matter.

"Mr. James, your sister is on her way," the nurse says when she returns.

She hands me a white paper cup with two white pills.

So much fucking white.

If I never see white again after this, I'll die a happy man.

***

"OH MY GOD ..." Claire stands in the doorway of my hospital room, her hands forming a peak over her nose and mouth. From here, she's nothing more than a mess of dark waves and shiny, tear-brimmed eyes.

She looks like shit, but I'm in no place to judge. Nor would I tell her that. She'd kick my ass, hospital bed or not. Claire may be pixie-sized, but she's scrappy.

Her neon green sneakers graze against the tile floor with muted shuffles as she hurries to my side, and she wastes no time sliding her cold hand into mine. Her hands are always cold, but in this moment, they're icy—a staunch reminder that I'm far from the warmth of the beach and the place I existed mere moments earlier.

"Of course you'd wake up the *one* time I stepped out." She forces a smile, but she looks at me the way a person looks at a ghost—uncertain if what they're seeing is real.

"How long have I been here?"

Her brows meet as she shrugs out of her jacket and

drops her bag on the floor. "Thirty-three days. Thirty-three terrifying days ..."

"What the fuck happened?"

She retrieves a guest chair and pulls it next to me, only in true Claire fashion, she opts to perch on the side of the bed instead.

"You were on one of your weird little weekend rental car drives where you go God knows where ... and we think you were maybe driving back to the Enterprise in Newark on a Sunday night." She gathers a long, slow breath. "Someone crossed the median on the 495 and hit you head-on—a drunk driver."

"Jesus."

"They didn't live ... in case you're wondering." Her voice is pillow soft. "Luke is working on getting a settlement from their insurance company for you, but these things take time."

We wallow in silence, and I let the gravity of the situation take hold. The settlement is the least of my worries at this point.

"It's a miracle you survived after all of your injuries." Her lower lip trembles, and she picks at a hangnail. "You lost a lot of blood ... your brain was so swollen... they had to put you into a coma ... I called Mom and Dad ... but I haven't heard back ..."

I place my hand over hers, pain shooting up my shoulder.

Her dark eyes are marred with sadness and relief, but she forces a tight half-smile.

"Have you talked to my wife yet?" I ask.

Claire's smile fades, and her expression morphs into the same one plastered on the faces of the nurses earlier.

"Don't look at me like that." I sniff. "Is she okay? What ... was she with me in the car when that happened?"

My stomach sinks as her eyes search mine.

My God.

That's it.

She was with me and she didn't survive ...

"Cainan, *you don't have a wife.*" Her words are careful and deliberate, and her head tilts and her gaze narrows as she surveys me.

"Of course I do." My hands ball into fists, though the grip is weak, pathetic.

"You're confused." She lifts her hand to my forehead, brushing away a strand of hair like a mother comforting her child.

I push her away.

She rises and takes a step back. "You had a head injury ..."

"I *saw* her, Claire. I was just *with* her." My jaw is locked, and I speak through clenched teeth. The more I recall being with her, the more it begins to slip away like an elusive dream that fades with each waking minute.

"You saw her *where?*"

"At our summer home in Calypso Harbor."

My sister stifles a laugh. "Cain, it's March. Your accident was in February. And you don't have a *summer home in Calypso Harbor*—you make fun of people with *summer homes*. Like all those assholes at your firm. You always say you're never going to be like them. Plus, where even *is* Calypso Harbor? I've never heard of it ... have you? Whatever you're remembering ... was probably a dream."

No.

It was too tangible, too sensory-rich to be a dream. As real as this moment, here, in the hospital, as real as the fire-poker pain searing down my back and the salty droplets leaving mascara-colored tracks down my sister's red cheeks.

"What about my kids? The boy and the girl?" I'll be damned—I can't remember their names either.

"You don't have a wife and you *definitely* don't have kids, at least none that *I* know about ..." She perches on the side of my bed once more. "You once told me ... and I quote ... *I'd rather stick my manhood in a vise grip than lock myself down with a wife and kids*. Granted, you were drunk when you said that, but you said it. And hell, Cain, you're a freaking divorce attorney. You make money on the fact that more often than not, marriages are a joke. Mine excluded, of course."

She winks despite her serious tone.

"Mr. James?" Nurse Miranda clears her throat in the doorway. "Sorry to interrupt, but I need to take you down to imaging. Claire, you can wait here. It shouldn't be too long."

"Yeah. Let's check out that head of his." Claire squeezes my hand before I'm wheeled away. "Apparently my brother ran off and got married while he was out of it ..."

My sister would *never* mislead me—and yet a part of me refuses to believe her.

I lie on my back as the muted fluorescent hall lights pass above me, one after another, alternating with stark white ceiling tiles.

More fucking white.

The instant I close my eyes, *her* face is the first thing I see—and in full detail, from the starry, Northern-Lights glow of her green eyes to the single freckle on the side of her nose.

Fullness invades my chest and warmth courses through my veins when I imagine her smile.

Maybe I'm dreaming now. Maybe, if I close my eyes one

more time, I'll wake up in our bed, her soft skin hot against mine as she kicks off the covers and laughs in her sleep.

If none of that was real, how do I know she gets teary during happy movies? How do I know she sponsors orphans in Third World countries and donates to no-kill shelters? How do I know her favorite author is Toni Morrison, with Stephen King coming in as an unexpected close second? Her favorite vacation spot is this hole-in-the-wall place we found in Greece on our honeymoon. She glows when she's pregnant. Pure radiance. And she's a phenomenal singer, even though she'll insist she isn't. Her thick, chocolate-brown hair gets frizzy in the summer and flat in the winter, but she'd be just as gorgeous if she sheared the whole thing off. She chipped her front tooth when she was twelve, though it's hardly noticeable unless she points it out. She loves Christmas more than a person should. Loves those disgusting hot dogs from the carts on the street, too. She's seen *Chicago* on Broadway more than anyone else I know. But more than anything, I know that I'm her whole world. The kids too. We only work when we're all together. And right now, I'd do anything to get back to them.

And I will.

I'll do *anything*.

"All right, Mr. James." The nurse brings my bed to a halt outside a set of double doors. "We're here."

This is all a dream.

No—a nightmare.

It has to be.

3

"I HOPE you weren't waiting long. There was a stalled semi on 15." His name is Grant Forsythe, and I met him in a hospital waiting room in Hoboken a month ago. He noticed my ASU sweatshirt and after a couple of minutes of small talk, we discovered we both live in the Roosevelt Row section of Phoenix, never miss the opening Cardinals game, belong to hiking clubs, and enjoy many of the same dive bars and local musicians.

He's also the best friend of the man whose life I helped save.

As an actuary and hobbyist statistician, I should be able to calculate the odds of such a chance encounter, but I'm trying not to overthink this. While I've never been the girl with the adventurous spirit and a go-anywhere-anytime attitude, something about witnessing a man cling onto his life last month has sparked something in me.

Life is short.

And it can be gone in the blink of an eye—zero warning.

I was on my way to catch a late flight out of Newark when I witnessed the accident happen in real-time—a red Ford truck crossing the interstate median, only to barrel into a black sedan head-on. The truck skidded into the ditch and proceeded to burst into flames, but the sedan came to a rolling stop upside down beneath an overpass. The screech of tires, the burn of rubber, the metallic crunch that followed—I'll never forget them as long as I live.

It all happened so fast. Blink-and-you-might-miss-it fast. Did-that-actually-just-happen fast.

But I slammed on the brakes of my rented Prius and pulled to the side, dialing 9-1-1 as I checked on the driver—a man, bloody and incoherent, fading in and out of consciousness.

I stayed with him until help arrived.

I held his blood-covered hand.

I begged him to hang on just a little bit longer ...

And when I saw him begin to lose consciousness, begin to let go, I squeezed his hand tighter and rambled on about anything and everything—myself mostly. A ridiculous little one-sided introduction. But I wanted him to focus on my voice.

To cling to the present.

To not succumb.

After all of that, it seemed wrong to head on to the airport, to carry on with my life like nothing happened, so I followed the ambulance to the hospital, and I waited in the waiting room—the scene from the accident replaying in my head over and over and over like a traumatic movie my head refused to turn off.

I couldn't visit the man, of course, since I wasn't family.

But I stayed at the hospital, waiting until the nurses assured me that his family was there.

I didn't want him to be alone.

And if he died, I didn't want him to die alone either ... like my twin sister, Kari, five years ago. If only someone had been there when she rolled her Jeep down a steep embankment at one o'clock in the morning, maybe she'd still be here.

To this day, we don't know if she was distracted or if she'd fallen asleep at the wheel. We also don't know what would've happened had help arrived sooner. The authorities said she'd been gone at least four hours before the sun came up and a passing driver noticed the garish red of her car contrasting against the muted tans of the desert landscape.

I've been thinking a lot these last few weeks, about chance and probability, about the likelihood of me being on that stretch of New Jersey interstate at that exact moment, of me camping out in the waiting room and running into an attractive stranger who happened to be visiting from my hometown—a stranger who just so happened to be the best friend of the victim.

"Not long at all." I lift my martini glass and give him a gracious smile. I don't tell him that if it were any other night, I'd be putting in a few more hours at the office. I find that sometimes men get put off by a driven woman. If he likes me enough to stick around after the first date, he'll figure it out on his own anyway. "So sorry it's taken this long for us to get together. My travel schedule has been crazy."

"You fly a lot for work?" He flags down a server and orders a beer.

"At least once a month, lately it's been more often than that. They've been sending me to our HQ in Hoboken and sometimes into one of our satellites in Manhattan, which I don't mind."

"Grew up in Jersey City," Grant says. "Not far from there."

He's handsome.

More handsome than I remember.

Broad-shouldered. Tall. Dark eyes. Darker hair. Deep-set eyes. Even deeper dimples.

A flash of a smile that plays on his lips when our eyes catch.

I'm no expert in menswear, but I'm willing to wager that his suit cost a pretty penny.

Also, I saw him pull up to the valet stand in a freshly-washed silver Maserati.

Not that any of those things matter.

They don't.

I do just fine on my own, and material things have never impressed me.

But if a girl's going to be approached by a stranger and asked on a date, it isn't the *worst* thing in the world if he's dashing, confident, and clearly unafraid to work his ass off for the things he wants.

The last guy I dated was respectably average in all areas, and I was beginning to think about introducing him to my family ... but eight dates in, he dropped a bombshell that sent me packing. Not only was he in the middle of a messy divorce, he was living with his mother and paying for our dates with funds from his weekly unemployment checks—which were about to run out (hence the confession).

Crazy enough, he was a step above the guy who came before him—a man who claimed he was a doctor when he was actually a "holistic animal chiropractor" and got bent out of shape when I would refer to him as "Liam" and not as "Dr. Jeppesen" in conversation.

I'd resigned myself to a much-needed dating sabbatical in the months leading up to my chance encounter with Grant.

"What brought you all the way out here?" I ask. Seems like anymore, Phoenix contains more transplants than locals, and everyone has a story. Most of them are along the lines of wanting to trade gray midwestern winters for sunshine and palm trees or 'just wanting a change,' but every once in a while, someone throws a curveball of a story my way.

"A job."

I don't love the vagueness, but I give him a chance to elaborate before lobbing questions at him like darts. I do that to people. I fact-gather. I can't help it. I've always been curious, always wanted to have all the information possible before I make my assessment.

He continues, "I graduated from Montclair State with a degree in Finance. My uncle knew a guy who wanted to hire someone fresh out of college, someone he could shape into the right fit for his company. Jumped at the chance and haven't looked back since. Best decision of my life. Bar none."

"You don't miss the hustle and bustle of the East Coast? Or the seasons?"

Grant shakes his head and makes a face.

"Think you'll ever move back?" I stir my drink with a skinny metal straw.

"Not a chance." His beer arrives and he takes a sip, eyes locked on me. "The views out here are ... *breathtaking*."

I don't think his comment was a double entendre directed at me, but for some insane reason, my cheeks flush with heat and my heartbeat reverberates in my ear. Maybe it's the way he's looking at me—like he's two seconds from devouring me. Like I'm the only woman he sees in this room full of distracting, prattling strangers.

It's not something I'm used to.

I tend to intimidate men, I think. Or I attract the kind of men who are easily intimidated, men who expect me to make the first move or throw myself at them like a sex-starved damsel in distress.

Something tells me Grant can hold his own in the sexual prowess department. But I'm not a sleep-with-a-guy-on-the-first-date kind of girl, so my assumption will remain unproven.

For now.

"I never had a chance to ask you about your friend," I say. "The one who had the accident ... is he okay?"

"Funny you should ask," Grant says. "His sister called me earlier today. They brought him out of the coma."

I lift a brow. "He was in a coma?"

"Medically induced. They were trying to get the swelling down on his brain or something like that. I didn't ask for details. Medical stuff makes me ... yeah." He offers a humble chuckle and sips his beer before peering around the crowded restaurant. "Anyway, Claire said he was talking, asking questions, getting his bearings. He was a little confused, but she said his prognosis so far is good."

I clasp a hand over my chest and exhale. "Oh, that's amazing. I'm so relieved to hear that."

"Yeah, same."

"My sister was in an accident several years ago ..." I say. "Unfortunately she didn't make it, but I'm happy for your friend."

Summarizing Kari's life in a single sentence hurts. Physically hurts. But I plaster over it with a winced smile.

"Jesus, Brie. I'm so sorry about your sister. I had no idea." He reaches across the table, places his hand on top of mine, but not for an awkward or uncomfortable length of time. "That must've been horrible."

"We were twins," I say. I don't get to talk about her that often, so I relish the opportunity. "Identical. Crazy close even though we were night and day. She was the wild one. I was ... not."

He offers a bittersweet smile as his dark eyes hold mine with full attention.

I ramble on about Kari longer than I should, telling him silly stories and painting her personality in vivid detail, from her neurotic obsession with peel-able nail polish to her affinity for pinpointing which indie rock bands were going to make it big before anyone else. Not once does his expression glaze with boredom. Not once does he interrupt or change the subject. He gives me his full, undivided attention.

"Are we ready to place our orders?" Our server interrupts our moment.

"Oh ... I think we're just doing drinks," I tell her—because that was the plan. We were going to meet up for drinks and conversation, nothing more, nothing less.

Grant's dark eyes soften as he peers across the table in my direction. "You hungry? I'm starving."

I try to tamp my excitement. "I mean ... a girl's got to eat, right?"

His bright grin fills the dim, candlelit space that environs us.

"Give us another minute to look at the menu, please," he tells her. "And in the meantime, we'll take another round." The server dashes off, disappearing behind the bar. Grant rests his elbows on the table and leans closer. "You were saying?"

He doesn't take his eyes off me. Not for a second.

My stomach somersaults.

Who *is* this guy?

When our second round arrives, he lifts his glass to mine. I don't know what he's drinking to, but for the first time in my life, I'm drinking to chance, to strange coincidences, and to the future—whatever it may bring.

4

Cainan

"IF YOU DON'T MIND, I'm going to take off early. My roommate's in a play tonight with Daniel Radcliffe, and we have tickets ... am hoping to get there early." My assistant, Paloma, lingers in my doorway, one rail-thin hand on her narrow hip. "Unless you need me to do anything else?"

I cover the Post-It note—the one I'd been scrawling on all afternoon, over and over, until the paper was more black ink than yellow.

Elle

Four imperfect loops: small, tall, tall, small—an exact rendering of the wrist tattoo from the girl in my dream—the dream I haven't dreamt since waking in the hospital six months ago, the dream that continues to haunt me every day. Some days it's murky and water-colored. Other days its crystal-fucking-clear. But it's always, always there.

"You're free to go, Paloma." I say. "Thank you."

Today was my first day back at the office. Someone gave me flowers—fucking flowers. Roses, no less. Don't roses mean "I love you" or "I'm sorry" or something? And someone else brought champagne cake from some French bakery and placed it in the boardroom. My partners, Trey and Graeme, welcomed me back with a short-but-sweet speech, and then dismissed the rest of the team, the paralegals and assistants anxious to get back to their workstations and hamster-wheel jobs.

It's ironic—I almost died. And yet, since the moment I was condemned back into my body, I've never felt more ... *dead*.

All the color, all the meaning, all the *joie de vivre* has been sucked out of my life.

For the past six months, I've been homesick for a person in a place I'm not even sure exists, at least not in the here and now.

On top of all of that, I'm dealing with short-term memory loss—mostly involving the months leading up to my accident. It's as if everything that happened during that time was wiped clean. Something like that can really fuck with you, if you let it.

My physiotherapist tried to refer me to a shrink, claiming I seemed despondent, borderline depressed—common symptoms after traumatic events, he assured me. But I'm not depressed. Confused, perhaps. Frustrated beyond all belief. But not blue.

My personal trainer gave me a bottle of 'mood-enhancing vitamins.' I chucked them in the trash the moment I got home.

When I tried bringing up that surreal experience to my doctor, he offered a polite chuckle, telling me the drugs they use to induce medical comas can produce "vivid and/or disturbing dreams."

But what happened was so much more than a dream, more than a series of exchanged words and crystal-clear visions.

I *know* this woman.

I know everything about her … everything but her name.

It's like the man I was before her no longer exists.

All I am, all I'll ever be … is hers.

I toss the sticky square in the trash beneath my desk, then I check my watch. I'm supposed to meet Claire and her husband for drinks tonight. She, too, felt it fitting to celebrate the completion of my recovery and my subsequent return to work.

I shut down my computer, lock my desk, and shrug into my suit jacket before heading out.

The office is quiet, half of it unlit. Most of the staff has gone home for the day ... home to their husbands and wives, home to their children, home to their lives.

I used to wear my workaholism like a badge of honor. My unrivaled work ethic was a thing to be feared, a thing to be treasured, a thing that filled my life with the only meaning it ever needed.

But six months of intense physiotherapy and friends who look at you like you're a shell of the man you once were will force humility in your veins faster than you have time to say sixty-hour-work-week.

And casual sex? It's a thing of the past. And not for lack of trying.

I've had my fair share of hook ups the last few months, the women as gorgeous as they were sexy, intelligent as they were skilled between the sheets—but it doesn't feel the way it did before.

I found myself going through the motions.

The gratification? The nirvana of a no-strings orgasm? Gone. And the instant I'd cum, I'd hate myself for it. I'd feel as if I betrayed the only woman I loved—even if she wasn't fucking real.

I hit the sidewalk outside, the early afternoon sun setting and the air turning unapologetically brisk with each step. Up ahead, a woman hails a cab. When she turns to climb in, her dark hair curtains the side of her face, but I manage to catch a glimpse of her sharp jawline and heart-shaped mouth.

My pulse hammers as the cab door shuts and the car takes off, merging into rush hour traffic and a cacophony of honking horns, idling motors, and bus fumes.

She glances out the window as they pass—but it isn't her.

It never is.

5

IT HAPPENS SO FAST—GRANT on one knee, a propped ring box in his hand with a diamond so large it throws sparkles on the wall beside us.

Six months ago, we met in a hospital waiting room.

Five months ago, we had our first date.

Five seconds ago he asked me to *spend the rest of my life* with him.

Now he's wearing the self-assured smile of a man who knows I'm going to say yes.

I mean ... how could I not? Literally. How could I not say yes in front of all these watchful people with happy tears streaming down their grinning faces?

My entire family is here—as well as a restaurant filled with dozens of patrons, their watchful gazes careened in our direction as our moment plays out for their entertainment.

My mother stands behind Grant, dabbing happy tears with her cloth napkin. My sisters circle us, all of them waiting with bated breaths. And my father—my father who doesn't like *anyone*—is readying his phone's camera and grinning as if the moment is one for his personal books.

None of them seem to care that our first date was a mere one-hundred-fifty days ago. Granted, we've been inseparable ever since, full-speed ahead. And everyone is loving this "newfound adventurous" side of me. I work less. I laugh more. I actually travel for *fun* sometimes—not just for work. Grant and I spend our weekends hiking, catching our favorite bands when on tour, checking out the newest restaurants and pubs, lazily ambling through farmers' markets and art venues, hands intertwined like that annoyingly-crazy-about-each-other couple ... but not once have we discussed marriage.

Marriage ...

Forty-five percent of first marriages in the United States end in divorce. The average age of divorce is thirty—three years from now. There have also been studies correlating the size and cost of an engagement ring to marriage survival rates, suggesting the bigger the ring, the bigger the likelihood of the marriage ending in divorce.

Should that last statistic hold true for us, we don't stand a chance.

"*Brie...*" My mother clears her throat.

Grant's proud smile falters. His eyes shine a little less bright.

"I'm sorry." I force myself into the present. "You caught me off-guard. I'm just ... wow."

We do family dinners all the time. Once a week at least. I had no reason to believe this was anything other than another run-of-the-mill reservation at one of my mother's favorite Scottsdale eateries.

"Say *yes*!" My sister, Carly, whisper-shouts in the background.

Another sister echoes her sentiments.

I nod before I speak. "Yes..."

But the word I've uttered hundreds of thousands of times in my lifetime suddenly feels sharp and foreign.

And something deep inside me regrets the agreement the instant it leaves my lips.

6

Cainan

"HAPPY FIRST DAY BACK AT WORK!" Claire throws her arms around me when I get to the table Friday night. An IPA in a frosty pilsner glass waits for me, and my brother-in-law, Luke, glides it in my direction.

I remove my jacket and hook it over the back of my chair as Claire takes her seat, bouncing with glee with the most ridiculous smile on her face. The woman will find any reason to celebrate anything. I blame it on the fact that we never had birthday parties growing up. And holidays like Christmas and Valentine's Day were forbidden in the James household. Now Claire will turn just about anything into a party if you let her.

"How was the first day?" Luke asks.

"Boring as fuck." I reach for my beer. "Would've been nice if they'd saved me some work to do ..."

I've been partners with Trey Renato and Graeme DuVall since we were wide-eyed sharks, fresh out of law school. We founded our practice together with the mindset that everything would be equally divided. But when I was decommissioned by the accident, the other guys happily stepped up to the plate. My caseloads were chum and those two wasted no time helping themselves to an easy feast, leaving nothing behind for me when I returned. Not even a crumb.

I don't hold it against them, though. My clients needed their services. Divorcing couples don't like to be kept waiting. God knows the New York courts make them wait long enough anyway.

"You look good," Claire says. A tea light candle flickers between us. It's dark in here, like the strange, cozy nightmare that has become my life.

"You saw me a week ago," I say.

"Yeah, but this is the first time I've seen you in a suit since before ..." She squints. "And you got your hair cut."

"I get my hair cut every three weeks." I take a bigger sip, scanning the room. If this was before, I'd be looking for a long-legged beauty to eye-fuck, but the mere thought of doing so holds zero appeal.

"Babe, try this." Luke slides his tumbler toward my sister, who takes a sip.

"Love it." She pushes it back before shooting him a lucky-in-love grin. "Want to try mine?"

I look away.

Those two have been impossibly in love, obsessed with one another since the moment he solicited her event-planning expertise to throw some gala for one of his charities.

Luke is one of *those*.

The silver-spooned trust fund kind.

The ones who used to try to kick my ass in high school,

only to have me hand it right back to them with a side of *never fucking go near me again.*

The ones with more money than God, who've never known what it's like to go to bed with a growling stomach or to use the same backpack five years in a row at school. He'll never know the satisfaction of organic ambition, of wanting to rise from the ashes and become a self-made man.

I don't fault him for it—we can't help the families we're born into or the cards we're dealt.

We are who we are.

And at least he's doing something with his life, even if it involves traveling to exotic places to throw his money at the less fortunate. I imagine it makes him feel better. I hope it puts things into perspective.

I'm happy for my sister though. I'm relieved she'll never have to want for anything in her life—*and* she's got a guy who gets dreamy-eyed every time she walks in the room.

We weren't born with silver spoons. We were born with rusty, tetanus-infected nails to parents who shunned the word "love" and screamed at one another so often the neighbors would call the cops just to make sure no one was getting murdered.

I suppose, in some ways, Luke is the antithesis of everything Claire was taught about love. He's gentle with her. I've never heard him raise his voice ... not with her or with anyone. Every time he looks at her, he's got stars for eyes. And the man can't take his hands off her for more than two seconds at a time, always brushing her hair out of her eyes or slipping his arm around her shoulders when they walk.

I'd be suffocated with someone like that.

But not Claire.

He makes her happy. And he's good to her.

We should all be so lucky.

"Oh, we didn't *cheers*!" Claire lifts her half-empty cocktail in my direction. Luke does the same. I swear those two are in full synchronicity ninety-five percent of the time.

I lift my glass against theirs. We drink in unison.

Scanning the room, I spot a handsy couple to my left. A bickering couple to my right. And a table full of middle-aged married couples on some kind of quadruple date.

I've never believed in love, never loved anyone, never wanted or needed or so much as considered pursuing anything remotely in that vein—but lately I wonder if there's something everyone else knows that I don't.

The only kind of love I'd consider would be the kind that knocks me to my knees and fills me with that indescribable fullness I get any time I think of the woman from the dream. I don't know what actual love feels like, but I can only imagine it feels something like that.

"I want to set you up with this new girl who moved into my building." Claire wears a twinkle in her eyes, and she squares her shoulders as she slicks her palms together.

"Hard pass." I exhale, ears tuned into the still-bickering couple. It would appear they're fighting over finances. If it were an appropriate thing to do, I'd slip them a business card as, clearly, they'll be needing my services in the near future. Sex and money are the top reasons people split. Speaking from professional experience, if the two of them don't rush home after this and have steamy makeup sex, their marriage is fucked.

"Her name is Hannah," Claire continues. "She's an accountant. She just moved here from Idaho. And she's super, super nice."

"You also claimed Lexie was *super, super nice*." I shoot her a look, dropping the name of the woman she tried to fix me up with several years back—the woman who tried to fucking trap me with a fake pregnancy when she sensed I was pulling away. And I was pulling away ... because she was *batshit-fucking-crazy*. Things were fine at first ... but they started going downhill the day I caught her going through my phone when I stepped out of the room. The next day, I caught her spraying my cologne on her clothes before she left one morning. I later found out she took it upon herself to make a copy of my apartment key without permission so she could hang out at my place while I was at work because she "missed" me. Six months after I ended things with her, she tried hacking into one of my social media accounts. And when that didn't work, she messaged every attractive female on my friends' lists and spread malicious lies about me. After slapping her with a cease-and-desist and threat of a restraining order, I shut down all of my accounts and haven't looked back since.

"In my defense, Lexie was really good at acting normal." Claire rolls her eyes. "But Hannah is really sweet. Promise."

"No." I take another drink. The fighting couple are attempting to settle their bill with their server, only now the two of them refuse to make eye contact. I'm going to go out on a limb here and say makeup sex isn't in the cards tonight.

Claire bites her lip. "Don't be mad ..."

"What?" I squint. "Why would you say that?"

"I kind of ... sort of ... already invited her to meet us here." She shrugs her shoulders, winces, and laughs. "And she just walked in, so act cool."

Before I get a chance to respond, Claire stands and waves the guest of honor to our table.

"Hannah!" Claire traipses out from behind the table and hugs a girl with mousy brown hair and shifty eyes partially obscured by oversized, thick-rimmed glasses. She's tall, thin, flat as a board on all sides. The instant our gazes meet, her pale complexion turns ruddy, and her stare flicks to the candle centerpiece.

I haven't said a word, and already I make her nervous.

Doesn't matter how "sweet" someone is, a severe lack of confidence is a deal breaker.

"Hannah, this is my brother, Cainan," Claire introduces us when Hannah takes the seat next to me. She smells like baby powder and drugstore perfume marketed to teenagers —a peculiar combination. "Cainan, this is Hannah. She just moved into our building last month."

"What's your drink?" I ask, but only because the girl is fucking trembling and she clearly needs something to calm her nerves. Hell, *I* need something extra to calm *my* nerves with all this shaking-poodle energy she's putting off.

"Oh. Um. Water is fine. I don't drink alcohol." Her voice is barely audible in the crowded bar.

"You don't want to jazz it up a bit? Maybe make it sparkling water? Add a lime or something?" Claire teases.

Luke flags down a server and holds up four fingers. "Can we get a round of waters?"

He's trying to make her more comfortable, but this entire thing is getting more painful by the second.

Hannah reaches for a napkin on the table and begins shredding it into tiny pieces.

Luke, Claire, and I exchange looks.

"Hannah's from Boise," Claire announces out of the blue. "She came here because she wanted a change of pace, isn't that right?"

Hannah nods.

"You went to Idaho State," Claire says to her, though this information is directed at me. "Studied finance and accounting."

Hannah nods. Again.

"You can talk, Han. He doesn't bite," Luke flashes a wide grin.

Han? Are they on a nickname basis?

Hannah's gaze flicks up at him, then back to the pile of napkin shreds on the table. I don't know what my sister was thinking inviting her here tonight, but I have to admit, it's amusing watching Claire try to salvage this shit show.

"Hannah's cousin is the director of that musical ... *The Emerald Canary*," Claire says. "The one that's impossible to get tickets to. I think they're going to make it into a movie, right?"

"Y ... yes," Hannah finally speaks.

"They're roommates," Claire adds. "I've been dying to meet him, but his work schedule is insane. Hannah says she doesn't even see him half the time."

Good God, this is agonizing.

I have to get the fuck out of here.

"Could you ... excuse me for a moment?" Hannah sweeps the pile of shredded paper into her hand, grabs her purse, and scurries off to the bathroom like the shivering mouse that she is.

The instant she disappears inside, I grab my coat.

"Whoa, whoa, whoa." Claire reaches across the table, a feeble attempt to stop me. "You can't just leave. What are we supposed to tell Hannah when she comes back?"

I shrug. "I'm sure you'll think of something. This is your mess to clean up, not mine. And please, for the love of God, stop trying to set me up. It never ends well for anyone involved."

Retrieving a twenty from my wallet, I place it in the center of the table.

Claire sighs, turning to her husband, and they exchange a wordless look, like *I'm* the asshole here.

I'd do anything for my sister—she's the only family I give a damn about. And while she can be a thorn in my side, she's *my* thorn. But I won't suffer through another minute of this.

If there's anything I've learned in the past six months, it's that life is too short. It shouldn't be wasted. And if you're going to waste it, at least waste it with the right person.

Sorry, Hannah ...

You're not *her*.

Ten minutes later, I'm two blocks from my apartment when I spot Serena McQuiston waiting at a crosswalk.

"Serena," I call out. She turns toward my voice, and I wave her down. "What are you doing all the way up here?"

I've known Serena since my freshman year at Montclair, when she spotted my best friend, Grant, and decided she had to have him. Grant, ever the opportunist, decided to make her his official fuck buddy.

"Just met some friends for dinner. How have you been? I haven't seen you since ..." her voice trails and her gaze averts. "You doing okay?"

"Better than ever," I lie. There are people who deserve to hear the truth and then there are people like Serena who pretend to care but only truly give a shit about things that involve them. "You seeing Grant when he comes this week?"

Her overfilled lips curl into a sly smile. "Always do."

The crosswalk sign flicks to white and she leaves with a wave and a wink.

7

Brie

"CAN'T WAIT to tell Cain the big news." Grant zips his suitcase and slides it off his bed, chuckling to himself as if he's privy to some inside joke. Outside, the blazing September sun scorches through an open window, baking this room ten degrees too hot. "The look on his face will be priceless."

"You haven't told him yet?"

It's been a week since we got engaged—the fact that he hasn't shared the news with his supposed best friend strikes me as strange considering the fact that he goes to New York for work once a month.

He laughs under his breath. "Actually, he doesn't even know you exist."

"Wait, what?"

"He's going to be shocked, I can tell you that."

"I'm confused." I perch on the edge of his neatly-made bed with its tucked corners and wrinkle-free coverlet. Grant is nothing if not pristine in every facet of his life. He's a details man, which is great, because I'm a details woman. "Why wouldn't you tell him about us?"

"Brie, love... he's gone through pure hell the last six months. Last thing he needed to hear was that I'd met the love of my life and was happier than ever. I didn't want to make the visits about me."

"Okay, but given the fact that we met because of his accident ... I don't think sharing that news with him would detract from his recovery ..."

"You're overthinking this, Miss White." He's trying to be playful, attempting to lighten this exchange. "Or should I say, future Mrs. Forsythe?"

He makes his way closer and dips to kiss the top of my forehead, cupping my face in his warm hand. "You'll meet him next month at the party. We'll give him the whole story then."

Ah, yes. The party celebrating the fact that Cainan didn't die. Grant said Cainan's sister is an event planner and wanted to get all of his friends and family in one room, sort of like an anti-funeral. He rolled his eyes at the concept, but I found it brilliant.

"All right," I tell him as I lie on my back and tuck my hands behind my neck. The ceiling fan above spins on low, its blades shiny and polished. The diamond on my left finger digs into my nape, so I readjust my position. "Wish I was going with."

As often as the two of us travel to New York for work, not once have our work schedules aligned.

Grant stands at the foot of the bed. "I know, babe. But you can't miss your sister's baby shower."

"Yes, I can. It's her fifth kid in eight years. She shouldn't be having baby showers at this point." I roll my eyes and sit up. "Send me pictures, will you?"

He makes a face, one I've never seen before. "What, like selfies? Of the two of us?"

"Yeah, why not?"

He chuckles. "Guys don't do that, babe."

When I discovered Grant was the friend of the man whose life I helped save, I wanted so badly to be able to put a face to his name. A non-bloodied face. After I learned his name, I performed a string of fruitless social media searches. Later, when I brought him up to Grant, he mentioned Cainan had some weird stalker situation several years back and closed down all of his accounts. Besides, he was hardly on them. He was too busy working hard, and when he wasn't working, he was playing harder.

I didn't press the photo thing after that.

I didn't want to seem weird or pushy or obsessed when it was nothing more than an innocent bout of curiosity.

"Walk me out?" He glides his hand up my arm before interlacing his fingers with mine, and then he helps me up.

With his suitcase in tow, we head out, locking up, and ride the elevator to the main floor of his condo building, which is so new I can still smell the heady aroma of fresh paint on the wall and the pungent tang of the grout between the marble tiles.

Growing up, my father got his start as a local home-builder, putting up half a dozen houses a year until he bankrolled himself into bigger and better projects. It took him less than twenty years to become one of the wealthiest real estate tycoons in the greater Phoenix area. Seemed like every couple of years, my mother would have my father build us another home, always bigger, always better. She loved change. My father loved her.

The scent of new construction, in a strange way, reminds me of home.

"I'll text when I land." He kisses me, and then he pops the trunk of his car open. "I love you."

I repeat the sentiment as I always do, secretly hoping one of these times I might feel it when I say it. So far, when I say those three little words, all I feel is a hopeful little ping … that quickly morphs into guilt.

If I could just make myself fall head over heels for him, everything else could fall into place. Instead, I'm stuck in neutral. Tires spinning. Waiting for a push that may or may not ever come …

I think the world of Grant. I do. He's a good man. He works hard. He's clever and energetic, and his mind is constantly churning. He's a people person. He's tremendously easy on the eyes. Beyond generous in bed. Cultured. Self-aware. Considerate. The man wields a larger-than-life persona that walks into the room long before he does. Impressive, truly.

And my family loves him. No—scratch that—they adore him. And everyone's been so proud of me for getting out of my comfort zone, for "finally living." My oldest sister even teased me once that they had a running bet about which one of us would be more likely to wind up a spinster and the money was *all* on me … until now.

Even my father, who doesn't much care for anyone, is all but obsessed with him.

They golf together.

Get drinks on Friday afternoons.

Talk shop (money matters mostly).

I've even caught them texting each other, like they're good pals. It's cute and it's strange and it's funny and it also complicates things ... because if I change my mind about marrying Grant, it's going to devastate my father.

I climb into my car as Grant drives off and blast the AC. My radio plays on low, some melancholy Bon Iver song, though if I'm being fair, that could describe ninety percent of their songs.

I've been missing Kari lately, thinking of her more than usual. Wondering if she'd like Grant or what kind of advice she'd have for me. She was always the best at giving it to me straight, at not projecting her life goals and expectations onto me (unlike the rest of my well-meaning sisters).

My ring shimmers aggressively in the blinding midday sun as I grip the steering wheel. Grant said it's three carats. I told him he didn't need to go all out. But he said he had a thing for the number three because it represented the past, present, and future. That and the day we had our first date was March the third ... 3/3.

I still can't help but think about that study that correlates ring size with divorce rates.

But, as with any study, there are always, *always* outliers.

I pull into traffic and come to a slow stop at a red light. A text from my oldest sister, Carly, dings from my phone. I don't need to read it to know that she's probably asking if I've picked up the cake for Alana's shower yet.

Another text comes through, this one from my mom. I imagine if this one isn't about the shower, it's about the appointment she made at Bridal Atelier downtown for ten AM tomorrow morning.

My mother is full speed ahead with the wedding planning, and she's tickled pink at the fact that my father doubled the wedding budget. Thought I can't help but wonder if he's giving me what would've been Kari's budget

...

The light blinks to green, and I head the three miles to my townhouse, the one my father's company built for me at cost when I passed my tenth and final actuary exam.

I pull into the garage seven minutes later and kill the engine.

When Grant gets back from his trip, we're supposed to set a date. Last night at dinner, he mentioned a New Year's Eve wedding.

I laughed at first because I thought he was kidding.

It's August now ...

I told him we should wait a year, minimum.

But he kept citing Cainan's accident, raving on about how short life is and how when you know what you want, why wait? And then he went on about babies and family vacations and all the memories we'd make together. He painted the loveliest of pictures that quelled my nerves for the remainder of the night.

But the next morning, the thought continued to loop through my head.

Grant Forsythe is perfect for me in every sense of the word.

I couldn't have dreamed a more ideal man into my life if I tried—and for the first time, I am living, *truly* living, and it's because of him.

So why, then, does all of this feel so wrong?

8

CAINAN

"YOU HAVE no idea how good it is to see you ... walking around, looking healthy again." Grant gives me a half-hand-shake-hug sort of thing, the greeting we've been using since we were inseparable six-year-olds living on Copper Street in one of the worst neighborhoods of Jersey City. "You're back, baby."

"You just saw me last month, asshole. Come in. You want a beer?" I change the subject.

As kids we dreamed of making it big in the city, running this town and taking names. Then the traitor bastard up and moved to Phoenix fucking Arizona several years back, taking a lucrative gig with some connection of his uncle's. Now he claims he never wants to leave, and every time he comes back for a visit, he sports a golfer's tan and hiker's calves. Any time he tries to convince me to trade my concrete jungle for palm trees, sunshine, and desert, I give him two words: translucent scorpions.

No. Fucking. Thank. You.

I grab him an IPA in a squat brown bottle with a skeleton on the label, pop the cap, and hand it off, stealing one for myself before we settle at my bar. Earlier I'd asked over text if he wanted to go out tonight to some of our old haunts seeing how it was a Saturday night and it's been a long time since we properly hit the town together, but he shockingly declined. Said he had something he wanted to talk to me about.

"How long you back in the city?" I take another swig.

"Just until Tuesday." He picks at the label on his beer—an old habit of his when he's got something on his mind.

"Here for work?"

"Psh." His dark gaze flicks up. "Nah. I'm here to see my best friend."

"Bullshit."

He laughs. "And there might be a conference at the Times Square Hilton ..."

"Don't fucking lie to me, Grant. You know I catch you every time." I tip my bottle and take a swig.

"You feeling good though?" he asks.

I roll my eyes at the question I've had to answer at least fifty-nine times in the past thirty-six hours.

"Like a million bucks," I lie. He's in a good mood. I'm in a good mood. I'd like it to stay that way.

"You gave us quite the scare." He studies me the strange way most people do these days, like they're lost in thought or having a profound internal moment. And then he sucks in a long breath, lets it go, and takes an even longer drink.

"What? What's wrong?"

He drags his hand along the top of his thigh.

Sweaty palms on Mr. Confident is never a good sign.

"You're freaking me out here. What is it?" I ask.

"There's actually, uh, something I need to tell you." He squints, biting his lower lip.

"What? Spit it out."

Silence weighs between us for far too fucking long.

"I'm getting married." A careful smile spreads across his mouth.

"Jesus." I exhale, and then I exhale a laugh. "You scared the hell out of me, prick. Good one. Now what'd you really want to talk about tonight anyway?"

His grin vanishes. "I'm being serious, Cain. I'm getting married."

"To *whom*?" I have no doubt my face is wincing and twisted, melded in disbelief. "Last month you were here for a week and you didn't mention you were even seeing anyone. And you were texting with Serena ... *Serena* ... I just ran into her a couple of days ago. She said she sees you every time you're in town. Said she was going to see you this time too ..."

"Dude." He throws his hands in the air as if I'm being too harsh on him.

Grant is a lot of things, but a man who turns down easy pussy attached to a beautiful woman ... is not one of them.

I only hope the married version of him feels otherwise.

He shrugs. "Yeah, well, you were going through so much with your recovery and all of that. I didn't want to make it about me. And the last time I hooked up with Serena, *was the last time*. Now that I'm officially engaged, I'm done with that. Planning to break that to her this weekend actually."

"Grant, I fucking love you, but you're not the marrying type. You're going to hate every damn second of it. Trust me. I see this on a daily basis. And you've never been faithful to a single girlfriend in your entire life, starting with Stacy Westrick in sixth grade."

"Thanks for the vote of confidence." He shakes his head, lifting the rim of his beer to his lips. "Why do I get the sense that you're upset about this? I thought you'd be happy for me?"

"I'm just trying to wrap my head around this," I say. "Think we can both agree this is a little out of the left field, especially for you."

"People change ... you don't think I'm capable of changing?" He lifts a hand and lets it slap on his thigh.

"You always used to say marriage was a trap. Next you're going to tell me that you want a house in the 'burbs with five kids and a golden doodle."

Grant shrugs, fighting a signature smartass smirk. "That wouldn't be the worst thing ..."

"Who ... even ... *are* you right now?" I rake my fingers through my hair. "And how long have you known this girl anyway?"

"Long enough to know she's *The One*." He rests his chin on his hand, his mouth curling into one of those lovey-dovey smiles Luke always gets whenever Claire walks into the room. This marks the first time I've ever seen it on Grant. "And if it doesn't work out ... that's what prenups are for."

All of this is fifty shades of fucking wrong, but it's on him—not me. He's never told me how to live my life, I'm not about to start telling him how to live his.

"Did she come with you on the trip?" I ask.

He shakes his head. "No, she had a family thing this weekend back in Scottsdale. But she's coming to your party next month. You'll meet her then."

I grab myself another beer, and I get one for him too.

"Any other questions, counselor?" he asks.

"Yeah. What prompted this?" I ask when I come back.

"You almost dying, that's what," he says. "Made me realize that life is fragile. That money, cars, status ... none of that stuff matters. You can't take it with you. People are what matter. Love is what matters. Nothing else."

I point to the diamond Rolex on his wrist.

He covers it with his palm. "Bought it two years ago."

"Fine."

"You want to hear the craziest thing?" he asks.

"There's something even crazier than you getting married?"

"I met her at the hospital, the day after your accident. The minute I found out what happened to you, I booked a redeye to Newark. Got there as soon as I could. You were in and out of surgeries, so they had a bunch of us in the waiting room. Anyway, in walks this hot-as-hell woman with the prettiest eyes I've ever seen and an ASU sweatshirt on. She sits across from me. Grabs a *Better Homes and Gardens* magazine. Clearly she was bored as hell. So I struck up a conversation with her. Turns out she was from Phoenix, in town for work—and get this ... she's the one who saw your accident and called 9-1-1. Crazy, huh? Anyway, we exchanged numbers. Got together the next month. I'm telling you, the connection was—"

"Wait, wait, wait." I lift a hand. "No one ever told me that the person who called 9-1-1 went to the hospital with me."

He squints, like he doesn't follow.

"Most people would've done their due diligence and went on their way," I say.

"Yeah, well, this woman isn't most people. That's why I've got to lock this down before someone else does."

"If my near-death experience led you to your soulmate, it will have been worth it."

"Smartass."

"Seriously though, if she makes you happy, congrats." I exhale, biting my tongue instead of pointing out the fact that he's only been seeing her for five months. "And I look forward to meeting her so I can personally thank her for saving my life."

He lifts a hand to his chest, fisting the fabric of his pristine button down and biting his lower lip. "God, you have no idea how happy she makes me. I've never met anyone like her, Cain. It's like she walked out of my dreams and into my life. Wicked sense of humor. Outspoken. Honest. Intelligent. Ridiculously hot, and she doesn't even know it. It's like we were destined to meet that day at the hospital."

"Do you hear yourself right now?"

"Yes. I do. And I know how I sound, but I don't care. I'm in fucking *love* with this woman, and I'm going to make her my wife. Just thinking about the life we're going to have together ..." His eyes roll to the back of his head and he pretends to salivate.

If I told him about my dream, that I haven't stopped thinking about some fantasy wife for the last six months, I'd sound just as crazy—so I keep my mouth shut. We don't talk about sappy shit like that. We don't discuss our love lives—imaginary or otherwise—on any sort of level beyond the surface.

Besides, this moment is all his, as insane as it is.

"All kidding aside, I'm happy for you." I reach across the bar top and give his shoulder a squeeze. "And I can't wait to meet her."

"Thanks, man. That means a lot," he says. "But there was one other thing I wanted to say. Or ask, rather."

"Shoot."

"Would you be my best man?" His dark brows lift as he waits. "Can't imagine anyone else standing next to me on the biggest day of my life. Besides, if it weren't for you, I never would've met her."

"You don't have to sell me on it ... I'd be honored."

9

"WHAT DO you think of a September wedding?" I dry my face on a hand towel. Or am I hiding it? Grant's been back from New York three days now and we've yet to discuss the wedding date.

"September ... as in next year?" He swipes a squirt of toothpaste across his ultrasonic toothbrush and meets my gaze in the mirror.

"Or even the year after that." I'm teasing.

Kind of ...

I retrieve my travel bag of toiletries from the drawer he gave me shortly after we started dating, and then I uncap a tube of moisturizer. We spent a rare quiet night in: pajamas, pinot, pizza, and a Pay-Per-View movie. But the wedding date topic has been on the tip of my tongue since I walked in the door tonight.

He rests his toothbrush aside. "What's going on?"

I shrug a shoulder. "I ... I love how excited you are to

marry me. I love that you're so sure about what you want ... I just ... I feel like we're rushing things."

"Babe." He exhales, smiles, and places a hand on my shoulder. "Tell me what you're worried about and then let me quash those concerns for you. I love you, Brie. I love you more than I've ever loved anyone."

"What's my favorite movie?"

"What?" He half-laughs.

"What's my favorite movie?"

Grant's brows intersect. "I don't see how that's relevant to this particular discussion, but okay. Um ... your favorite movie is Die Hard."

"Grant."

He smirks. "I'm kidding. It's Splendor in the Grass."

"Okay. What's my favorite book?"

"The Bluest Eye," he answers without hesitation. "Your favorite color is indigo. Your favorite day of the week is Sunday. Your favorite lipstick is called Crimson Crush. You're a Gemini. Fittingly. And your favorite childhood vacation was when your grandparents took you and Kari to Mackinac Island for a week, just the four of you. Next question ..."

"You proved your point," I say. "I just ... don't you want to get to know each other at least a little more before we make it official? I've only met your parents once."

"And wasn't once enough?" He winks.

"Stop." I swat at him. "Your parents are wonderful."

And they are. His father tells the corniest jokes and complains about how expensive everything is, and his mother carries a knitting bag with her everywhere she goes, working on blankets she sells on Etsy and donates to local church fundraisers.

They're wholesome, perfectly imperfect.

And they love their son more than all the stars in the sky.

"Look," he says. "I get that you're scared. You're an intelligent, self-made woman. You're independent. You don't need me, and I love that about you. Brie ... for the first time in my life, I feel like I've met my match. If I made a list of all the things I wanted in an ideal partner, it would describe you right down to the way you laugh in your sleep and the to-die-for omelets you make on Sunday mornings. Your family? They're amazing. I know your sisters can be a little much sometimes, but your mom is like this ... glam hippie. And your dad is this badass businessman that encompasses all the things I want to be as a father someday. God willing. Your family is the loud, crazy, thick-as-thieves family I never had. And if I can't have you, can't have *this* ... I don't want it at all."

"Grant ..."

"Now, I know I just rambled on about all the things I'm getting out of this." He takes my hands in his and turns me to face him. "So let me tell you all the reasons I'm going to make this the best decision you'll ever make in your life ..."

My phone chimes from the kitchen, where it's been resting on the charger for the better part of the night.

"I'm so sorry," I cut him off. "It's probably work. I'll be right back ..."

Ordinarily I wouldn't take a work call in the middle of a heartfelt speech given by my soon-to-be-husband, but my company is in the process of hiring a temporary CEO after the board voted out the last one unexpectedly earlier this week, and I've been tasked with leading the hiring committee.

I trot down the hall and jerk my phone off the charger

just in time to catch the call before it goes to voicemail. "Hello?"

"Miss White? This is Barb at Fairway Recruiting. You have a moment?" the woman asks.

"Of course."

"I found you two highly competitive contenders. Both interested. Both highly qualified. Neither of which are able to fly to Phoenix in the next week. Conveniently, they're both located in New York. I know you have a satellite office out there. I could have them come in and interview with someone on location there or you could do a Skype interview ... let me know what you prefer."

"Actually, I'm headed east next week. I could fit in a couple of interviews while I'm there." I swipe a pen off the counter as well as an envelope from a nearby pile of mail and flip it over. "What are their names?"

So I can Google them ...

"Lucinda Meyers and Robert Goldberg. I'll send you everything in an email," she says.

"Great. Thank you, Barb." I place the pen aside and return the envelope to the stack of mail, only something catches my eye—an unfolded contract on DuVall, James, and Renato PC letterhead.

Grant—

This is our boilerplate prenup. I took liberties and added in a few fitting clauses based on what we'd talked about. If everything looks good, give me a call and we'll finish the rest. I'll need your future wife's identifying information at that time as well.

See you next month.

Cainan

A prenuptial agreement?

And what exactly had they talked about …

"Brie?" Grant's velvet voice from behind sends a shock to my heart, and I grab at my chest, sucking in a startled breath before turning to face him. "Everything okay?"

Once I compose myself, I take the papers off the counter and hand them over. "What's this?"

He accepts them, folding them in half. "Just trying to protect us both. Everyone does it. Especially people like us."

"People like us?"

"You know, professionals who are established in their careers and have a lot to lose should things go south." He places the stack aside and pulls me against him. "I know it's not the most romantic thing in the world to talk about, but it's in both of our best interests. No one ever gets married thinking things are going to blow up in their faces."

I pull away.

I'm not upset about the prenup.

And I agree it's smart and necessary.

But shouldn't he be discussing clauses and specifics with *me* first?

"What did he mean by adding some clauses based on what you two had talked about?" I ask.

Grant's full mouth tugs into a half-smirk. "Standard stuff. Retirement accounts. Assets. Those kinds of things. You'll see the contract when it's finished and you're welcome to take it to your attorney. Have her go through it with a fine-tooth comb."

"I don't want to talk about this anymore." I lift my hand to my temple, which is beginning to throb. I haven't had a tension headache in months, but lately I'm getting them every other day. "Should probably go to bed … we've got that hike in the morning and then brunch with my sister and her husband."

"Babe, please don't sweat it. We can talk about it more tomorrow if you want."

Grant hits the light switch and follows me to his room, where we burrow under the covers in a pitch-black room, beneath a whirring ceiling fan.

"Next September, okay?" I ask before I drift off.

"What?"

"I want to wait a year. At least." Maybe longer …

"I'd elope with you tomorrow if you gave me the word," he says. "And I'd also wait for you forever if I had to. Anything you want, okay? I want you to enjoy this."

I nuzzle into his arm and press my cheek against his muscled shoulder, wondering if I'd miss this—miss him—if it were all gone tomorrow. Within minutes, his breathing slows and steadies. He's out cold, not a care in the world, I presume. But me? I'm wide awake. Alone with my thoughts.

With the truth.

Am I delaying the wedding?

Or am I delaying calling the wedding off?

10

CAINAN

"DID YOU FINISH THOSE CONFLICT CHECKS?" I ask Paloma Wednesday morning.

She cups the receiver of her phone with her left hand—revealing a humble diamond engagement ring on her fourth finger.

"When did that happen?" I point.

"Yes," she says, "And three months ago. Oh, and Claire's on her way here."

Paloma returns to her phone call and I head to my office, digging my keys from my pocket. Before I have a chance to unlock my door, the sound of a baby cooing echoes from down the hall. I abandon my post and investigate, partially out of boredom but mostly out of curiosity.

Four doors down, one of our junior partners is bouncing a pink-clad infant on his knee. His wife—whose name escapes me—turns to give me a dainty finger wave.

I hadn't the slightest idea they were expecting, and

judging by the age of the infant, it was clearly born while I was out.

"Cain, you want to meet the future partner of DuVall, James, and Renato PC?" he turns her to face me, and I'm met with two blinking blue eyes with a spray of dark lashes —followed promptly by an impressive stream of white projectile that misses me by mere inches.

His wife makes a grab for a flower-covered diaper bag, grabbing wet wipes by the handful, dabbing up ivory vomit from the navy blue carpet, and the junior partner looks horrified, holding his daughter out as if she's contagious.

"I'll let you two tend to this ... we'll catch up later. Congrats on the new addition." I show myself out, and on the way to my office, I'm reminded as to why I've never wanted children in the first place.

It's ironic when I think about that dream with the wife and kids—how protective I felt of them, how proud I was watching them. How natural it all seemed.

Perhaps I've given that dream too much credence these past several months. Or maybe something in me truly changed when I hit my head in that accident. I've always been pragmatic, a man who knows exactly what he wants and makes no apologies for it. But now I find myself daydreaming more than a man should, searching faces in crowds for a woman who likely doesn't even exist.

I've got to let this go.

I need to get my life back.

Within five minutes of getting settled, Paloma rings my phone.

"Your sister's here," she says.

"Send her back. Thank you." I clear a couple of junk emails while I wait and scan the conflicts checks Paloma sent me this morning. Six new client appointments this afternoon. Twice as many as yesterday. And thank God. At this rate, I'll be back to my old pace by the end of next week.

"Knock, knock …" Claire sing-songs from the doorway, a three-ring canvas-covered binder tucked beneath her arm and two coffees in hand. "Ready to go over the details of your big night?"

"Only if you agree to stop calling it my big night …"

She shuts the door and takes a seat across from me, splaying the binder across the middle of my desk and flipping to a section with my name on the tab.

"Fine, we can call it your *little shindig*. Is that better?" Claire sits taller, legs crossed and hands daintily resting on the top of her knee.

"Smartass." I sniff. "Hey, did you know there was some woman at the hospital after my accident?"

"You're going to have to be more specific than that."

"Grant said the woman who called 9-1-1 also came to the hospital and waited in the waiting room."

"Yeah. Now that you mention it. I think there was someone there, but I didn't get a chance to talk to them. It was all so crazy. But how would Grant know her?" Claire wrinkles her nose.

"Because he got her number and now he's marrying her …"

She bursts into laughter. "What? Say that again? I don't think I understood you."

"It's weird, right?"

"Which part?" she asks. "Grant getting married or some random woman waiting in the hospital for you?"

"All of it." I slump back into my chair. "It's all fucking weird as hell."

Not unlike what my life has become since that fateful night …

"Grant's going to make the worst husband ever. Does he realize that?" she asks.

"I tried to tell him. Then I got accused of not being happy for him." I shrug. "He's bringing her to the party."

"Yeah, I saw he RSVP'd for two, but I just assumed he was bringing Serena ..."

We marinate in silence, though I'm positive we're thinking matching thoughts. "Anyway, enough about your mentally-insane best friend. I've got another meeting right after this, so let's get down to it." She clears her throat and flips to the next page. "So the venue I got us is in the East Village. It's called The LaGrange Experience. Brand-new upscale casual hybrid restaurant with outdoor space and a private dining room that can hold up to a hundred people. Just opened two months ago. I held a wedding reception there last month and it was breathtaking. You're not going to find anything nicer than this at a month's notice, so the fact that they're working us in is incredible."

"How many people did you invite?"

She lifts a finger before flipping to the next page. "Which brings me to the next item—the guest list. So far we're at a hundred and five RSVPs"

"Claire." I exhale and bury my face in my hands. "A hundred and fucking five? You said it was going to be a few friends ..."

"I'm sure not everyone will show up. You always need to account for the flaky ones. Anyway, it's not my fault you have so many friends."

"I have a lot of *acquaintances*. I have a handful of people I'd actually consider true friends."

"Well apparently dozens of people feel differently about you, so maybe you should reexamine some of those relationships before you go writing them off ..."

I lean back in my chair. "Whatever. Go on."

"The bar is crafting a special drink menu in honor of the occasion. I gave them a list of your favorites. I think it's only fitting that we celebrate your life by drinking your go-to cocktails."

"Claire … this sounds more like a funeral after-party than—"

"—Cainan." She tilts her head. "Hear me out. Six months ago, we were almost planning your funeral. Your friends, your family … we could've lost you. Why can't we celebrate the fact that you're alive? There are people flying in from San Jose, Seattle, Houston, Ontario, Liverpool … they want to show that you mean something to them, that they're glad you're alive. Don't rob them of that opportunity."

"You're fucking nuts. And I say that with love."

"Thank you." She winks and then sticks her tongue out. She's a James and that means she doesn't give a fuck what anyone thinks of her. We're cut from the same cloth that way. "For the record, when you were in the hospital, my phone was constantly buzzing and chiming and ringing. Texts, calls, emails. Everyone was worried sick. Praying, rooting, whatever. Believe it or not, for some insane reason, people give a shit about you, Cain."

I lift my brows.

"I know. I was shocked too," she chuckles. "But seriously, thank you for letting me put this little thing together for you."

I've known my sister all of her twenty-six years, which means when she initially approached me about doing this, I should've known damn well that "little thing" was code for "big-ass party" and "handful of people" was Claire-speak for "you, me, and everyone we know."

"You're literally a walking miracle." She leans close, placing her hand on mine. "You could have died. And honestly, except for the fact that you've got the tiniest scar above your right eyebrow, it's like nothing happened."

She neglects to mention the small limp in my walk—the one I'm still working five days a week to eliminate with the help of a physical therapist and personal trainer. Another month and it'll be practically gone, they tell me. Like it was never there at all. Two more months, and I'll be bench-pressing more than I could before the accident.

But I'm keeping the scar.

"I'm sorry, I need to take this." Claire digs into her bag and retrieves her vibrating iPhone. "Hey, yes, I'm leaving here shortly and I'll be headed that way. I wanted to tell you, I wasn't able to get a hold of ..."

I rise from my chair and head to the window, watching the people below trail up and down the sidewalk like ants on a farm. I think about Paloma and her engagement ring. The junior partner down the hall and his new baby. Fucking Grant getting engaged completely out of the blue.

It's like everyone's leveling up, moving forward in life, and I'm treading the same waters I was six months ago—only instead of the waters being tropical and the color of lapis lazuli, it's murky, brown, and void of human life.

Never have I wanted to "settle down" or live any kind of life that consists of mowing the lawn on Saturdays or waking up in the middle of the night to change diapers.

But I don't know that I want this life anymore ... either.

"Earth to Cainan ..." Claire's sharp tone pulls me out of my reverie. "Whatcha doing over there? Anything interesting?"

I'm less than a week back into my old routine, and

already I'm dying on the inside a little more with each passing day because something is missing.

I thought it was the woman from my dream.

Now I'm not so sure she exists.

For all I know, I was clinging onto that shred of hope like a crazy person, believing she was out there somewhere because being with her was the first time I truly felt alive.

Or loved, for that matter.

Something's got to give.

I can't wade these stale waters forever.

I won't.

"What's this?" She reaches for a Post-It next to my computer mouse before I have a chance to snatch it out of her hands. "Is this that tattoo from your dream?"

I made the mistake of telling her about the dream in full detail shortly after I woke in the hospital, when I wasn't one-hundred percent lucid and still refusing to believe it was a dream. I described my wife and kids in vivid detail, and then I scribbled the tattoo on a napkin with a teal gel pen Claire fished out of her bag.

Claire assured me I wasn't married, swore on her life that I didn't have any kids (that she was aware of anyway), and then confirmed with my doctor that these kinds of high-def dreams are completely normal and commonplace with patients in my circumstances.

In the weeks that followed, whenever I'd try to bring up the dream, she'd laugh it off, tell me to let it go.

And she was right, I suppose.

It's done me no good to ruminate, to obsess, to mourn the loss of someone whose name I can't even conjure despite knowing every minute detail about her.

"Why did you draw this?" she asks.

I steal it back, crumple it, and drop it in the waste basket beneath my desk.

"Cainan ... answer me," she says.

"What's it matter?"

"You haven't mentioned that dream since you were in the hospital. Do you still think about it?"

Every second of every fucking day.

"No," I lie. "Rarely." I lie again.

She examines me through half-squinted eyes, and she appears to be mere seconds from calling bullshit on me when her phone vibrates.

"Ugh. I have to take this. I'll call you later." Claire answers her phone, gathers her things, and shows herself the door.

And it's for the best. I don't know how I could possibly explain something to her that I can't even explain to myself.

I pull up my calendar and enter the location of the party while it's fresh in my mind. I'm nothing if not organized. While this isn't the sort of thing I'd ordinarily subject myself to, I remind myself that I'm a lucky son of a bitch to have this many people want to celebrate the fact that I didn't die.

They say everything happens for a reason.

Before the accident, once a month, I'd rent a car for the sole purpose of getting out of the city. Breathing fresh air. Driving through winding roads and cruising through scenic country valleys. Losing myself on unknown roads. Listening to music at top volume—or sometimes not listening to anything at all. I'd never have a destination. I'd simply drive until I got tired and then I'd book a nearby hotel, catch some sleep, and start again first thing the next morning. Occasionally I'd pick a location and stay there for the weekend.

What are the odds that out of all the roads and bridges

and highways, of all the millions of cars, it was mine that got hit at that exact moment on that exact road in that exact city?

I blew through a yellow light earlier that night.

What if I'd slammed on the brakes?

What if I'd waited another two minutes?

It's easier to stomach everything I've been through if I tell myself it happened for a reason. But until I know that reason, nothing makes sense.

11

"CAN I TELL YOU SOMETHING?" I ask my oldest sister on a comfortably warm Monday afternoon. Her kids are at school, and I took the afternoon off to pack for my flight tomorrow. She begged me to come over for prickly pear margaritas by the pool, which is usually code for Carly-Needs-to-Vent-About-Her-Husband.

"Brie, don't ask if you can tell someone something ... just tell them." She sips her half-finished drink. "But go on."

"I want to call off the engagement." I clear my throat. "I'm *going* to call off the engagement."

She slides her legs off her Newport-style pool lounge and swings around to face me. "No."

"What?"

"Don't do it. You can't. Dad will be devastated. *I'll* be devastated. My dimwit husband who can't start a load of towels without breaking the washing machine will be devastated." She slides her oversized sunglasses down. "Grant is *per-fec-tion.* I don't think you realize how lucky you are. You have what most women only dream of. Postpone the damned thing, but don't call it off. It'll be the biggest mistake of your life."

Carly rises, straightens her black sarong, and struts toward the mini bar to grab the pitcher of margaritas. She returns and tops us off.

"Brie, for as long as I can remember, you've been ... how do I put this nicely?" She exhales. "A risk-averse fraidy cat. You let everything and anything scare you. Rollercoasters? Not a chance. Sleep-away camp? Terrified you. Boyfriends? Good God, if they started to like you too much, you went running for the hills." Carly takes a seat and a sip.

"Okay, but I was a child then. I'm not afraid of every-thing anymore ..."

"You read the same books over and over. You watch the same movies a hundred times. When you travel for work, you book the same hotel and the same kind of rental car and you eat at the same restaurants. You gravitate toward what's safe and familiar. But since you met Grant, you've stepped out of your sheltered little box. You're trying new things, abandoning your old routines. You smile more than you have since ..." her voice falters. "Since we lost Kari."

"I'm not saying Grant isn't great."

"So you're saying he isn't great ... enough?"

The dog next door barks, and the lush palm trees filling her backyard oasis sway in a gentle breeze.

"I'm saying he's great." I shrug. "He's great and I don't want to marry him and that's all I'm saying."

Carly is quiet for a beat—no easy feat for a woman who *can't* hush half the time.

"Do you love him?" she finally asks.

"That's the thing. I don't think I do. But I like him a lot."

I reach for my cactus-shaped glass. "Part of me is like ... what's the catch?"

"What do you mean?"

"He's almost too good to be true," I say. "I find it hard to believe that anyone is *that* perfect *and* wants to lock me down by New Year's Eve."

"What? You never said you guys had set a date."

"We haven't. But we've talked about it, and he mentioned a New Year's Eve wedding."

"That's in, like, four months." She slides her sunglasses to the top of her head, pushing her blonde hair back. "What's the rush? I mean, yeah, it was a quickie engagement, and I'll be honest, for a while we were all wondering if he'd knocked you up, but clearly you're drinking tequila, so our mother and sisters will be interested to hear that's not the case."

I stare at the drink in my hand, and then set it aside now that I know it was more of a test than the offering of a proper hostess. I should've known ... Carly's always been tricky like that. Even more so since her three little angels turned into pimply, sneaky, hormonal teenagers with cell phones and cars. But, in their defense, if Carly were *my* mother, I'd be just as much of a pain in the rear. She helicopters the heck out of them, and it's only gotten worse as they've grown more independent. The more they push, the more she pulls. And they're all miserable for it.

"I will say it's strange how much he wants to seal the deal. I had no idea he was talking four months from now." Carly nibbles on the acrylic earpiece of her sunnies before setting them down and pacing the terra cotta tiles under the cabana roof. Her gaze is locked on the ground, the wheels in her head likely turning faster than she can keep up.

"See? It's a red flag."

"Absolutely it is."

"He did say he'd wait though," I add. "He said he'd wait as long as he had to. But that doesn't change the fact that I'm not in love with him."

"Agree."

"And you can't force love."

She stops pacing. "There's got to be something in it for him. Something more than … you."

"Like what?"

"He's been spending a lot of time with Dad, right?" she asks.

"They golf and get drinks …"

"Maybe he's trying to cook up some kind of business deal?" She's pacing again.

"Dad deals in real estate. Grant knows nothing about any of that. In fact, I'm pretty sure I know more about it than he does."

"Maybe he wants to learn from the best? Maybe he wants Dad to take him under his wing?"

I wave my hand. "Okay, let's stop. I don't like all this speculating. It's not fair to him, especially when we have no proof of anything."

Carly takes a seat in the lounger again, gathering the fabric of her sarong in her hands and kneading it between her spray-tanned fingers as she stares into the lush distance of her pristinely-landscaped backyard.

"Fine," she says. "Let me do some digging. In the meantime … what are you going to do?"

"I leave for New York tomorrow and I'll be gone a week. When I get back, we'll have a week together, and then we're supposed to fly back to New York that following weekend for his friend's party …" I sigh. "Really want to meet this friend of his, too. It's the man from the accident."

She claps her thighs, defeated. "Maybe a week apart will give you some clarity, some real time to think this through so you're not deciding your future from such an anxious place. When you get back, see if you still feel the same. And, hell, go to the party. Meet the guy. Who knows if you'll ever get a chance to meet him again? It's pretty amazing what you did, staying with him on the scene and everything. I don't think most people would do that."

"Okay, so I go to New York with Grant, meet his friend, and then, what ... break up with him after?"

"If that's how you still feel, then yes," she says. "But I will say ... many a long and successful marriage has been built on a loveless foundation. Sometimes knowing someone's going to be an amazing father and dependable provider is enough. Besides, look at Rob and I. We were insane for each other in the beginning. Now we rarely sleep in the same bed unless he's had too much whiskey and thinks he's going to get his dick sucked. Sometimes I wish we had more of an understanding. Instead we're just two frustrated jerks mourning the chemistry we used to have."

On that note, remind me never to get married and definitely scratch having kids off my to-do list ...

I rise. "I should probably get going. Have to leave for the airport at five AM, and I haven't started packing."

Carly pouts. "All right. My teenage terrorists are going to be home in about thirty minutes. I should probably start thinking about what I'm making for dinner or something ..."

I love my sister and all of her quirks and imperfections, but she has got to be the most miserable stay-at-home wife and mother I've ever met in my life. Growing up, our mom made it look easy. She breezed through her sunshine-infused days and greeted us with a smile on her face and freshly-squeezed lemonade at three o'clock sharp every afternoon, her citrus-colored Pucci sarong trailing behind her.

Carly was definitely not cut from the same cloth as my mother.

But to be fair, the man she married is nothing like my father.

Not even close.

And they only got married because he got her pregnant their senior year of high school and his old-school parents freaked out and guilt tripped them into becoming insta-adults.

I wonder if she ever resents the path her life took. She always says her kids are her earth, moon, and stars—and I believe her. But I also know she doesn't have anything else. The day the youngest one leaves the nest is going to be a day of reckoning for her, a day she'll be forced to look in the mirror and see herself in a new light. She won't be a PTA Mom or Cheer Club parent volunteer. She won't be spending her days doing heaps of never-ending laundry or grocery shopping for a family of five. She'll have no need for the extra-long suburbitank that hardly fits in their oversized garage.

As I leave my sister's house and head home, I try to picture my future with Grant. Not the one he describes with the kids and the dog and the house in the 'burbs and the Fourth of July cookouts and the family vacations to Disney with all the grandparents and cousins.

Only my mind refuses to conjure up a damned thing.

It's all ... blank.

12

CainanN

SIX MONTHS AGO, I'd be sending a drink to the straw-berry blonde in the fuck-me heels at the end of the bar, the one who hasn't taken her come-hither gaze off me since I walked in tonight.

But I'm a changed man—whatever the hell that means.

I order a double Laphroaig Lore single malt on the rocks and check my email on my phone. This place is busier than I expected for a Tuesday night. Then again, there's a hotel next door with limos parked out front, so there must be some event going on. Limos in Midtown always bring foot traffic—tourists mostly. All of them lured like wide-eyed magnets in case they might see a celebrity they can tell someone back home about. Bonus points if they can snap a blurry, zoomed-in cell pic. Extra bonus points if it's an anchor from The Today Show.

Someone takes the spot to my right.

I don't bother glancing away from my phone.

"Pinot noir, please," she says to the bartender. "Thank you."

Her voice is velvet soft and honey sweet—with a hint of familiarity, too. A soft yet spicy perfume radiates off her jacket as she slides it down her arms and hangs it on the back of the stool.

The bartender places a stemless glass before her and then pours the red wine halfway to the rim, then gives her an extra pour. An inch maybe.

"What's the craziest thing you've ever done?" The sound of a woman's voice in my ear and the weight of a stranger's stare captures my attention.

"I beg your pardon?" I don't look up from my phone.

"What's the craziest thing you've ever done?" she repeats her question, as if it's perfectly normal to ask a complete stranger a random question.

I lift a shoulder, gaze still fixed to my phone screen. "I don't do crazy things."

"Sure you don't." She exhales, lifting her glass.

"I'm sorry, but ..." I'm two seconds from asking her to leave me the fuck alone when I finally lay my eyes on her and all the oxygen is sucked from my lungs.

I can't breathe.

I can't speak.

I can't fucking think.

It's *her*.

It's the woman from my dream.

She lifts her dark brows, peering at me through a fringe of even darker lashes. The sour-apple green of her irises glimmer even in the dim light of this Midtown tourist trap bar.

"You're sorry but *what*?" she asks, blinking.

"I'm sorry, but ... do I know you?"

She studies me, head tilting from side to side. "There is something familiar about you ... are you on a billboard in Times Square?"

Her serious expression turns into a teasing smirk.

"I'm kidding. But only sort of. You look like a model. Or like you could be a model." She hides her face in a sip of her drink. "I'm sorry. I'm making this weird. I'll stop talking."

Please don't.

Please never stop talking.

My heart is two seconds from exploding in my chest as I search for the right words to suit this serendipitous moment, but I'm speechless, wishing I could press pause on this surreal reality long enough to wrap my head around it.

"I come here for work about once a month," she says. "Here and Jersey. And I always stay at that hotel." She points next door. "Maybe you've seen me in passing?"

"This is my first time here."

And I only stopped in because I was on my way to my sister's place on 72nd and needed to kill some extra time since she was running late.

She sips her wine, which is halfway finished already. Maybe she's got somewhere to be.

I take in every inch of her from the freckle on her nose to the square line of her jaw to her nervous, bouncing ankle. My gaze shifts to her left wrist in search of the tattoo from my dream, but it's covered by her blouse sleeve.

"Are you from around here?" she asks. Every word that leaves her pillowed lips sends tingles reverberating to every part of me.

"I am."

"And what do you do?" She blinks twice. I could lose myself in those bright greens for days.

"Divorce attorney. You?" I ask.

"I'm an actuary."

She doesn't strike me as someone who sits behind a desk and plays with numbers all day. I suppose I pictured someone a bit paler. Someone in a boring, three-piece suit. Someone allergic to smiling. Zero personality.

"What made you want to become a divorce attorney?" She takes another sip.

"It's a long and boring story," I lie. I'm not about to tell her about my parents' shit-show marriage. No one cares about that. Besides, I'm more interested in getting to know her. "You're a lot younger than most actuaries I know."

"I fast-tracked." She swirls the remaining wine in her glass before freezing and placing it down in a hurry. Turning to me, she splays a hand on the bar top. "Wait. Oh, my god. I know why you look familiar."

"What? How?" My ears burn as I wait. Never in my life have I been so dumbfounded, so incapable of uttering more than a few fucking words, but here I sit, paralyzed, in utter awe with a side of disbelief. "How do we know each other?"

Her heart-shaped mouth curls up at one corner. "We met earlier this year. In a bar. You hit on me."

Her words don't compute. Not at first. "I'm sorry—I think I'd remember hitting on someone like you."

"Wow." Her brows lift and she takes a sip. "Silly me for thinking you'd remember after that mouthful you gave me."

"Mouthful? What are you talking about?"

"You told me you could last longer than seven minutes ... that you could give me an orgasm ... that you wanted to know what my mouth tasted like ..." She's blushing, hiding an embarrassed half-smile.

Those sound like exactly the kinds of things I would've said *before*.

"I'm sorry," I say.

"Sorry? For what?"

"I'm sorry for coming onto you like that."

Her head tilts and her dark hair drapes over one shoulder. "Don't be. It's not like you got any anyway. I don't do strangers, remember? Wait. You don't remember hitting on me so you definitely wouldn't remember my stance on one night stands ..."

I take a drink of whiskey and settle back.

"When did we meet?" I ask.

Her brow lifts and she studies the wall behind me. "February. thought it feels like a lifetime ago at this point."

Her gaze falls to the fourth finger on her left hand, which is bare, but shows the indentations of a ring. My heart sinks, and I feel the color bleed from my face by the second, but I maintain my composure.

"Are you ... married ... now?" I swallow the hard lump in my throat and clear my throat.

She tosses back the rest of her drink.

My heart is heavy and arrhythmic, and my chest constricts. It feels like forever before she remotely reacts to my question.

She nods, eyelids heavy and gaze pointed at the wine glass before her. "I'm technically engaged, but I'm planning on ending it."

I release a hard breath. Obvious. Loud.

"What are you waiting for?"

She turns to me with glassy green eyes. "Have you ever broken someone's heart before?"

"More times than I can count."

"Well, I haven't. Not like this," she says. "He's crazy about me. He'd marry me tomorrow if I'd let him. And he's so good to me. So sweet. I have to let him down slowly. I have to handle this with dignity. It's the least I can do."

"Rip the fucking Band-Aid. Trust me, you'll both be better for it in the end. No sense in dragging out the inevitable."

Her lips waver and she offers a bittersweet smile. "You make it sound so simple."

"Isn't it though? If you don't want to marry him, tell him." *So you can marry me ...*

"He's a person. He has a heart. I'm treating him the way I'd want him to treat me."

"With kid gloves?" I snort.

"With compassion and respect for his feelings."

Her phone lights up beside her with a call, though I don't catch the name on the Caller ID before she swipes it away. "Shoot. It's him actually. I have to go."

Digging into her bag, she retrieves a twenty and places it on the bar top before sliding off her chair and tossing her jacket over her arm and her bag over her shoulder.

"Wait." I stand.

"I'm so sorry—it was lovely meeting you—again." She gives a distracted wave before disappearing out the door. As soon as she gets outside, she lifts her phone to her ear and vanishes into the throng of tourists gathered around a black limousine.

I drag my hand through my hair and sit back down, deflated.

I never got her name.

But she's real.

She exists.

I pay my tab and book it uptown, all but banging down Claire's door when I arrive.

She answers with a hand on her hip. "Dude, chill. What's going on? Why are you—"

I show myself in. "She's real, Claire. She's real. I just met her."

"What?" She locks the door behind me. "Who's real?"

"The girl. The girl from that dream."

"The one with the tattoo?" she asks.

Fuck. I never had a chance to check for it, but I know it was her.

I know it was.

I know it with every fiber of my fucked-up soul.

"Yes," I say. "*Her.*"

Claire's brows narrow as she studies me, and then she cups a palm over my forehead. "You feeling okay?"

"Please don't patronize me right now."

"Did you get her name?" She takes a seat on the sofa, adjusting the mountain of throw pillows behind her.

"No."

"Did you even talk to her?"

I pinch the bridge of my nose. "Yes. We talked for five, maybe ten minutes. I don't know. My mind was going a million fucking miles an hour. It happened so fast. And then she took a call and had to go."

"Where did you find her?"

"At the bar attached to the Mondauer Hotel in Midtown. Said she was in town for work and that she always stays there. But get this—we met before. Right before the accident. I don't remember it, but she says we did."

Claire is quiet for a moment, and without saying a word, trails down the hall to Luke's home office. The click of the door closing follows.

They're talking about me, I'm sure.

I bet she thinks I've lost my fucking mind. And maybe I have.

A moment later, the two of them emerge—hand in hand, a united front.

"I think we should call Dr. Shapiro," Claire says.

"What? No. Absolutely not."

"I could call my cousin? He's a shrink in Seattle," Luke offers.

Claire pulls up her phone. "I actually found this really interesting article on déjà vu the other day. Let me see if I can find it. It said something like when we think we're repeating an event, it's really just the memory loops in our brain getting tripped up. Or something like that. Two secs."

"This is *not* déjà vu, Claire. This is real fucking life." I pace the pre-war parquet floor of their living room. "You know what ... forget it. Forget I said anything."

The two exchange concerned expressions.

They want to help. And they mean well. But no fucking thank you.

I can do this on my own if I have to. I can find her. I can make sense of all of this. And I don't need Dr. Shapiro on speed dial to do so.

"We should probably get going if we're going to make our dinner reservation," Claire says. "We can talk about this more over drinks if you want ..."

"No. I need to go back to the Mondauer."

Claire laughs. "And do what? Hang out in the lobby like a stalker?"

"No. I'll be at the bar."

"Then we're going with you. We'll just cancel our reservations," she says, turning to Luke. "Right, babe?"

"Of course," Luke says. "I'd love to meet this mystery woman myself."

"Because you don't believe me ..." I roll my eyes when they aren't looking.

"Cainan." Claire comes to my side, taking my hand. "Put yourself in our shoes. If I hit my head, woke up, and told you I was married to the King of Jamaica and then six months later told you I found him in a bar in Manhattan ... you'd tell me I was batshit freaking crazy and you'd have me committed."

She isn't wrong.

"You guys better get going," I say, "or it'll be three months before you can get another table at Centro Pietro."

With that, I show myself out.

I hail a cab back to the bar.

And I wait for her until closing time.

But she never shows.

13

Brie

"YOU'LL HAVE to let me know if there are ever any openings at the Phoenix branch," my Manhattan counterpart,
Maya Delgado, says in her thick accent Wednesday
morning over lunch.

Carly would be proud—I'm eating at a restaurant I've
never tried before and I switched to a new hotel just to try
something different for a change.

"You're looking to move?" I ask. My gaze moves to my
naked ring finger. I left the ring at home before I flew out
here. It was an unintentional move. I was washing my face
and sat it next to the sink. I was already through airport
security Tuesday morning when I realized I'd forgotten to
put it back on.

She twirls a mound of pesto-slicked linguine into a
spoon. "My grandparents live in Mesa. They're in their
eighties and Gram's not getting around as well. I've already
lost one set of grandparents, and my biggest regret was not

spending more time with them. Would just be nice if I could be closer, you know? At least temporarily. New Yorker for life, baby."

She places a fist over her heart then makes a peace sign.

"Yeah." I dab my mouth with a cloth napkin. "I don't know if there'll be any openings soon ... but maybe we could trade locations? Maybe for a few months or something?"

"Seriously?" Maya's eyes smile before her mouth does. "You would do that for me?"

I nod. "Yeah, why not?"

Who even am I right now?

I chuckle to myself.

I'm a crazy woman, that's who.

"We'd have to get it cleared with HR and a couple of the higher ups, but I don't think it'd be an issue. We do the same jobs. And we can keep our caseloads. We'll just be trading offices essentially," I say. "Maybe we could start at the end of the month? Go through the end of the year?"

I check my watch. The first candidate's interview is in two hours. The second interview is tomorrow. Brenda at Fairway Recruiting managed to line up a third for this Friday morning, five hours before I'm set to fly back home.

"You realize you'd be trading arguably the best weather months in Phoenix for some of the worst ones in New York, right?"

Shrugging, I say, "I've always wanted to see New York around the holidays. It'd be nice to experience a white Christmas too."

"All right." Maya sips her water and lifts her dark brows. "Let's do this."

On our way back to the office, we pass the little bar connected to my original hotel, and I think about the guy from yesterday, the one who hit on me in a Hoboken hook-up bar earlier this year. There was something different about him. A quietude, a lack of sexual aggression perhaps? He kept studying me. And he claimed to have no recollection of ever meeting me before, of ever hitting on me.

My cheeks heat for the next block when I realize that maybe I had the wrong guy.

Maybe he wasn't the same one from the bar?

By the time we're back to the office, I snap out of it. It was definitely the same guy.

I could never forget that chiseled jawline or iridescent copper gaze.

But it's only when I'm sitting down, that I remember the words he said to me as I walked away from him the first night we met: *Next time we meet, we won't be strangers.*

I never thought there'd be a next time.

I'm willing to bet he felt the same way.

"It was just a pick up line," I whisper to myself under my breath as I prepare for our first interview. "And it meant absolutely nothing."

14

Cainan

"MR. JAMES?" My assistant says over the loudspeaker Friday morning. "I have Grant Forsythe for you on line three."

"Thanks." I swipe the receiver and grunt a hello into the phone.

"You sound like fucking ass. What's your issue?" he asks.

I'm losing my damn mind. That's the issue.

Tuesday, Wednesday, and Thursday I stayed at the hotel bar until close, hoping, praying, waiting, and wishing for that woman to come back— but she never did.

And in a city of almost two million people, there was no way of finding her. Besides, for all I knew, she flew back to wherever she was from.

"Did you get my email?" Grant asks.

I turn to my computer screen, the brightness searing my tired eyes. "Yeah."

"And?"

"I haven't had time to go over it yet," I say.

"Rough week?" He chuckles into the receiver.

"Something like that."

"All right, cool. I get it. Not every day can be rainbows and sunshine … unless, you know, you live someplace that actually has sunshine most days of the year," he says. "Anyway, I looked over the boilerplate prenup you sent and I made some notes. I wasn't sure if there was a way we could address the post-marital assets in a more … subtle way? Like aggressive but not aggressive?"

I double-click on the attachment in his email. His handwriting over my typed contract is almost impossible to decipher, so I zoom in.

"So her dad is this ridiculously-loaded, residential real-estate fat cat," he says. "Estimates put him at just under half a billion dollars net worth."

"And you want to make sure you get a piece of that if the marriage falls apart?"

"I mean … let's say we're married twenty years, her parents pass, and she gets a fourth of that since she's got three siblings," he says. "I want to make sure I don't walk away empty-handed."

"And why would *you* be entitled to any of her parents' fortune?"

"Because I'm about to double it for them," he answers without hesitation. "I've been talking to her father about switching his long-term finances and capital gains accounts to my company. Once he signs with me, the yearly management fees alone could top seven figures. He could be my one and only account and I'd be sitting pretty. Virtually retired."

"I see."

"I'm going to make that wealthy bastard an even wealthier bastard, and I want to make sure everything is allocated in a fair way—without coming off ..."

"... without coming off as a self-serving douche?"

"Cain, stop ..." he exhales into the phone, dramatic and exhausted. "You know what it's like to have nothing. To come from nothing. It's not like I'm trying to *steal* anything. And for the record, I treat this woman like the freaking queen that she is."

"Except for the part where you've been flying to New York once a month and hooking up with Serena McQuiston ..."

"I'm not perfect." He snorts. "And I told you last time, I'm done with Serena. I'm taking this engaged thing seriously."

Famous last words ...

"You realize there's a cheating clause in this prenup," I remind him. It's standard. I left it in knowing damn well he'd gloss over it because I'd hoped I could bring it up personally. Best friend to best friend, I still don't think he's making the right decision, but unfortunately, it's not my call.

"Can we take that out?"

"She'll notice if it's not there. Spouses *always* notice. If she takes this to her own attorney, they'll notice too. And with the verbiage you want me to add, any lawyer with half a brain cell can see this thing is tipped generously in the husband's favor."

"Damn. Okay. Get creative then."

"You want me to write a prenup that looks fair at first glance, but secretly gives you an out so you can cheat and still walk away a rich bastard in the end." I pinch the bridge of my nose. I do this sort of shit all the time for other clients.

It shouldn't be that hard to do it for my best fucking friend. But there's a weight in the pit of my stomach. A hesitation.

"Exactly."

My cell phone vibrates next to my computer mouse.

"Grant, my sister's calling. Let me get back to you about this later." I return the receiver to its cradle and take Claire's call. "What's up?"

"Hey! So your party is next weekend ..."

"Yeah?"

"But we've had a handful of guests who originally RSVP'd yes but have since had to cancel ..."

I lean back. "Okay. And you're telling me this why?"

"Well, the party invite is on Facebook," she says. "And you no longer have a Facebook account. But a bunch of people are posting old pictures of you in this group and writing well-wishes and asking questions about you. I just think you should reactivate your account so you can respond to some of them."

"No."

"One week," she says. "Reactivate it for one week then you can go dark again."

"No."

She laughs. "Then give me your password and I'll reactivate it and post as you."

"Hard no."

"Seriously though. Some of these pictures on here are freaking hilarious. I forgot you used to get highlights. You looked like a boyband-er. And remember when you used to tan all the time?"

Good God. "Who the hell posted those?"

"If you logged on, you'd see ..."

I groan.

"Oh, and have you seen Grant's new fiancée? She's

freaking gorgeous. They're going to make beautiful babies someday. They look really happy together."

I bite my tongue, unable to tell her about Grant's attempt to fuck her over in this prenup.

"Oh! Gotta go. Luke's beeping in." My sister ends the call, and I slump back, dragging in a ragged breath as I tap on the App Store icon and re-download the Facebook app I swore off a lifetime ago.

Three minutes later, I'm logged in and welcomed back.

I wade through a hundred notifications until I find the invite to the party, and I accept it.

A flood of images, most of them older than fucking time and would be embarrassing as hell if I were the kind of guy who gave a damn what people thought of me.

Halfway down the page, I click on an image Grant posted eleven hours ago—one of the two of us in London our senior year of college, when we had a competition to see how many English girls we could bag. For the record, he won because his standards were arguably looser than mine. But to this day, I get hard anytime I hear a beautiful woman speak with received pronunciation.

I smirk at how young, stupid, and piss-poor we were at the time.

Never would've believed we'd have both come so far in such a small amount of time, but here we are ...

I click on Grant's profile to check out his pictures since Claire said his bride-to-be was drop-dead gorgeous and I'd like to see the face of the woman we're about to fuck over— should I agree to trash my morals.

I expect to find a generically beautiful stranger with a sun-kissed glow and desperation emanating off her body in the form of fake tits and an exercise addiction—because historically that's been Grant's type.

Only the woman smiling ear to ear in his profile pic, her arms wrapped around Grant's shoulders identified as "Brie White" ... is the woman from the bar last week—who also happened to be the woman from my dream.

And now she's marrying my best friend.

I sink back. Gutted. Hollowed.

She told me in the bar that she was planning to leave her fiance—but now that I know it's Grant and now that I know how thirsty he is for a drink of her family's fountain of wealth ... he'll never let that happen.

And even if he did—it wouldn't change the fact that I could never have her.

I would never do that to him.

No amount of justifying will ever change the fact that she's off-limits.

15

Brie

I RETURN to my apartment Friday night with every intention of chucking my suitcase into my closet to be dealt with later, uncorking a bottle of sweet red, and drawing myself the hottest, bubbliest bath in the history of mankind while I rid myself of airport grime. When I was finished with all of that, I fully intended to crawl into bed solo and lose myself in the book I started on the plane but didn't have time to finish thanks to the chatty man across the aisle.

Only I'm greeted with Grant in a navy suit, bearing a bouquet of two dozen ice-pink roses wrapped in rose gold paper and tied with a lace ribbon.

"Surprise, babe." He goes in for a kiss, his hand parking on my hip as he breathes me in and tastes my lips. "Missed you."

"You didn't have to do all of this ..." I take the extensive bouquet and leave my bag by the door. "I thought we weren't getting together until tomorrow?"

"I couldn't wait another day." He leads me into the living room, where two massage tables are draped in linens and two female masseuses greet us with smiles. Handing me a robe, he says, "Go get changed, babe. After this, I'm having your favorite dinner from Hollow Tree delivered, then I thought we could catch that indie flick you've been wanting to see."

I have to hand it to him—Grant is going to make someone an amazing husband someday. An impressive amount of thought and foresight goes into his every gesture.

I slip away to my bathroom, freshen up, and change into a robe.

But in the hour that follows, I'm silently grateful I don't have to look into the eyes of the man whose heart I'm about to obliterate.

16

Cainan

HER NAME IS BRIE WHITE.

All day, I've been repeating those two words in my head on a loop. Like a mantra.

So much fucking white ...

When I woke up in the hospital, everything around me was white.

It's a coincidence, I'm sure. White is a common last name. It's even more common as a color, particularly where hospitals are concerned.

I lock my office Friday afternoon and pass Paloma on my way out. "I'm taking the rest of the day."

I'm too wound up to get anything done.

I need air. I need a walk. I need a drink. Hell, maybe even a fucking cigarette with a side of Ativan—anything to calm myself so I can make sense of this.

Grant said he met her at the hospital, that she was the one who saw my accident and called 9-1-1. Not only that, but she followed the ambulance and stayed in the waiting room ... which was where she met *him*.

But according to Brie, we met before that fateful night.

I saw her first. I wanted her first. I put my sights on her first—even if I don't recall any of it. And now, none of that matters.

No one ever said life was going to be fair.

But no one ever said it was going to be fifty shades of fucked up.

17

BRIE

GRANT'S SIDE of the bed is empty Saturday morning. The scent of coffee wafts from the kitchen into my room via the half-opened doorway. But the house is silent. He isn't making breakfast. He isn't watching the news in the living room. He isn't clicking away on his laptop.

I drag myself out of bed, freshen up, and find him seated at the kitchen table, facing the sliding glass door to the back patio.

He's still, unmoving save for the slow rise and fall of his shoulders.

He wanted to make love last night, but I rebuffed him. I told him I was tired. He kissed me and rolled over, sleeping soundly in a matter of minutes while the wheels in my head spun with a thousand guilt-laden thoughts.

Perhaps he feels me pulling away? Perhaps he knows what's in the cards for us.

I have to end it.

It's not right to drag it out, to delay the inevitable. Originally, I'd planned to go with him to Cainan's party later this week since the tickets were already purchased, but I don't want to feel like a fraud, playing the part of the doting fiancée when really I'm two seconds from calling the whole thing off the instant we're back on desert ground.

"Hey." I shuffle to the coffee maker and pour myself a mug. "You okay over there?"

It's not like him to be so sullen, so paralyzed.

Finally, he moves, his head turning to the side. "Hey."

I take the seat next to his and clear my throat. "I wanted to talk to you about something."

I wrap my twitching fingers around the warm ceramic. I've always hated confrontation, hating hurting people.

Dragging in a long breath, he turns from the glass door and faces me. It's then that I catch the dampness in his dark eyes and the thick tear sliding down his cheek.

"My dad died this morning," he says.

Grant buries his head in his hands, shoulders jerking with each silent sob.

"Oh my God." I go to him.

I wrap him in my arms.

He may not be the man I want to marry, but he still means something to me.

And I'm no stranger to loss.

"I'm so sorry," I whisper as I hold him.

"Had a heart attack in his sleep ... I ... I just talked to him two days ago ... he and Mom were getting ready to go on a cruise in the Bahamas ... he sounded great ... he ..." Grant's words trail into nothing.

I wrap him tighter.

I don't tell him about my decision to move to New York. Now's not the time.

Instead, I swallow the breakup speech I'd gone over a dozen times in my head while he lay sleeping all night.

I can't kick the man when he's down.

Cainan

"THANK YOU SO MUCH FOR COMING." Grant's mom wraps me in a powdery lilac-scented hug that takes me back to my youth. A pitch-black dress hugs her pleasantly plump figure, and she accessorizes with a gold cross necklace and teary eyes.

The place is packed, throngs of visitors making their way toward the lifeless body of Grant's father in the front of the church, his casket surrounded by a hundred floral arrangements and potted peace lilies.

If I have half the turnout at my funeral, I'll die a lucky man.

"Oh, I wanted you to have one of these." She reaches toward a table behind her and retrieves a white and blue boutonniere, pinning it on the lapel of my jacket with shaking hands. "There you go. You were like a second son to him. You deserve to be recognized as such."

"Thank you, Georgette."

Michael "Big Mike" Forsythe was a tough-as-nails son of a bitch who'd have done anything for anyone. He'd survived two back injuries from his career as a construction foreman. A boating accident as a teen. A bout with early stage lung cancer. *And* a pulmonary embolism ten years ago. But in the end, a widow-maker heart attack took him in his sleep at sixty-three—a year and two months after he retired.

"I'm so sorry for your loss," I say. "Really going to miss him."

Guilt gnaws at my insides. I should've spent more time with them. Growing up, I thought of them as my second set of parents while secretly wishing they were my first and only.

She swipes at a tear before running her hand along my arm. "Me too."

"How's Grant doing?" I've only been here a few minutes, but I've yet to run into him. When he called me two days ago and told me the news, he sounded numb and the entire phone call lasted less than sixty seconds before he said he had to go.

Her thin lips press flat. "He's trying to stay tough. You know how he is."

"I do."

"Last I saw him, he was in the church library talking with our pastor." She points to a hallway to the left. "Brie is with him. Have you met her yet?"

I don't know how to answer that question in a concise, uncomplicated manner, so I shake my head.

"Oh, Cainan, she's the sweetest thing." Georgette clasps at her heart, a crumpled tissue in her hand. "You're going to *love* her."

The irony of her words isn't lost on me.

"I'll see if I can track them down," I say. "You let me know if you need anything, all right? I'm less than an hour from here."

I leave Georgette as she greets an older couple, and I make my way to the hallway to locate my best friend and his *intended*. My heart lurches in my throat with each step. My sister's unmistakable voice trails from the other room. Up ahead, a group of guys we used to run around with in high school stand in a circle, half of them almost unrecognizable thanks to their thinning hair and bulging beer bellies.

Up ahead, I spot Grant through an open doorway. There's a woman on his arm. Brie, obviously, though I can't see her face from here.

My stomach knots with each step that draws me nearer.

The pastor shows himself out.

I linger in the doorway, the two of them oblivious as she cups his face in her hands and whispers something to him. Sweet, tender. Compassionate.

It's a special moment, one that guts me from the inside out for a myriad of complicated, contradicting reasons.

"Hey ..." I interrupt their moment because standing here any longer would be creepy.

They turn to me in unison, a team.

Grant's eyes grow light when he sees me.

Brie lets out a quiet gasp, but her preoccupied fiancé doesn't seem to notice.

"Hey, man. Thanks for coming." My best friend doesn't give me his famous handshake-side-hug and his eyes are a dull shade of brown, the whites bloodshot as if he's been crying.

I've known the guy almost twenty-five years and not once have I seen him shed a single tear—except when the

Ravens defeated the 49ers in Super Bowl XLVII and he lost five thousand bucks to a guy at work.

"Brie, this is Cainan." He slips his hand around her waist and pulls her into a makeshift circle. Or is it a triangle?

"Nice to see you again, Cainan." Her shiny chocolate curls bounce with each relaxed step. And she extends a hand. "Looking much different than the last time ..."

I squint, confused, until I realize she's referring to the night of my accident—which means she's completely skipping over our brief exchange at the bar two Tuesdays ago. We didn't flirt. We didn't do anything wrong. Hell, we didn't even exchange names. I can't imagine any reason for her to feel guilty—unless she found herself attracted to me and has decided not to call off the engagement?

"Thank you." I slide my palm against hers, bracing for the electric jolt that follows when I catch my gaze on her heart-shaped mouth—the one that can never be mine. "Grant told me what you did, and I'm extremely grateful."

"I'm just glad you're okay." Her bright green eyes hold mine and her voice is library-soft. "I'll let the two of you catch up. I'm going to see if Georgette needs anything."

"Thanks, babe. I love you so much." Grant squeezes her hand as she walks away.

I love you so much ...

My jaw is clenched as the brain-squeezing tautness of a tension headache forms.

"She's amazing, isn't she?" Grant asks. His gaze drops as he watches her go, and he bites his lip, though I don't think he realizes he's doing it.

Old habits die hard.

"Yeah. You two seem really ... in sync."

His brows rise and he scratches at his temple. "Don't know how I got so lucky."

Our recent prenup conversation floats through my mind. I resist the urge to ask if he's referring to *her* ... or her father's money.

"You doing okay?" I change the subject. "So sorry about your dad. He was one of the best."

"Thanks, man." He nods. "It's hard, but just taking things one day at a time. That's all you can do. At least he got to meet Brie. That's the little bit of solace I've found in all of this."

"Yeah? Did he like her?"

"Psh. No. He *loved* her. He's the one who told me to lock her down," he says with a teary-eyed chuckle. "Told me a woman like that only comes around once in a lifetime if you're lucky." Grant shrugs. "I guess after watching what you went through and talking to my dad, I realized I wanted more for myself. A wife who loves me like my mom loved my dad. A couple of kids. Family vacations. All that stuff."

I can't help but wonder if he was waxing poetic about his dream life while he was balls-deep in Serena McQuiston, but I keep that question to myself.

The man just lost his father.

He's feeling nostalgic and wistful.

I'll let him have his moment.

"Excuse me. Sorry to interrupt," an older woman in a pinstripe suit stands in the doorway. "We're about to begin the service."

Grant gives me a tight-lipped nod. "I should find my girl. Oh, and hey. We're still good for Friday."

"Friday?"

"Yeah. Your party ..."

"You guys are still coming?" I squint.

"Of course we're coming. You're my best friend. Wouldn't miss it for the world."

19

Brie

RAUCOUS LAUGHTER BURSTS from the kitchen and fills the entirety of Grant's childhood home. He and his uncles and cousins are playing cards while his mother serves up a buffet line of reheated leftovers that neighbors and friends have been dropping off left and right all week.

I'm seated in the front room on a floral sofa with plaid pillows. A Terry Redlin picture adorns the wall behind me and a brass corner lamp gives off a cozy glow as I page through one of the photo albums his mother left sitting out.

Grant had a happy childhood from what I can tell. Lots of trips to the shore. Carnivals. Fourth of July ice cream socials. Colorful birthday parties with rented clowns. An abundance of family and friends. Growing up with four sisters, I can't wrap my head around life as an only child.

I haven't had the chance to ask if he was an only child by choice, and given the fact that we only buried his father yesterday, it doesn't seem like it'd be an appropriate question to ask in the near future.

I close the burgundy album and reach for the smaller one with the powder blue cover. The first picture inside is from Mike and Georgette's wedding day. They're almost unrecognizable with their full, youthful faces, wide eyes, and big hair, but I grin, happy for them as I page through their memories.

If I have half of what these two had, I'll consider myself fortunate.

"Hey. There you are." Grant stands on the other side of the room. "Went looking for you. Thought maybe you were upstairs. Mom wanted to know if you were hungry?"

A rupture of laughter flows from down the hall.

So many of this week's events have taken me back to Kari's death five years ago.

The phone call you never want to get.

The beautiful flowers that seem to never stop coming.

The scent of food that's been reheated far too many times.

Perfume. Tissues. Tears.

The carbon-copy greeting-card phrases everyone gives one another because we never truly know what to say in situations like these.

A swell of emotion has resided in my chest all week. And I intend to keep it there. None of this is about me.

"I'll grab a plate in a few," I say.

"What are you doing in here all by yourself anyway?" His gaze falls to the wedding album in my lap. Before I answer, he takes a seat next to me, peels the photo book from my hands, and begins to flip through the plastic-covered pages. "I haven't seen this in ages ... wow. Look how young they were."

More laughter trails from down the hall, which only makes this moment all the more painful. He has a wonderful family. They've been nothing but supportive of Grant and Georgette, and they've welcomed me with open arms while grieving their beloved patriarch at the same time.

Tomorrow we leave to spend a couple of days in the city—kicking things off Friday night with Cainan's party. And Cainan, as it turns out, is the same man who hit on me at a singles bar in Hoboken this past February. Of course I didn't know that when I came across his car accident two days after that night. And then when I saw him again at that Midtown bar the other week, I didn't know he was Grant's friend.

Everything is cross-crossing and intersecting in the strangest of ways, and I don't quite know what to make of it. The only thing I am still sure of—is that I still intend to end the engagement when the dust from all of this settles and we're back home in Phoenix.

I wish I felt differently about Grant. I do.

But you can't force yourself to love someone any more than you can make yourself to un-love someone.

Either you do—or you don't.

There's no such thing as in between.

"We're going to have one of these someday." Grant closes the album and places it on the coffee table with the others. "Can't wait to fill it with memories of our own."

His dark gaze holds mine captive.

Grant cups my cheek in his hand and deposits a slow kiss, one I have to force myself to return even if his lips are ice cold and his breath tastes of beer and marinara.

"I love you so much, Brie," he whispers in my ear as he cups my cheek.

An apologetic ache burns in my chest.

And then I say the words he needs to hear because the man has had enough pain and suffering for one week. "I love you, too."

He returns to the kitchen, turning back once to give me a sleepy smile.

The bitterness of my lie remains on my tongue long after he's gone, and while I'm lying in bed later that night, unable to sleep, my mind is inexplicably fixed on the strangest thing.

No, not thing—person.

Grant's best friend.

20

Cainan

"HOW MANY OF those have you had?" Claire points to the empty tumbler in front of me.

"It's my first." I push it toward the passing bartender and nod when he asks if I'd like another.

"Jesus, Cain. The party doesn't even start for another twenty minutes. Pace yourself. I can't have my guest of honor stumbling and bumbling around like a drunken idiot."

"When have I ever stumbled or bumbled?" I shoot her a look and accept my refill.

"Fair point." She glances toward the door. "Okay, people are arriving. I just saw Mia Taylor and her husband. And DuVall is here with his wife. You should probably head to the private dining room ... oh, there's Serena. *Aaaand* Grant and Brie."

The latter two follow a line of well-dressed guests down a dimly-lit hallway. His hand rests on the small of her back, her body enveloped in a little black dress that makes me want to eat my fucking fist.

Like the good brother I am, I head to the private room to *receive* my guests—beginning with the Taylors, old college friends of mine who flew all the way here from Seattle, and moving onto DuVall before Grant interrupts by squeezing between us to order two drinks.

"Hey, man," he says, inadvertently butting DuVall out of the equation.

"Glad you guys could make it." Although I saw them two days ago, in some ways it feels like a lifetime.

I've been doing my best to emotionally distance myself from whatever mental hold my mind had on that woman.

Guests arrive in full force. Singles. Pairs. Groups. An hour into the event, Claire tells me everyone who RSVP'd has officially arrived and instructs the wait staff to start handing out champagne for the toast.

She's *officially* insane.

But whatever.

A hundred people lift their glasses to me.

They celebrate the fact that I'm alive—I smile as if I share their enthusiasm.

But the truth is, I've never felt so dead inside.

In some ways, I suppose I've come full circle.

The woman I believed I was destined to love ... belongs to my best friend.

She can *never* be mine.

So while he's been mourning his father, I've been mourning her.

And the life we'll never have.

21

BRIE

I GATHER a breath of chilled city air into my lungs and pull Grant's linen suit jacket tighter around me. The restaurant signage glows above me. Passersby converse along the sidewalk.

Inside, Cainan's party is still going strong. We've been here three never-ending hours, and somewhere along the line, Grant did four too many shots and drank three too many beers and forgot that he was here with a plus-one.

If this were a viable engagement, I'd be livid.

But instead, I wandered outside, indifferent, to get some space and take a break from watching The Grant Show. I also needed a breather from the pretty girl in the Boho dress who hasn't stopped shooting sad-eyed daggers my way since we arrived.

If I had to guess, she and Grant have a history.

I lean against the brick façade and dig my phone out to

respond to a half-dozen texts from a couple of friends back home, my mom, a colleague, and two of my sisters.

"You never told me about the craziest thing *you've* ever done." A man's voice sends a sharp start to my heart, and when I settle down, I find Cainan to my left.

The door behind him floats shut.

He dips his hands in his pockets, taking his time moving closer. He studies me, his chiseled features shadowed in the dark. I inhale his cologne—recognizing it as the same one he wore the first time we met.

"Excuse me?" I ask.

"At that Midtown bar last week. You asked me about the craziest thing I'd ever done," he says. "But you didn't tell me yours."

He's beside me now, back against the brick, arms folded as he stares toward the street. His entrancing brown-gold gaze flicks to mine for a second, and I lose my breath.

"So?" he asks.

"Shouldn't you be inside with everyone?" I change the subject. Force myself to look away so I don't have to revel in his magnetic stare or the way my heart hiccups when he points his attention my way.

It's wrong to feel that way about someone you can't have and shouldn't so much as consider wanting.

He exhales through his nose, taking me in from his periphery. "Probably. What are *you* doing out here?"

"Same thing you're doing—getting some air." A brisk shiver runs through me, but I'm not ready to go inside. It's so loud inside that it's impossible to hear myself think, and after a while, being shoulder to shoulder and elbow to elbow with drunk and uncoordinated strangers becomes draining.

We linger in silence, but it isn't awkward or uncomfortable—it just ... is.

"I wanted to thank you," Cainan breaks our wordless moment, "for what you did during the accident. For staying with me. For calling for help. For following up at the hospital."

My mind goes to my sister. "Of course."

"No, I mean it. Thank you." From my periphery, I observe as he turns to me. "You saved my life."

If it wasn't me, it would've been someone else, I'm sure.

I just happened to be in the right place at the right time.

"I'm glad you're okay," I say, turning toward him for a fraction of a second, as if looking into his hypnotic stare any longer than that would rob me of my breath once more.

"I wish I could remember meeting you before the accident," he says out of nowhere. "The month or so leading up to it ... it's like it didn't happen."

I've heard of that happening with brain injuries and accidents. I'm inclined to believe he's telling the truth.

My focus settles on the scar above his right eyebrow, a remnant of the night he almost died.

In a way, it's like a demarcation on a timeline.

"I hope I didn't make too big of an ass of myself when I hit on you." He fights a smirk.

I return one myself. "You definitely have a way with words. That's for sure. But I forgave it all when you chased after me to give me my phone."

"Really?" His head cocks. "I did that?"

"You did. Is that not something you'd typically do?"

Cainan juts his chin forward. "Not back then, no."

We linger in silence for a second, and I contemplate a question to which neither of us will ever have an answer—why'd he make an exception for me?

I suppose it doesn't matter now.

"You said the strangest thing to me before I walked

away that night," I tell him. The wind lifts a strand of my hair and brushes it across my cheek. I swipe it away. "You said, 'Maybe next time we meet, we won't be strangers.'"

He blows a quick breath through pursed lips. "I said that? Really?"

Nodding, I add, "You did. But then we met again—and we kind of were strangers anyway. I didn't recognize you at first. You said I looked familiar but that you didn't remember ever having met me in that bar ... it makes sense now. With the memory loss, I mean. Nothing else makes sense though."

He lifts his brows, as if he's agreeing but only with his eyes.

"This whole thing is crazy, isn't it?" I ask. "The way we've crossed paths all these different ways. Small world, I guess."

Cainan faces the street again, his back against the brick. Lost in his thoughts, perhaps. There's something deep and quiet about him—the way he looks at people, the weight of his presence.

Grant is effervescent, a people person. He's charming and charismatic and he wields a brilliant smile that can light a room from a mile away.

But Cainan is reserved. There's an undercurrent of intelligence in his eyes, but he's not boastful. I get the impression he's quietly loyal. Unquestionably trustworthy. And being around him reminds me of this lake my family vacationed at one summer—surrounded by ancient oaks, the water so unaffected it looked like glass.

"I called a psychic," I say, cringing.

"What?"

"The craziest thing I ever did." My cheeks warm, but I continue with my confession—one that flows like water from a broken faucet in his presence. "Five years ago, my sister passed. And ... I guess ... you know, people do weird things when they're grieving. Me? I called a psychic. And then I called another one. And another. We've got them all over back in Arizona—especially in Sedona. I must have spent thousands of dollars trying to connect with her. All I wanted was a sign."

I exhale, an unexpected lightness taking over me.

"Did you get one?" he asks without missing a beat.

I appreciate his reserved judgement.

The wind lifts my hair into my face again. He reaches to brush it away, the soft pads of his fingertips tracing my mouth. Instantly, I think of what he said that first night— about orgasms, about using his tongue and fingers ...

I clear my throat and redirect my thoughts.

"They were all frauds. They were all cold reading me." I shake my head, and then I add, "Anyway. That's the craziest thing I've ever done. And you're officially the only person who knows, so ..."

My family would laugh if they knew. Maybe not back then, because they were grieving too, but now. In retrospect. Because I'm the pragmatic one. I'm logical. I'm a numbers girl. Give me facts. Real things rooted in reality. Not woo-woo psychic mediums claiming they can see through some invisible spirit veil and talk to dead people.

I've yet to tell Grant. I don't suppose it's worth mentioning at this point, seeing where our engagement is headed. And who knows how he'd respond? He doesn't strike me as anyone who believes in anything he can't see, feel, hear, or touch.

"What kind of sign were you wanting?" he asks.

I'm comforted by the fact that he isn't snickering, rolling his eyes, or offering a sympathetic cringe. He's simply standing there, listening, interested in the insanity coming out of my mouth on this chilly fall evening.

In a city of millions, right now, it feels like it's just him and me.

"I don't know. Something only the two of us would've known. We were twins. We had all kinds of inside jokes. Secrets. Nicknames. Things no one else could possibly know. I just wanted to know she was out there ... somewhere. I guess. I know this sounds crazy."

I don't tell him about all the books I secretly devoured on my Kindle about seemingly everyday people having brushes with the ghosts of their loved ones. I don't tell him about lying in bed at night poring through stories online from people claiming their deceased grandmother was leaving pennies all over their house, or that they smelled their late father's cologne everywhere they went, or that they woke to find a transparent apparition of their dead best friend at the foot of their bed.

I wanted so badly to believe the stories, as strange and implausible as they were.

I wanted so badly to stumble across a sign that Kari was on the other side—wherever that is—having the time of her life and missing me as much as I missed her.

He sniffs. "No, I get it. Sometimes we just want answers, and we do what we have to do to get them. Sorry you got ripped off. Maybe you'll get your sign someday ... maybe when you least expect it."

"Eh. It's all right. I stopped looking a long time ago."

The door opens, and for a moment, I find myself bracing for Grant's unwelcomed interruption. But it's only a drunk couple. Stumbling, they turn left, disappearing into the dark halfway down the street.

"So I have to ask ..." he says. "When I met you at the bar

the other week ... you said you were going to end your engagement."

Shit.

I twist the glistening ring that rests secure on my finger. "Yeah. I did say that."

"You realize he's crazy about you." He speaks with a tight tone, like he's merely stating fact.

"I know."

"Never seen him like this about any other woman before, and I've known the guy since we were a couple of kindergarteners with matching Superman lunchboxes."

A bittersweet smile claims my lips when I imagine the two of them as chubby-cheeked little boys with ripped jeans and grape Kool-Aid mustaches. They were inseparable, Grant told me once. Closer than brothers. Grant's mother told me she always thought of Cainan as her second son, that every year she baked him a single chocolate cupcake on his birthday because his parents never celebrated it. A handful of times they took him along on family vacations. And his senior year of high school, after his parents kicked him out of their house, he moved in with the Forsythes, where he lived until he went off to college the following fall.

"You're his best friend," I say. "And I don't think we should be having this conversation. I'd appreciate it if you'd keep what I said to yourself. He just lost his dad and—"

Cainan lifts a hand. "Your secret's safe with me."

I exhale.

I plan to end things once we get back to Phoenix and Grant feels well enough to return to work. While I hate the thought of hurting him, I also think it's cruel to drag it out and lead him on any longer than necessary.

The door to the bar swings open once more, this time nearly smacking against the brick until the hinge catches it.

This time it *is* Grant.

He steadies himself against the wall, his gaze unfocused as he attempts to study the two of us. Music thumps behind him, growing faint as the door coasts shut.

"Where was my invite?" he asks, slurring. Stumbling toward me, he loops a muscled bicep around my shoulders, tugging on my hair and nearly dragging me down in the process. "What's up, guys?"

"You should get him home." Cainan gives me a look, apologetic almost, laced with a hint of sadness, though I can't figure out why. Maybe he, too, was secretly and guiltily enjoying this alone time? "I'm going to get you a cab, man. We're cutting you off."

We're. He said *we're.* Like *we're* a team.

The fiancée and the best friend.

He heads to the curb to hail a cab, and when we get one, he and I hook our arms around a man who can hardly keep himself upright, and place him carefully in the backseat. Sliding in beside him, I close the door and roll the window down.

"Thank you," I tell Cainan.

He stands on the curb, hands tucked into his front jeans pockets, and he leaves us with a nod. We're halfway down the street, when I steal a glimpse behind us and catch him watching as we drive off, like he hadn't moved an inch.

Two minutes later, we're en route to our suite at the Peninsula, the traffic stop-and-go the entire way. Grant slumps against me, head on my shoulder, and I crack the rear window to catch a break from the stale cab and alcohol spores invading my airspace.

I've never seen Grant drink this much. I've also never seen him so careless or irresponsible. But given what happened this week, I give him the benefit of the doubt.

He probably needed an escape.

He needed a good time with his friends.

He needed to smile.

He needed to forget that sometimes life sweeps the rug out from under us when we least expect it.

Fifteen minutes later, I'm paying the cab driver and helping Grant out of the backseat. A handful of curious onlookers watch as the hotel doorman approaches with an outstretched, white-gloved hand. We manage to make it inside and board the elevator to the seventh floor when Grant decides it's a good time to press his mouth against my neck and shove his hand up my skirt.

Never mind that we're not alone.

Never mind that we've never so much as gotten frisky in public before.

I brush him away and he laughs, slumping against the wallpapered interior as the elevator cart deposits the first load of passengers on the third level.

The doors close.

Grant burps.

A woman in head-to-toe Chanel with penciled-in eyebrows whips around and gives him a dirty look.

I ignore her and count the seconds until we arrive at our stop.

One ... two ... three ... four ...

"This is us." I loop my arm in his and drag him through the parted doors, down the hall, and to our suite.

I swipe the keycard and tug him in, watching carefully as he staggers to the king-sized bed and collapses in a heap. I fully expect him to pass out—which is why it catches me off-guard when he rolls to his back and shoots me the lopsided grin of a man with one thing on his mind.

"Baby, you looked so fucking hot tonight." His compliment jumbles together, like one big, long word. And then he pats the comforter before unzipping his slacks.

"You're drunk." I turn my back to him, unearthing a pair of pajamas from my suitcase. "Get some sleep. We've got brunch with your friends in the morning and then we're flying out."

"Come on. Don't leave me hanging ..."

I shimmy out of my dress and unclasp my bra and get changed. When I turn back, I find him passed out, mouth open, semi-hard cock in his hand.

Exhaling, I slide his shoes off, followed by his pants, and then I return his manhood back to his silk boxers before covering him with a blanket and climbing in beside him.

Rolling to my side, I bury a hand under my pillow and shut my eyes.

The mattress shifts a moment later, and the warmth of his body presses against mine, followed by his arm anchoring over me as his body melds against me. The sharp tang of liquor lingers on his breath with every heavy exhalation.

The heater by the window hums.

A neighboring door slams.

People laugh from the hallway.

The night replays like a movie in my head: Grant introducing me to his friends from college. Grant doling out topshelf tequila shots like it's his job. Grant making a toast. Grant snapping pictures, beautiful women dripping from his arm, grinning into their iPhone cameras with pouted lips and sexy gazes. Grant striding past me to say "hi" to someone—and completely ignoring me the rest of the evening.

But there are other scenes from the night that creep through: Cainan greeting his guests with the reserved smile of someone who doesn't crave the spotlight like oxygen. Cainan obliging his sister's every request. Cainan sipping his Old Fashioned, peering around the room until our eyes catch and my stomach somersaults.

Cainan joining me outside for some fresh air.

Cainan soaking in my secrets without a hint of judgement.

While I hardly know the man, I can't help but notice the way I feel when I'm in his presence. It's an instant calmness. An inexplicable connection. An overwhelming and undeniable sensation of being at ease ... of being *at home*.

But it wasn't like that the first night we met, when we were true strangers.

Funny how quickly things change without any sort of explanation.

I like the way I feel when I'm around him. Grounded. Serene.

It's a strange war we wage against ourselves, trying to convince our heads of things our heart knows to be true. Our head loves reason, logic. Our heart rejects it. Only one will win.

Squeezing my eyes tighter, I force myself to go to sleep so I can stop thinking about Cainan.

At the end of the day, he's Grant's childhood best friend, practically his brother—and entertaining anything between the two of us would be a reckless daydream, a frivolous waste of time, and quite simply: wrong.

22

CAINAN

"HOW YOU FEELING?" I slap Grant on the back before taking a seat across from him at a Madison Avenue brunch spot called Tangerine—Claire's suggestion, naturally.

Rumbling, he slides a pair of dark Ray Bans down his nose and gifts me a bloodshot scowl.

"That's what I thought," I say. "You forget you're old now."

"Since when is thirty considered old?" Claire's husband, Luke, quips from across the table before flagging a waitress. "Let's get the poor guy some more water. A couple of Advil, too, while we're at it. Think we've all been in his shoes before ..."

I steal a glimpse of Brie, soaking in the way the sunlight paints her dark hair in warmth and gives her creamy-tan skin an exuberant glow.

In an instant, I'm transported to that dream.

And then I shove it from my mind's eye as if it's nothing more than a pesky intrusive thought.

All last night, she nursed one cocktail. Maybe two. She lingered by the bar, alone for the most part, smiling at anyone who imparted their eye contact for more than a second or two. Occasionally making small talk with a handful of randoms. Mostly, she kept to herself while Grant made his rounds. Not once did she appear bored or resentful.

A class act.

Our eyes catch from across the table. She smiles. I smile. A white peony centerpiece rests between us, one that matches her gauzy blouse.

More *white*.

Like her last name.

Like everything that surrounded me the instant I woke up in the hospital.

A server with an off-white apron doles out the brunch menu, which is printed on ivory cardstock, and then she greets us with a smile before taking drink orders.

Four still waters.

One freshly-squeezed pineapple juice.

Zero mimosas for this crowd.

"So you guys fly out later today?" Claire asks Grant and Brie as she unfolds a cloth napkin across her lap.

Grant grunts, his hand resting across his forehead, eyes still covered by his dark sunglasses.

"We do," Brie answers for them. "Wish we could stick around longer, but we're both back at work tomorrow."

Claire pouts. "You'll have to plan another trip out here again. I'd love to talk wedding planning with you ... did you guys set a date yet?"

Brie's gaze shoots to mine for a fraction of a second

before returning to my sister, and I recall our conversation last night. She needn't worry. Her secret's safe with me. I'm not going to be the bearer of bad news. More than likely, I'll be the one picking up the pieces when he wants to go on an all-you-can-fuck Vegas bender in an attempt to get her out of his system.

"Oh. Um. Nothing in stone," Brie almost stumbles over her words.

Our waters arrive in pristine crystal stemware, silence consuming us for a few seconds.

Grant chugs half of his before sighing and slumping back in his seat. "She's having second thoughts."

Claire gasps.

Luke glances at his lap, blowing a hard breath between rounded lips.

Brie's jaw turns slack as she studies him. "*Grant ...*"

I don't know how she's going to salvage this. The way I see it, she's got a couple of options. She can deny his statement to save face in front of all of us or she can tell him he's correct and dump his hungover ass here and now.

She's too well-mannered to do the latter.

Too soft-hearted to do the former.

"Think I'm going to order the eggs Benedict." Luke peruses his menu, speaking to no one in particular.

The faintest flush resides on Brie's cheeks. Grant whips out his phone, disconnecting from the rest of us as he taps out a text to God knows who.

"If you'll excuse me, I'll be right back." Brie tucks a small bag under her arm and disappears around the corner to the restrooms.

Claire, Luke, and I damn near sigh in collective relief.

Grant doesn't seem fazed in the slightest.

"Dude." I reach across the table and yank his phone out

of his hand to get his attention. "Not cool putting her on the spot like that in front of us."

He reaches for it—and misses. "Not cool taking my fucking phone out of my hand. What are we? Twelve?"

I don't remind him that neither of us had cell phones at that age. I don't remind him of our humble roots, though maybe someone should. The older we get—and the fatter his bank account— the more he seems to forget where he came from.

Placing the phone down in front of me, I lean forward to say something ... only I stop when a distracting text fills his screen.

Snatching it up, I shove it at him.

"Seriously?" I wrinkle my nose at him. The image of Serena's *au naturel* teardrop tits is now forever burned into my memory. "Thought you were done with her?"

He examines the text, his lips lifting into a half-smirk. "She's obsessed with me. What can I say?"

"How about you take responsibility for your part in that?" I shoot him a look. "Maybe, I don't know, tell her to stop texting you because you're engaged to the love of your life?"

I use air quotes around *love of your life*.

"The hell is your problem? Who died and made you the relationship police? You've never given two shits about this kind of stuff before ..." He taps out a response to Serena, and judging by the full-on smile engulfing his face, it's fair to say he isn't telling her to stop sending him nudes.

Claire places a hand on my forearm.

"Are we ready to order?" Our server returns with a chipper grin that fades the instant she realizes she left for a few minutes and returned to a war zone. "Looks like you could use a few more minutes ... I'll check back in a bit."

"Grant, maybe you should go find Brie? Make sure she's okay?" Claire sips her water.

He doesn't look up from his phone. "She's fine."

He doesn't know that though. And he obviously doesn't care.

Grant hungover *and* in a mood is a combination I haven't seen since college. It can only get uglier from here.

Rising, I toss my napkin on the table.

I'll fucking do it.

Before anyone has a chance to protest, I stride toward the restrooms, a man on a mission. I stop short when I find her leaning against the wall, her phone pressed to her ear. Perhaps she didn't shy away because he put her on the spot. Maybe she had to make a simple phone call.

"Hey," she says when she sees me, covering the receiver on her phone. Lifting a finger, she adds, "Give me a second. Just finishing up a work call."

A few seconds later, she hangs up and turns back to me.

"Just wanted to make sure you're okay," I say, embracing how bizarre it is that I'm the one checking on her while her fiancé sits back at the table, feasting his eyes on a buffet of nudes from his longtime (and ongoing) fuck buddy.

Her dark brows gather, but then her expression softens, and she waves a hand. "Oh. Yeah. No. I'm good. Everything's good."

"Is it?" I keep my voice low, intimately so.

She tilts her head, studying me through squinting emerald eyes. "For now, yes."

All the things I want to say in this moment are all the things I can't say.

You're making the right decision leaving him ...

Grant is notoriously self-centered and unfiltered when he's in a mood ...

If he truly loved you, he wouldn't be fucking another woman behind your back …

He doesn't deserve you …

You should be mine …

But I say none of those things because Grant's relationship shortcomings aside, he's still my best friend. My brother. The most loyal friend I've ever had. And we're not the kind of men who have ever let a woman come between us.

He would never throw me under the bus.

I'm not about to do it to him.

Besides, Brie's mind is made up. She's leaving him. My opinions and Grant's secret second life are irrelevant. They won't make a difference either way.

"I'll be back to the table in a minute. Just have to make one more work call," she says. "Go ahead and order without me if you need to."

I return to the scene of the crime and take a seat. Grant's phone is buried and out of sight, and he and Luke are now talking finances and long-term investment vehicles —like none of that shit show happened.

I survey the hall for Brie. While I hardly know her, the table feels incomplete in her absence. I'd almost say I *miss* her, but that would be absurd. Besides, I couldn't even begin to explain why I have these feelings.

It's easier to ignore them.

So I do.

When Brie comes back, we place our brunch order. The five of us spend the hour that follows talking current events, upcoming trips, and exchanging old memories. When we're done, we split the tab and go our separate ways—Grant and Brie hailing a cab so they can collect their bags from the hotel and head straight to JFK to catch their flight, and Claire and

Luke debating whether or not to hit up an art fair in the East Village or jog off their heavy breakfast in Central Park.

"You doing okay?" Claire prods me in the arm with her elbow. "You got kind of quiet after you checked on Brie ... I swear you maybe said all of twenty words over the last hour. Not like you."

"I'm fine." I do my best to convince her with my words, but my voice must fail me because she rolls her eyes.

"Liar," she says. "What's really going on?"

Without saying a word, Luke excuses himself to a newspaper stand half a block away. As Velcro'd as he is to my sister, he always knows when she needs a moment away from him.

"Does it bother you that Grant's getting married?" She folds her arms, hips cocked. "Is that what this is about? I know you two had this grand plan to be bachelors for life or whatever, but if—"

"—no."

"Okay ... then what was that about earlier? With the phone and the text message and the freaking air quotes. I don't think I've ever seen you use air quotes in my life. And your tone with him. Yeesh." Claire exaggerates a shudder.

"It doesn't matter."

She scoffs. "Of course it matters. So tell me. You know I won't let this go until you do. What was that really about?"

I debate whether to give her a satisfying enough response that'll send her on her way for now ... or to just tell her the truth, which she's bound to pry out of my sealed lips sooner or later.

"I don't even know how to say this," I begin.

Claire lifts a shoulder. "Just say it."

"Brie ..." I swallow a lungful of crisp, late morning air,

only it tastes like bus fumes and dying leaves, "is the woman from my dream."

Claire is quiet for a rare beat. "That Brie?"

"Yes. *That Brie.* I just … this is so fucked up, Claire. This entire thing. I've spent all this time searching for someone I wasn't even sure existed … and when I find her, she's engaged to my fucking best friend." My jaw clenches. I leave out the part about Brie confessing she's going to end her engagement because, it's a secret she's entrusted me with. But I don't hold back the next part, "And not only that, but he's been screwing around on her with Serena the entire time they've been engaged."

Not to mention the prenup bullshit—another detail I'm not at liberty to share due to attorney-client privilege.

"He doesn't love her," I continue. "And he sure as hell doesn't deserve her."

Sliding her hand into the crook of my arm, she leads me to a nearby bench and forces me to take a seat.

"Okay, so the way I see it," Claire says, "this can only be a good thing."

"How so?"

"Grant met Brie because she was the one who came upon your accident, called 9-1-1, stayed with you, followed you to the hospital. All that stuff. Right?"

I nod.

"So when you were fading in and out of consciousness in your mangled car, she was probably the last face you saw, the last voice you heard before you passed out completely. Also, you said you met her in a bar the other week, right? And that you'd met before but you didn't remember meeting her?" Claire's eyes light and her words spew faster, as if she's on the cusp of her own personal eureka moment.

"Oh my God. It all makes sense. *That's* why she was in your dream!"

Her theory makes sense.

"The actual dream itself meant nothing," Claire says with convincing insistence. "And Brie just happened to be in it because she was fresh in your subconscious." Taking a seat beside me, she covers my hand with hers. "Cain ... this is a good thing. We've figured it out. We've cracked the code. You can move on with your life now. Your *real* life. You can forget all about that stupid dream because now we know it was nothing more than mental gibberish."

Luke returns, taking slow and cautious steps our way, this month's issue of the New Yorker tucked beneath one arm as he waits for Claire to give him the all-clear.

"I have to go. We can finish this talk later though, okay?" She rises. "But seriously. Think about it. *You're finally free.*"

I don't tell her I disagree.

I'm not free.

I'll never be free until I can make her mine.

And making her mine will never be an option.

23

Brie

"HEY, BABE." Grant greets me with a kiss Wednesday night as I step across the threshold of his front door.

I tense at his touch.

The time has come.

I'm ending this.

My throat constricts, and my mouth is dry. The words are there, on the tip of my tongue, ready when I am.

We landed late Saturday evening and went our separate ways from Sky Harbor. The last few days we've been catching up at work, too busy to send more than a handful of scattered texts throughout the day.

I take a seat on his sofa as he opens a bottle of pinot noir in the kitchen, pouring two glasses almost to the top.

After that comment he made at brunch last weekend—about me having second thoughts, I excused myself to make a call, hoping the topic of conversation would be diverted by the time I came back. And it was. On the plane ride home,

Grant slipped his headphones on and crashed for four straight hours.

"I've missed you." He hands me a glass and takes the cushion beside me. "Work's been insane this week, playing catch up. It's like they're incapable of functioning without me telling them exactly what to do twenty-four-freaking-seven."

There are circles under his eyes that weren't there ten days ago—before his dad died, before he missed a week of work, before he got so hammered at a party that he made an ass of himself and showed his true colors the next morning.

"You're quiet." He rubs my shoulder. "And tense. Jeez, babe. What's wrong?"

I place my untouched wine glass on a coaster and clear my throat. "There's no easy way to say this, so I'm just going to—"

I don't get to finish my sentence before Grant pops up, dragging a hand through his hair and pacing the spot between the coffee table and fireplace.

"I knew it," he says under his breath. "I knew you were going to do this."

He stops pacing and turns to me.

"Brie ... babe ... please. Don't ..." His glassy eyes are darker than I've ever seen before.

"I'm sorry." I rise. "I think we rushed this, we got carried away ... but I don't want to get married. And not just to you—to anyone. It's not something I want. I don't even know if I want kids."

"You're scared." He comes around the coffee table and clasps my hands in his, peering so intensely it feels as if he can penetrate my soul. "It's normal. Everyone gets scared. Cold feet. Whatever. We can do counseling. We can talk through this."

He's speaking so fast it's a wonder his mouth can keep up.

"I don't think counseling can change my mind about wanting to get married ..."

"I thought we were in love? Isn't that what you do when you love someone? You take it to the next level? You commit?" His eyes search mine. "We can postpone it. How much time do you want? A year? Two? Whatever makes you comfortable. The last thing I want to do is scare you into walking away because I'm so damned crazy about you."

"Grant ..."

"I've never felt this way about anyone." He swallows, his gaze glassy. "I know ... if you walk out of my life, there will *never* be another you. I swear to you, I'll do whatever it takes to make you happy. Tell me what you want and it's yours."

"You *do* make me happy. You're a good man. And you've always been wonderful to me ..." Save for him completely ignoring me at Cainan's party last weekend. "This isn't about you. This isn't about anything you've done. It's just the way I feel."

"Seriously, Brie? You're going to pull this shit right after my fucking dad died?" His tone changes. The glassy eyes turn dry. The painful wince on his face is replaced with scowling lips and ruddy cheeks.

Grant releases my hand. He scoffs and steps back.

Suddenly it's as if I'm arguing with a teenager and not a thirty-year-old, self-made man.

"I don't think it's fair for you to use *that* card." On instinct, I fold my hands across my chest, but I keep my shoulders pulled back as I maintain my composure. "Would you have preferred that I strung you along?"

He tries to speak but nothing comes out.

"There was never going to be a perfect time to do this. I'm sorry," I say. "I really am. I hate that I'm hurting you. But I want you to know that I adore you as a person. I think you're an amazing human being, and I have nothing but respect for you."

His hands go to his hips, and he squints out the window. "How many times did you practice that one in the mirror?"

"Excuse me?"

"You sound rehearsed."

My arms fold across my chest. I take a deep breath and remind myself that he's deeply hurt, that sometimes people get this way as a defense mechanism, that hurt people *hurt* people.

"I've given this a lot of thought, yes. But I haven't rehearsed any of it. I'm speaking from my heart," I say. "Anyway, I hope we can stay friends after—"

Grant collapses on the sofa, his head buried in his hands. I can't tell if he's actually crying or if he's faking it—all the more reason to assure myself that I'm doing the right thing. I've seen countless sides of this man in the last week that I never knew existed.

"I fucked this up." His voice is muffled against his palms. "I'm so sorry, Brie. I'm so sorry."

I hesitate before taking the spot next to him, and then I place my hand onto his back to let him know I'm still here. "You didn't ... fuck anything up."

"What can I do?" When he turns to me, his eyes are red and glossy. But his cheeks are dry. "Tell me what to do. I want to make this right. I can't lose you."

The words are on the tip of my tongue, but I stop myself.

We're going in circles.

"I'm sorry." I collect my bag. "My mind is made up— for a couple of weeks now."

The color drains from his face as he watches me stride to the door. Half of me expects him to rush to my side, to try to capture me in his arms, to fall to his knees in an act of last-resort desperation.

But he remains planted on the sofa, still as a statue.

"I'm moving to Manhattan," I say, because I know that as long as he believes I'm in town, he'll relentlessly pursue me.

"What? When?"

"Next week," I say.

"How long have you had this planned? And when were you going to tell me? Is this why you're ending things?"

"I just decided the other week. And it's a temporary arrangement. I'll be moving back after the first of the year. I'm doing a favor for a colleague."

He exhales, as if he's relieved that I'm coming back. Though, if I'm lucky, he'll have moved on by then.

Grant is an attractive man. He's successful and driven. He's ambitious and hard-working. He's an outgoing people person. Phoenix is filled with beautiful, intelligent, driven women who'd be happy to scoop him up in a heartbeat.

"Why don't we just take a break then?" He stands, shoulders back. There's a confidence in his tone that doesn't belong. "Three months apart. Three months to think about things. To really think about them."

"I've already thought about them ..."

"Think about them some more then," he says. "You might be surprised. You might miss me. You might change your mind. And when you do, I'll be here. Waiting."

24

Cainan

"CAN YOU BELIEVE THIS SHIT?" Grant blows a breath into the receiver Thursday morning. I check the clock—my nine AM should be here any minute.

This is the first we've talked since brunch last weekend, and I have to admit I'm relieved he's pretending like our heated little moment never happened. Moving on is in everyone's best interest.

"I'm so sorry ... I know you really liked her." I drum my fingers against my desktop. Pretending to be shocked at this news and lying to my best friend isn't my finest moment, but the truth would make things ten times worse.

"I just ... she blindsided me," he speaks slowly, as if he's dumbfounded with disbelief. I picture him slumped over his desk, head in his hands, staring at the wall with wide eyes.

"You really didn't see this coming?" As much as I want to remind him of the fact that he literally said she was having second thoughts a few days ago, I opt not to go down that road.

"I mean, maybe? She'd been kind of quiet the last couple of weeks; thought maybe she was pulling away. Then I thought it was my imagination. Guess I didn't want to believe she was having a change of heart."

"She could still change her mind." I say the kind of thing I'd want to hear if I was on the other side of this. "You never know."

"She's moving to New York for a few months."

I almost choke. "What?"

"Some job trade thing with one of the actuaries at the Manhattan branch. It's just until the first of the year."

My heart races as fast as my thoughts. I've spent the past several days wrapping my head around Claire's dream theory, ignoring the lingering pull that remained, and convincing myself to let the whole thing go because it was as unrealistic as it was impossible.

"I need you to keep an eye on her for me," Grant says. "Make sure she doesn't meet anyone else."

"And how exactly do you propose I do *that*? You realize I've met her all of twice." Another necessary and pseudo-harmless little lie I'm not proud of.

"I want you to date her."

His words land like a lead anvil. For a moment, I'm certain I misheard him.

"What?"

"I mean, don't *fuck* her," he says with a casual chuckle. "Just ... fill that void so she doesn't have time to date anyone else."

"Absolutely not."

He's out of his goddamned mind.

"I'll pay you," he says in a tone that borders between mild ribbing and serious-as-a-heart-attack.

"The hell is wrong with you?" Screw Grant if he thinks he can pay me to be a goddamned heartbreaking con man in this innocent woman's life.

"You'll do it. You know why? Because I'd do it for you." His words are the God's honest truth, and we both know it.

"Look ... you know I love you like a brother, and I'd do *almost* anything for you—but I'm not going to fake date your ex-fiancée."

It's an insane plan that will never work, not to mention wrong on a myriad of levels.

"Fine," he says. "Then just ... befriend her. Keep an eye on her for me. Let me know what she's up to and all of that."

"I'll be here if she needs anything. But this whole thing is between the two of you. You have to leave me out of it."

My desk phone chimes, and Paloma's voice comes over the intercom.

"I have to go. Hang in there, all right? You'll get through this," I say.

"Fine. But my offer still stands. I'll pay you ..."

"Fuck off with your offer." I snort, rising and fastening my suit coat.

Even if he dumped ten million dollars in my lap, I still wouldn't do it—and for reasons I could never begin to explain to him.

"You're a good man, Cainan. Best friend a guy could ask for."

I just wish it felt that way.

25

Brie

"I THINK THAT'S IT." Maya stands in the center of her living room, hands tucked in the back pockets of her five-hundred-dollar mom jeans. "If you think of any other questions, just shoot me a text."

It turns out, all this time I'd been working alongside the daughter of a famous billionaire.

She's a *Delgado*—as in the Park Avenue Delgados.

As in the media mogul Delgados.

As in her mother was once the mayor of New York City and her father golfs with Bezos, Gates, and Zuckerberg every summer on some private island in the Pacific.

I try not to gape too hard at the apartment I'll be calling home for the next three months. I also tried not to foam at the mouth when she told me this was *the* apartment they used in the *Sex and the City* movie—the prewar unit with the custom closet that Big purchased for Carrie before the whole wedding fiasco.

Maya leaves a set of keys attached to a platinum Cartier key ring on the table as well as a list of important numbers, all of them scratched out on monogrammed stationery with rose gold leafing on the edges.

So I guess she's an actuary for fun?

Either way, I have a newfound respect for a woman whose work ethic already rivaled mine.

"Thanks again for doing this. My grandparents have no idea I'm moving to Phoenix for the rest of the year. Can't wait to surprise them." She wheels two enormous designer suitcases to the door. I hand her my house keys. I'd offered to let her use my car as well, but she promptly informed me that she'd never driven in her life, that she intended to use a driver to get around. I nodded and acted like it was a completely normal thing to do where I'm from.

"Let me know if you have any questions when you get there," I say. "Though I think it's all pretty self-explanatory ..."

What my place lacks in old world charm, it more than makes up for with efficient, new construction amenities. My water heater will never break down. My windows are airtight with pristine screens. The laundry is conveniently located off the master bedroom. And kitchen appliances gleam with a pristine factory finish, seldom used since I spend most of my time at the office.

Maya leaves with a wave, and I lock the door behind her before heading to one of the windows in her living room to watch the world below. Horns honk. People shout across the street. A small dog yips before doing its business against a trash can.

I'm no stranger to this city, but living here is going to be an exciting change of pace. One I welcome with open arms.

I crack the window and let in an early autumn breeze,

one that smells of crisp leaves and chilled earth from way up here.

From the counter, my phone chimes with a text, pulling me from my reverie. While I'm ninety percent certain it's my mom or sisters making sure I made it all right, I check anyway.

Only it isn't my mom or my sisters.

GRANT: HEY, JUST CHECKING TO SEE HOW NYC IS TREATING YOU? TODAY'S THE DAY, RIGHT?

It's been over a week since I ended things. While he's been giving me space, he's still holding onto a thread of hope that things are going to work out. He texts every other day or so, mostly touching base, asking how my day was, that sort of thing.

He wants me to know he still cares—as if I could possibly forget.

ME: JUST LANDED A COUPLE OF HOURS AGO. GETTING SETTLED. SO FAR, SO GOOD!

I keep it neutral. Short and sweet. I don't want to lead him on, but I don't want to ignore him either. We're adults. We can act like it. Break ups don't have to be messy or dramatic. And honestly, I wouldn't mind staying friends with him. We have fun together. There's no reason we can't continue to hike together, catch games, and see live shows at our favorite venues.

GRANT: I'M GOING TO SEND YOU CAINAN'S NUMBER. IF YOU EVER NEED ANYTHING, HIT HIM UP.

A second later, Cainan's contact card comes through.

I shove my phone into my bag and grab Maya's keys before changing into tennis shoes and heading out to explore my new neighborhood. No one smiles in passing, not that I expect them to. Everyone's glued to their phone, staring straight ahead, lost in their own little universe.

I don't mind.

I'm just here to soak in the scenery, reveling in the fact that there isn't a cactus to be seen. Not a single javelina demolishing the contents of someone's garbage. No angry sun beating down.

In many ways, this feels like strolling through a movie set. Every awning, every street light, every front stoop in its perfect place.

Dreamlike almost.

I'm fully engulfed in this moment—until someone calls my name.

"Brie?" It's a man's voice. Vaguely familiar.

I stop in my tracks, my gaze fixed on the tall drink of water standing in front of me. "Cainan?"

If I wasn't so stunned, I could calculate the odds of running into him on this exact street in a city of millions of people.

"This is so crazy—Grant literally just texted me your number. And then I walk outside and run into you."

If I didn't know better, I'd suspect that Grant orchestrated this whole thing as a way to keep tabs on me, only it's not conceivable. I never told him Maya's name. And even if he did figure it out, her address is private and registered under one of her father's many LLCs. Besides, Grant would have no way of knowing that I was going to go out for a stroll at this exact moment.

It's nothing more than a strange coincidence.

"Oh, yeah? He mentioned you were moving here. You staying close by?" he asks.

I point behind me. "A couple blocks that way."

His full mouth tugs at one side and he points to the building beside us. "Guess that makes us neighbors."

My stomach trills, and my heart misses a couple of beats—not unlike what happened at brunch the other weekend, when Cainan came to check on me. It was a kind gesture. Surprising too. One I had to force myself not to read into.

He's nothing more than a nice guy.

"You know of any good coffee shops in the neighborhood?" I ask.

"Was actually on my way to Atlantis over on 65th. Best coffee this side of Midtown and bonus points—it doubles as a bookstore ... if you're into that sort of thing ..."

I lift a palm to my heart. "Are you kidding me? Books and coffee are life."

"Oh, yeah? Favorite author?"

"Toni Morrison. No question. *The Bluest Eye* is a masterpiece," I say without pause. "Also, don't judge me, but I've read just about every Stephen King book in existence."

I wait for him to laugh as some 'book' people do when I gush about my love of commercial fiction, but his expression is strangely unreadable.

"Mind if I tag along?" I check my watch. It's too early for dinner and unpacking my one suitcase will take all of thirty minutes, if that. I've got nothing but time on my hands. "Unless you're headed somewhere ..."

He studies me. "Not at all."

"YOU TALK to Grant much these days?" I ask when we're settled at a corner high-top in the back of Atlantis. My hands are wrapped around a warm mug filled with café au lait sprinkled with brown sugar and cinnamon.

Cainan drinks his coffee black. Straight forward and unfussy.

"He's called me every day since you broke his heart." His gaze falls to my wrist for a second.

I think he's being sarcastic, though I can't tell for sure. He's guarded. Slightly unreadable. And given the fact that this is only our fifth time meeting, if I count his accident, we're still barely more than strangers. Though now that I'll be living here the next few months, I expect that to change.

"How do *you* think he's doing?" I ask.

"Do you care or are you just making conversation?"

I frown. "I care."

"Not good. You really did a number on him."

My shoulders deflate, weighted with guilt. "My parents are beside themselves over this. My sisters are all disappointed, telling me every chance they get what a huge mistake I'm making. My mom cried. Real tears. And my sisters clucked around like angry hens. My father hasn't spoken to me for a week. Anyway, Grant calls or texts me at least every other day, and every time I hear his voice ... it's equal parts sad and hopeful."

"So you ran off to New York so you wouldn't have to deal with all of that?"

I shake my head. "Me being here has nothing to do with Grant or ending the engagement. My counterpart at the Manhattan branch wanted to trade locations until the end of the year. Her grandparents live in Mesa. We traded houses and offices. It's temporary."

"Grant's under the impression that you'll be back together once you return."

I sip my coffee, the taste bitter on my tongue. "I know he is."

"So there's no chance you'll take him back?" His attention lands on my wrist once more. A nervous twitch, perhaps?

"The likelihood of me changing my mind is ... less than zero." I shrug. "I don't love him. Not like that. And I don't even think I want to get married."

He winces. "Why didn't you just tell him 'no' when he proposed?"

"Because he organized this whole thing at this packed restaurant and my entire family was there. And I liked him a lot. I liked being with him. Everything was so new and exciting. And Grant's a fun guy. You of all people should know that. And he treats me like a queen. It seemed like a safe bet at the time."

"So you decided to tell him 'yes' and then play it by ear?"

I take another drink. "I'm not proud. I wish I were better at saying no to people. My twin sister always called me a sugar-coater. But she was a Band-Aid-ripper. She was brutally honest and it came natural to her. She'd tell you to your face exactly what she thought of you, and she made no apologies for it."

"Sounds like she'd have fit in great out here."

I snort under my breath.

"That was Kari for you." I say, allowing myself to miss her so badly it hollows my chest for a moment. "Anyway, I really did a number on Grant. And my family, too."

"You can't live your life for anyone else."

"I just hate hurting people I care about."

"I'd be concerned if you didn't," he says.

"You probably know him better than anyone," I say, "so

tell me ... what does everyone else see that I don't? What am I missing here? Why does he seem so amazing, and yet walking away from him feels like a weight's been lifted? Like I've averted some kind of crisis?"

Cainan starts to say something but stops, and instead gifts me with an apologetic, closed smile. My curiosity is piqued, but my respect for his quietude remains.

"I'm sorry. I'm way out of line here. You're his best friend. I shouldn't put you in the middle of this." I wave my hand. "You're just really easy to talk to."

He rests an elbow on the table, his hand wrapped around a navy mug as he drinks me in. My heart forgets to beat again when our eyes lock. In this light, his hazel eyes are almost entirely golden with the tiniest flecks of brown. Mesmerizing, hypnotic. And in a way I can't explain, they almost feel like home.

"You sugarcoat because you think softening the blow can control the outcome," he breaks his silence. "But we can't control other people's feelings or reactions. We can't control anything beyond our own reactions. The sooner we accept that, the easier it gets."

"Wow. That's ... deep." I attempt to downplay how impressed I am with his sage advice.

Grant and I never had conversations that dug beyond the surface. He's easy to talk to, but his topics are shallow and safe. I never realized it until now. Perhaps that's one of the components we were missing. There was no connection beyond the physical and external—the superficial. It was never intellectual. Never profound.

Never like this.

There's a depth to Cainan, a rare quality this day and age. He's an old soul. Classic and reserved yet as strong as corded steel. I imagine many people mistake his aloofness for cold-heartedness.

"You won't believe how many divorcing couples try to sugarcoat the hard truths because they feel guilty and don't want to hurt their partner even more than they already have. Nine times out of ten, it only makes things worse."

"Let me ask you this ... if you don't believe we can control anything besides our reactions, what made you want to become an attorney?"

"Fair question ... to which I would say you can control things like divorce. Nobody has to stay married to anyone if they don't want to. My reference was more along the lines of not being able to control the way other people respond, other people's actions," he says.

"Do you believe in marriage?" It's a bizarre question to ask someone you hardly know, but given the topic of conversation and his profession, surely it's not completely out of line.

"Most days, no," he answers without hesitation.

"What do you believe on the other days?" I'm overwhelmed with the urge to pick his brain, to peel back his mysterious layers.

I was wrong about him the night we met. He wasn't some married man from the suburbs taking part in his secret double life. He wasn't a liar. He was exactly who he said he was.

A rarity.

There aren't enough people like him in this world.

Cainan's phone buzzes on the table. Glancing down, he exhales. "I'm sorry. I have to take this. I'll be right back."

Cainan swipes his phone and hauls himself outside, pacing in front of the shop windows as he talks to the mystery caller. He rakes a hand through his dark, sandy blond hair, his back toward me. I take the opportunity to drink him in. Shamelessly..

He's tall, but not too tall. Wields a runner's build. Broad-shouldered. Chiseled features that belong on bill-boards. Cainan James is sexy in every sense of the word—but his beauty is merely a bonus, second to the rest of his charms. It's his intelligence, his soul, the unshakable tranquility he exudes that does all the heavy lifting.

And then there's the way he looks at me—as if I'm the only person in the room.

Grant did that on our first date, and while it sent the butterflies in my middle into a feeding frenzy, it was nothing compared to the chaotic flurry I experience when Cainan does it.

I watch as he ends his call, slides his phone into a side pocket, and returns inside.

I shift my thoughts back to neutral, clear my throat, and sip my latte.

It's self-indulgent, maybe even masochistic to fantasize about a man I can't have.

"Brie, I'm so sorry, but I'm going to have to cut this short." He glances at his half-empty coffee and grimaces. "I've got an emergency client mediation to attend. Anyway, it was great seeing you. Truly. Now that we're neighbors, don't be a stranger."

With that, he's gone.

I finish my drink, forcing myself to deny whatever it is I'm feeling with each and every swallow.

When I'm done, I pass a book display by the cash regis-ter. This month's pick is Paolo Coelho's *The Alchemist*.

On a whim, I buy a copy. Then I make my way back to Maya's apartment, losing myself between the pages of a novel about a man inflicted with a reoccurring dream and his search for its meaning. But every few chapters, my mind tiptoes to Cainan, a man who seems so quietly sure of himself, of who he is, and what he wants.

Someday he's going to set his sights on someone and never look back. She'll get lost in the depth of his eyes, find herself intoxicated with the velvet in his tone and the way he smells like pure masculinity with a touch of sandalwood. He'll woo her with his intelligence and charm her with his peaceful confidence.

I don't even know this woman, but I'd give anything to be her.

26

Cainan

"WHAT THE HELL happened with Grant and Brie? I just saw he changed his status from engaged to single? Did you know about this?" Claire greets me Saturday morning with a barrage of questions.

"Hello to you too." I shut her apartment door behind me.

"Seriously, when did that happen?"

"Over a week ago."

"When were you going to tell me?" She plops down on her mid-century modern sectional and hugs a pillow. "They were so cute together."

"Brie changed her mind. It happens."

She nibbles a painted thumbnail. "I guess ..."

"He'll get over it. In fact, he's already planning a guys' weekend in Vegas."

"Of course he is." Claire rolls her eyes. "Sounds like his comment at brunch that weekend had some truth behind it after all. Brie must've been having second thoughts, and Grant must've been aware of that."

My phone buzzes in my pocket with a text. The number on the screen is unfamiliar.

602-555-9945: HI! IT'S BRIE. HOPE YOU DON'T MIND ME TEXTING YOU … GRANT GAVE ME YOUR NUMBER. ANYWAY, JUST WANTED TO SAY IT WAS NICE CHATTING WITH YOU THE OTHER DAY. LOVED THE COFFEE SHOP. WILL DEFINITELY BE BACK. ALSO, I GRABBED THIS BOOK WHILE I WAS THERE. SO GOOD! IF YOU EVER WANT TO BORROW IT, LMK!

A photo comes through of a book with a bright orange cover.

The Alchemist.

I've seen it before, but I've never read it.

"What're you grinning about over there?" Claire interrupts my moment.

I wipe the expression clean off my face. "I wasn't *grinning*."

"Like hell you weren't. Who texted you?"

"Does it ever get exhausting for you? Being all up in everyone else's business?"

She leans off the sofa, swiping at my phone. "Tell me or I'm going to have to see for myself."

"Brie moved here this week. I ran into her a couple of days ago and we had coffee. She was texting me a book recommendation."

I'm met with crickets.

"It's completely innocent," I add before she has a chance to insert her opinion.

"Brie as in … Grant's Brie?"

I nod.

"Jesus, Cainan. What the hell is wrong with you?" She rises from the sofa and strides the length of her living room. "Is there something you're not telling me?"

"Of course not."

She gathers her messy hair into an even messier bun, securing it with the hair tie from her wrist. "Your supposed *dream girl* met you, dumped your best friend a week later, then moved to your city a week after that ..."

"I know how it sounds, but it's not like that. At all."

"It better not be. You can't do that to Grant. I know he's a douche sometimes, but he's your best friend."

Spending time with Brie was so natural—as if we belonged together. The conversation was never stilted or awkward. Her eyes never left mine for a moment, intense and curious as she gazed at me through a frame of dark lashes and latched onto my every word like she was hungry for more.

And then there was the disappointment in her voice that she tried to hide when I told her I had to go. I didn't show it, but I felt the same.

I didn't want to leave.

I wanted to cancel the meeting, tell one of the junior partners to cover for me, and spend the rest of the day just the two of us.

I opt not to share those particulars with my sister.

"I would *never*." Which is why I also don't bother sharing with Claire the fact that I knew Brie's favorite authors before she even told me. And I knew because of the dream. The dream Claire insists was nothing more than *mental gibberish*. "I'd never do that to him."

And I mean it.

I can't. And I won't.

27

Brie

"HAVE A GOOD WEEKEND, BRIE!" Denise, our front desk manager, bids me farewell Friday afternoon. A group of ladies from accounting and HR follow her in a small herd toward the elevator. I overheard them talking about getting drinks later. Paulina, the other actuary, invited me to her daughter's ballet recital at some private fundraiser, though I think she was simply being nice because I told her I didn't have much planned for the weekend.

I've been here two weeks, and it's no easier to make new friends here than it was back home. Everyone has their cliques. Everyone has to be one-hundred percent sure they can trust you before they let you into their inner circle. And I get it. I'm not offended. It just means I'll be spending another quiet weekend in the confines of Maya's beautiful apartment.

Except for tonight.

Tonight I'm seeing *Chicago* on Broadway. It's just about

the touristiest thing a non-New Yorker can do, and I have zero shame about it. I've seen the movie about a dozen times, and I saw the show four times when it came through Phoenix a decade ago, but I've never seen it here.

I check my email for my ticket confirmation code before shutting down my computer and locking up Maya's office. I'm halfway to the elevator when Grant calls.

"Hey," I answer, but only because I ignored his last two calls. Ever since I moved here, he's been calling and texting daily. I think it makes him anxious, me being so far away. It's like he's convinced I'm going to meet someone else and get swept off my feet. Never mind that it's an irrelevant fear. Regardless of what may or may not happen while I'm here, it changes nothing back home with him.

We're friends. It's all we'll ever be.

I stop at Atlantis on my way home and grab a coffee. The show isn't for another couple of hours, and the whirl-wind week I've had is catching up with me.

Being here is unexpectedly bittersweet. Two weeks ago, Cainan and I sat at the table in the back and had coffee. Two days later, I texted him about *The Alchemist.*

He read the text, but never responded.

Radio silence.

Maybe it's a loyalty thing. Perhaps he felt guilty afterward for hanging out with his best friend's ex? Maybe he thinks he's doing the right thing?

"What are you up to tonight?" Grant asks as I leave the coffee shop.

"Just catching a show later." I try to keep our conversations vague, short, and neutral at all times. I don't want to give him false hope. I don't want to foster any kind of conversational intimacy.

"Oh, yeah? Which one?"

"*Chicago*. What are you doing this weekend?"

"The usual … " He keeps his answer vague as well, though I'd guess his intentions are different than mine. I think he wants me to wonder, to assume the worst, to imagine him painting the town and hooking up with beautiful Phoenician women. "Actually, I was thinking of laying low. Cainan's planning this insane Vegas weekend next month."

"Is he now?" There's a twinge in my chest, though I'm not sure what it means. Jealousy, perhaps? Though I have no right being jealous of Grant chatting with his best friend.

"Yeah. Says he wants to cheer me up."

"I'm sure the two of you will have a lovely time together."

He chuckles. "Oh, there'll be eight of us total. Going to rent out this suite at the Waldorf Astoria. Hit up a bunch of clubs. Get crazy."

Grant is definitely trying to make me jealous. Only instead of picturing Grant covered in stunning, gorgeous, half-naked women … I'm picturing Cainan.

My middle turns tense, and my skin is blanketed in a hot flash of displaced jealousy.

"Sounds like a good time," I say, forcing an upbeat tone.

"Hey, I have a work trip coming up in a few weeks," he changes the subject. "I thought maybe … if you were cool with it … I could stay with you?"

My jaw turns slack as I search for the right words. Cainan's words from the other week, about not sugarcoating, come to mind. "Grant, I don't think that's a good idea."

The old me would've fed him a bunch of excuses, would've told him it's not my place, and I don't feel comfortable allowing someone else to stay there with me. Instead, I zip my lips and leave it at that.

Grant utters some kind of protest on the other end, but I'm no longer listening ... because up ahead, rounding the corner is none other than Cainan James himself.

"Hey, I'm sorry," I tell Grant. "I have to go."

"Everything okay?"

"Of course," I say, thumb hovering over the disconnect button. "Talk later?"

"Yeah, sure." He doesn't mask the frustration in his voice before hanging up.

Cainan spots me, and my stomach caves as I wait for his reaction. Holding my breath, I remind myself to breathe.

"Hey, stranger." His smile almost makes me forget he's ignored me for the past two weeks.

Did I text the wrong number by mistake? There's a chance Cainan didn't get my text. It might've gone to some random person instead, and I've gotten my panties in a wad over nothing.

"Hi." I force a smile. And then the question comes before I have a chance to stop it. "Did you get my text the other week?"

He sucks in a breath through clenched teeth, wearing an apologetic mask. "Yeah. I did."

I lift my brows. "And?"

His eyes search mine. He's trying to come up with an excuse, I can tell. Only, doing such a thing would be an act of hypocrisy given his strong stance on not sugarcoating the truth.

"If this is about Grant ..." my voice trails off, half of me willing him to assure me it isn't.

Only that isn't what happens. At all.

"I'm going to be completely honest with you," he says. "It's *absolutely* about Grant."

His words are a swift blow, a sucker punch to the ego. But I don't let it show.

"I don't understand," I say. "Grant gave me your number. He told me to reach out to you if I needed anything. I don't think he'd be upset about us having coffee or talking books ..."

Silence weighs between us, heavy with a thousand unsaid words.

Did he feel it too? And if he did, would he ever admit it?

Does he not trust himself around me?

"You know what, don't worry about it." I wave him off and check my watch. "I've got to get going. I've got plans tonight, so ..."

I won't beg him to be friends with me.

I also won't stand around and pretend I didn't fall asleep last night imagining the intensity of his kiss against my mouth or the way my body would melt against his without a single protest, no matter how wrong it would be.

"What are your plans?" he asks.

"I'm catching a show on Broadway."

"Let me guess ... *Chicago*."

I smirk. "Either you're psychic or you're making fun of me for being a predictable tourist ..."

"What time is it?"

"Five fifteen."

"No—what time is your show?"

"Seven thirty. Why?"

His lips press together and his brows meet. He looks like a man on the cusp of a bad decision. "You want to come over for a drink before? Maybe tell me a little more about that book?"

I nod before I have a chance to talk myself out of it.

HIS PLACE IS as quiet and impressive as he is.

Marble floors in the entry. Tall ceilings. Oversized lime-stone fireplace. Pristine chef's kitchen. The faint scent of bergamot and sandalwood baked into the walls. Dark wood accented with burnished metal. Leather wrapped every-thing. Comfortable but not gargantuan or in-your-face.

He takes me to what appears to be a bedroom converted into a library, and, for the first time in my adult life, I'm weak in the knees—a term I'd always thought was an expression until now.

"I've never met a man with a library before," I say, drag-ging my fingertips along a shelf sectioned off by poetry and bookends shaped from black quartz. "Favorite poet?"

"I don't know that I could pick just one, but Pablo Neruda is definitely top five." He slides a small book from his collection, flicks it open to a page in the middle, and clears his throat. "*I do not love you as if you were salt-rose or topaz or the arrow of carnations ... I love you as certain dark things are to be loved ... in secret ... between the shadow and the soul.*"

A body-tightening shiver runs through me, followed by a spray of knee-weakening goose bumps.

"Anyway." He inserts the book back to its rightful posi-tion. "What's your drink?"

"What do you have?"

"Everything."

"Vodka cranberry. I'm a simple girl." I give him a wink.

His mouth pulls up. "Something tells me you're anything but."

Disappearing down the hall, he leaves me to my own devices in the comfort of his suede-and-walnut scented library with its floor-to-ceiling shelves chock full of poetry, philosopher's tomes, and all the classics.

Cainan is a renaissance man.

Grant was never into books. He told me once that he'd paid underclassmen to write his World Lit papers in college and he'd maybe finished one book in his entire life—a biography on Michael Jordan. He said he could never sit still long enough to focus.

Cainan's inherent tranquility is all the more fitting now that I've seen this side of him.

"Here you are." He returns a minute later with my vodka cranberry and two fingers of an amber-hued liquor for himself, and then he makes himself comfortable in a cognac club chair. "Help yourself. You can borrow anything you'd like."

I select an antique copy of The Picture of Dorian Gray and carefully flip through its fragile pages, making my way through the initial chapter while working on my cocktail.

When I glance up several minutes later, Cainan is staring at my wrists again. Just like he did that day at Atlantis.

"Why do you keep looking at my wrists?" I half-laugh.

His brows meet. He hesitates. "No reason."

Maybe it's a nervous tic? Though he doesn't come across as a nervous man in the slightest ...

I check the time and remember I still have a show to catch.

"I should probably get going." I fold the book, set it down, and take one last sip of my drink. As much as I want to borrow it, it's clearly a first edition, signed by the author, and probably worth thousands. "Thank you for inviting me up. Next time don't wait two weeks ..."

"Don't forget your book." He hands it to me. "It's due

back three weeks from today. If you need to renew, let me know."

Our hands brush in the exchange. My heart trills.

If this is all it takes to get me going, I can only imagine the way my body would react if things were ... different ... for us.

He's a good man.

I wish I wanted him less ...

"You ever going to read *The Alchemist?*" I ask as he shows me out, book pressed against my breathless chest as if it could possibly disguise my current state.

"What makes you think I haven't already?" He winks before closing the door.

I swoon all the way to *Chicago*.

And when it's over, I swoon all the way home.

Walking the sidewalks of New York in a daydream haze, I'm flattered that Cainan took time out of his busy schedule to read a book I recommended—but now I can't stop wondering: as he flicked through the soft manila pages, did he ever think about me?

28

Cainan

I'M LOSING MY MIND.

I take a seat in the living room as soon as Brie is gone, and I slide my copy of The Alchemist off the coffee table. I didn't want to read the book when she recommended it to me two weeks back. In fact, a handful of times over the years, I'd tried ... desperate to know what all the hype was about but never making it past the first few pages, because it read like a poorly-translated Aesop's fable, choppy and simplistic in places.

This time I pushed through.

I finished the first chapter.

Then the next.

And the one after.

By the time it was over, I'd read it in one sitting, my neck kinked and my hands stiff from holding the same position for hours.

Perhaps in the past, the message of the book didn't resonate. I couldn't relate. I didn't want to take the time to wade through the jerky paragraphs to find the heart of the message.

If timing is everything, this book couldn't have smacked me in the soul at a more perfect chapter of my life. In fact, there are many ways Santiago's journey mirrors mine. The dream that haunts him. His relentless quest. His obsession with destiny.

In my dream, I knew Brie's favorite authors. I knew she loved *Chicago* on Broadway.

There's no explanation for that. I highly doubt she was spouting off her verbal autobiography as I lay dying in my mangled car that fateful night.

But there's also no explanation for the missing tattoo.

She caught me staring at her wrists earlier, and on instinct, she covered them with her sleeves and said she had to get going.

That has to mean something.

My phone buzzes beside me. A text from Grant fills the screen.

GRANT: JUST EMAILED YOUR VEGAS TICKET. CAN'T FUCKING WAIT. YOU HAVE NO IDEA HOW BADLY I NEED THIS.

I check my email, confirm the eTicket is there, and send him a thumbs' up emoji.

GRANT: HAVE YOU SEEN HER AROUND YET?

He's asked this on a daily basis, ever since I made the mistake of mentioning we had coffee together. I also casually mentioned she's staying in the neighborhood. Now he's hell bent on using me as his personal extra set of eyes, diligently checking to see if there've been any new sightings or developments.

I chew the inside of my lip.

Two weeks ago, Brie texted me. Two weeks ago Claire preached to me about the perils of playing with fire—not that I needed the sermon. And every fucking day for the past two weeks, Grant reminds me of his broken heart in some way, shape, or form.

For that reason, I ignored Brie's text about the book. I've avoided Atlantis like the plague. And I've drowned out my thoughts of her with anything and everything—mostly work.

I convinced myself I was doing the right thing, even if it made my insides twist and knot, even if my thoughts pricked through at three o'clock in the morning without explanation.

ME: SAW HER ON THE SIDEWALK A LITTLE BIT AGO.

I wasn't going to invite her up initially—until she mentioned she was going to see *Chicago*. It made me think of the dream. About all the things I knew about her that I wanted to confirm. I'd fully intended on working a few of those details into small talk, but I wasn't expecting her visit to be cut so short.

GRANT: HOW'D SHE LOOK?

I huff. I imagine he wants me to tell him she looks hopeless and miserable and despondent, that she's a shell of the woman she was when she was his. But the truth was, she looked fucking beautiful. Glossy dark hair, livewire green eyes, chunky sweater over skintight leather leggings, a guarded smile she wore only for me.

ME: IDK. NORMAL?

GRANT: BTW I TOLD HER YOU PLANNED THE VEGAS TRIP.

ME: WHY DID YOU LIE?

GRANT: BC I DIDN'T WANT TO SOUND LIKE A FUCKING LAMEASS. BESIDES AS MY FORMER BEST MAN AND LIFELONG BEST FRIEND YOU SHOULD'VE BEEN THE ONE PLANNING THE TRIP ANYWAY.

GRANT: DID SHE SAY ANYTHING ABOUT ME?

ME: NOPE. WE TALKED BOOKS THEN SHE HAD TO GO. SAID SHE'S SEEING A SHOW TONIGHT.

GRANT: WHAT TIME WAS THIS?

ME: MAYBE TWENTY MINUTES AGO?

GRANT: INTERESTING. I THINK SHE HUNG UP WITH ME SO SHE COULD TALK TO YOU ...

ME: AND YOUR POINT?

My question is idiotic. I know his point. He's still on that kick about me "wooing" her so I can keep tabs on her and ensure she doesn't date anyone else while she's in town.

GRANT: TEXT HER AND ASK HER TO HANG OUT THIS WEEKEND.

I place my phone aside, followed by my copy of *The Alchemist*, and I walk away. Grant can get really fucking persistent sometimes, and I'm not in the mood tonight.

Vegas is the antithesis of my scene, but the poor bastard is hurting and duty calls, even if I have to ignore the fact that he claimed Brie was the love of his life yet still had his hands down Serena's pants while simultaneously scheming to fuck Brie over with the prenup. Multitasking at its finest.

I retire my judgement.

It's not my place to play judge and jury.

But I'd be lying if I said I wasn't happy she dumped his ass.

Brie deserves better.

She deserves someone more like ... me.

29

Brie

"EXCUSE ME. I ordered this without mayo and it's drenched …" A skinny blonde in a silk Boho duster and knee-high boots slaps her deli sandwich on the counter Tuesday morning. "Hello? Does anybody work here?"

She scoffs and checks her phone before rising on her toes and flagging down a poor deli worker slicing a hunk of turkey breast.

"Hey! You," she calls to him. He pretends not to hear her. Turning to me, she rolls her eyes. "They act like their job is so damn hard. Maybe a—"

She stops speaking the instant our eyes lock.

"You're Serena, right?" I ask. "From Cainan's party?"

Her Alaskan-blue eyes size me up from top to bottom, but before she can say anything, a middle-aged man in a white apron approaches her from behind the counter. I stand back, averting my gaze as she gives him the what-for over her turkey sandwich on rye. He takes it back without a word, making a show of tossing it in the trash before instructing one of his minions to make her a new one.

"So you live here in the city?" I ask.

"Brooklyn." She watches as a girl who can't be older than eighteen or nineteen makes her a dry turkey replacement sandwich. No cheese. No condiments. As soon as she wraps it in brown paper, Serena peels her stare from that direction and steals a glance at my hands.

I imagine she's looking for my ring—for proof that the engagement is officially over.

"Here you go." The young girl hands Serena her sandwich, and just like that, she's on her way. Not so much as a *see you around* or *nice running into you.*

Weird ...

I refuse to take it personally, given the fact that she knows nothing about me other than the fact that I was once engaged to a man she knows.

Ten minutes later, I dive into my soup and salad combo at a table-for-two.

Wonder what Cainan is up to today...

ME: I FINISHED DORIAN GRAY OVER THE WEEKEND. ALSO JUST RAN INTO SERENA AT THE HIGH MARKET DELI. SHE COULDN'T GET AWAY FROM ME FAST ENOUGH. I GET THE SENSE THAT SHE AND GRANT HAVE A HISTORY?;-)

CAINAN: YOU HANG AROUND THIS CITY LONG ENOUGH AND YOU'LL REALIZE THAT EVERYONE "HAS A HISTORY" WITH GRANT FORSYTHE.

ME: DAMN. AND HERE I THOUGHT I'D JOINED SOME EXCLUSIVE CLUB.

ME: WHEN CAN I RETURN YOUR BOOK? DO YOU HAVE AN AFTER-HOURS DROP BOX?

CAINAN: I'LL BE AROUND SATURDAY MORNING IF YOU WANT TO SWING BY.

ME: WILL DO …

I check the time and finish my lunch so I can get back to the office for my one o'clock Skype meeting. It isn't until I'm boarding the elevator and riding it to the tenth floor that the ache in my cheeks pulls my fingers upward.

Holy crap. I'm grinning like an idiot.

I wipe the ridiculous expression off my face, compose myself, and duck into my office to check a few emails before the meeting starts. While I'm at it, I make a note on my calendar to return the book to Cainan on Saturday morning.

Not that I'll forget …

Something tells me it's all I'm going to think about for the next four days.

Even if I shouldn't.

30

CAINAN

BRIE SHOWS up shortly before eleven Saturday morning. "Feel like a walk? It's *gorgeous* outside."

It's gorgeous inside too—the credit all hers.

Satin waves the color of dark chocolate frame her face, and her emerald irises light from within as she bites a smile and hands me the book she borrowed.

She isn't wrong. It's a fine October day. Crisp weather. Not too breezy. Trees turning the color of olives and rust and burnished gold, painting picturesque autumn portraits along every avenue.

"Fine." I tease her with a wink as I grab a jacket and slip into a pair of sneakers—not unlike Mr. Rogers, though I'm a tad sexier if I do say so myself.

I place the book aside and lock up on the way out.

The instant we hit the sidewalk, the breeze brings me her perfume—a simultaneously sweet and dark number.

"What do you think of city life so far?" I ask as we head north, hands in our pockets, ambling ahead with destination-less strides.

"Definitely different than popping in once a month," she says. "But, it's also everything I expected and more. Sometimes I feel like I'm just some character living out a fantasy."

"You're giving this place way more credit than it deserves. It's not *that* dreamy."

"Tell that to my inner teenager who can't stop walking around Maya's apartment like I'm Carrie Bradshaw." She chuckles under her breath and tucks a loose lock behind one ear, revealing a single dimple.

"Who's that?"

She shoots me a look. "Please tell me you're joking."

I shake my head.

"Carrie Bradshaw," she says the name harder. "Sex and the City ..."

Shrugging, I shake my head once more. "You're going to have to be more specific than that."

"It was this show from, like, twenty years ago. My sisters used to let me watch it when I was probably *way* too young," I say. "It was about these four best friends who lived in Manhattan and they had these crazy love lives."

"Ah." I recall a handful of billboards around the city and the occasional tour bus showing four middle-aged women dressed in outdated clothing. "I think I know what you're talking about now."

"I'd tell you to binge it, but something tells me it's not your kind of show."

"I don't really watch TV."

"Oh." She rolls her eyes, though I get the sense she's kidding. "You're one of *those*."

"My parents didn't believe in TV growing up, so we never had one. When I got to college, I was too busy to even care about what was on TV, and it wasn't something that interested me. I moved to the city right after finishing law school, and I've been building my career ever since. I can't imagine sitting down and doing nothing but staring at a screen like a zombie. I'd much rather be staring at a book."

"I love that about you," she says as we round the corner. As soon as she realizes what she said, her cheeks turn rosy and without hesitating, she adds, "Grant said you're not on social media either."

Trying to change the subject?

"Correct. Tried it. Hated it." I don't get into the whole hacked-by-a-psycho-ex thing because it's neither here nor there. "I've never understood the obsession with other people's lives. Who the hell cares what some random person from your high school is up to these days? I'd much rather be living my life than watching everyone else live theirs."

"I don't disagree with you," she says. "Though sometimes when you come from a large family, it's just easier to keep in touch on a website. If my sisters want to post pictures of their kids, it's easier to post them there than to send out two dozen text messages."

"I suppose," I say. "Guess I wouldn't know what that's like."

She's quiet for a beat.

"You have a sister, right? Claire?"

"Yep."

"And you said your parents didn't believe in TV? That must have been an interesting childhood."

I chuff. "To say the least."

"What else didn't they believe in?"

"You name it," I say. "Christmas, birthdays ... getting along with each other for more than five seconds at a time."

She flinches. "I'm sorry."

"Don't be. They were assholes. And I haven't seen or spoken to them in over a decade," I say. "I've moved on. Life's too short to hold onto the past."

"Do you ever miss them?"

"Hard no." I'm not even sure if they're still living in Jersey. Don't know. Don't care.

"What about your sister? Does she still talk to them?" she asks.

I shake my head. "She invited them to her wedding a few years ago, only because it seemed like the right thing to do. They RSVP'd yes—and then they no-showed. I ended up walking her down the aisle."

"Wow."

We finish the current block in silence.

"What's your family like?" I change the subject.

"Big," she says. "Loud. Opinionated. Traditional. They could make a sitcom out of us. My parents have been married almost forty years and still adore each other like lovesick teenagers. I have three older sisters ... Carly, Alana, and Megan. We lost Kari five years ago. Carly has three kids. All teenagers. Alana is pregnant with baby number five and due any day. Megan is the most indecisive soul you'll ever meet in your entire life. She's had four fiancés and six careers in three states over the last ten years. My family can be intense, and we've had our fair share of disharmony, but there's never been a shortage of love."

"Sounds nice"

She pulls in a slow breath. "Yeah. It is."

"You miss them?"

Brie smirks. "Not yet."

We round the next block. Up ahead a hot dog vendor gabs into his phone, and the scent of all-beef franks fills the air.

"Confession time," Brie says, "I really love hot-dog cart hot dogs—also I'm really hungry right now because I skipped breakfast—so I'm going to get one. Please reserve any and all judgement. I don't know what's in the water, and I don't want to know what's in the water."

My blood turns cold, cracking like ice in my veins. The dream comes around again. This small detail about her isn't news to me in the least.

Before I have a chance to respond, she's ordering.

"You want one?" Brie turns back to me. "You know you do …"

"I'm good. Thanks." I wave her off and shove my hands in my pockets, hardly able to feel them.

For a moment, I'm not sure if any of this is real.

What if *this* is a dream?

She returns with a steaming hot dog slathered in ketchup and mustard and a handful of napkins. We take a seat on a nearby bench. A city bus roars past us, as well as pockets of people, many of them tourists snapping pictures as they draw closer to Central Park.

"So what are you reading these days?" she asks between bites.

"Contracts. Mostly."

"No. For fun."

"Just finished *The Alchemist* for the fourth time," I say.

She slaps my shoulder. "See! I told you it's amazing."

"*So I love you because the entire universe conspired to help me find you.*" The line has been resonating in my mind lately.

Brie nearly chokes on her bite. "What?"

"It's a line from the book …" Oops. Maybe I should've thought about my choice better.

The color returns to her face. "Ah. I've only read it once. I guess maybe if I were an overachiever who'd read it four times, I'd have known that …"

"I'm hardly an overachiever. Intense maybe—if something captures my interest. Overachiever, nah."

"That sounds exactly like the kind of line my sister, Kari, would've tattooed on herself." Brie takes a small bite. "She had eight of them. My parents only knew of three."

"You have any tattoos?" I steal a glance at her wrist, half-expecting there to be something this time despite knowing it's impossible.

She sits up taller. "Nope. Too permanent."

"Afraid of commitment?" Seems like a safe bet to me, given the status of her engagement.

Brie gives me side eye, glancing up through a fringe of dark lashes. "No need to analyze it. They're just not my thing."

A dab of ketchup rests on the side of her mouth. I swipe it away with the back of my thumb before stealing one of her napkins to clean myself.

I had to touch her. *Needed* to touch her. I couldn't resist.

I wanted to know if she's real.

If this moment is real.

We linger on the park bench long after her lunch is finished, chatting books and art, travel and history. I've never considered myself talkative or "chatty." I don't tend to speak unless the words about to leave my lips are profound or worthwhile to the listener. But with Brie, the conversation flows. The words don't stop. I want to tell her everything about me. And I want to know everything about her.

It's as though my soul has been waiting for her to come along my entire life.

Now here she is.

What I wouldn't give to make her mine ...

31

Brie

I STEP out of the shower Saturday night to find a text message waiting.

GRANT: HEY, BEAUTIFUL. HOW WAS YOUR DAY? WHAT DID YOU DO?

I wrap a towel around my dripping body and contemplate my response. Do I tell him I returned a book I'd borrowed from his best friend and invited him on a walk? Do I tell him we palled around the city, wandering for hours upon hours with no destination, the conversation flowing like delicious wine? Do I tell him about how we talked about our families? Spent an hour people-watching in Central Park? Do I tell him about the buskers we stopped to listen to on Bleecker Street? Do I tell him about the little Thai place Cainan took me to for dinner? How it was the size of a postage stamp but had the best Som Tam I'd ever tasted?

Do I tell him that being with his best friend inexplicably breathes life into my heart and soul in ways he never could?

I wipe the fog from the mirror, re-secure my towel, and inhale a steamy breath before making my decision.

ME: HAD A GREAT DAY ... WANDERED THE CITY, TRIED A NEW RESTAURANT, WALKED FOR HOURS.

I decide to leave Cainan out of it. I don't want to hurt Grant any more than I already have. I don't want to make him worry about nothing.

Then again, if I'm leaving him out—I know damn well he isn't *nothing*.

32

Cainan

I'M HEADED out to meet a few friends for drinks Saturday night when my phone buzzes in my pocket. My heart stutters in the moments before I read it, half of me hoping it's her.

Maybe she forgot something at my place?

Maybe she has a question?

Maybe she's bored and wants to know what I'm doing tonight despite the fact that we spent the entire damned day together—glued at the proverbial hip yet doing our best to keep our hands to ourselves and our conversation painfully platonic?

But it isn't her.

GRANT: WHAT'S UP? WHAT'D YOU DO TODAY?

I'm not in the business of lying. Not to myself. Not to my best friend.

I'm also not in the business of being a woman-thieving asshole.

But telling Grant that I spent the entirety of the day aimlessly traversing city block after city block because every step away from my neighborhood equaled more time with Brie ... would crush him.

If I told him I saw the city today through her big green eyes, wiped ketchup from her full mouth because I wanted to know what it was like to touch her, if I told him I didn't look at my watch for hours, ignored a handful of phone calls and texts, and gave her my undivided attention because as far as I was concerned, she was the only living, breathing woman in all of Manhattan—it would devastate him.

ME: SHOWED BRIE AROUND THE CITY A BIT. TOOK HER TO THAT THAI PLACE ON SPRING ST.

I decided to go with the cleanest, most scrubbed version of the truth.

A second later, my phone rings.

"Hey," I say to Grant. "Everything okay?"

I cringe at the overt paranoia in my tone. He's going to see through me.

"So," Grant says. "I was texting with Brie a little bit ago. She told me all about her day ... but not once did she mention she spent it with you."

A heavy silence bridges the thousands of miles that span between us, and a lump settles in the back of my throat.

"Why do you think she'd leave that out?" he asks.

I clear my throat. "Your guess is as good as mine. You ready for Vegas?"

I change the subject. It's a cheap move. Desperate too.

"Don't you think that's weird?" he asks. "Why wouldn't she mention you?"

"Who the hell knows. You're reading into it," I say.

He hesitates. "Am I?"

I'm not sure if he's asking the universe a rhetorical question ...

Or if he's asking *me*.

"That trip can't come soon enough," I tell him. "We've got to get her out of your system."

The instant I speak, I know those words aren't meant for him.

33

"THE DOCTOR SAYS she's dilated to a three. Been having contractions all weekend, but they're still a ways apart. We're thinking it'll be any day now," my mother says from her side of the phone Sunday afternoon as I'm leaving an adorable little uptown eatery called Cielo.

Paulina from work invited me for brunch earlier today, but it turned out all she wanted to do was vent about a couple of ladies from the marketing department. For two solid hours, I was nothing more than an earpiece, but at least I got a free meal out of it.

"You might want to pack a bag and start looking at plane tickets just in case," she adds.

"Will do …" I take my time heading home, belly full of sugared sourdough French toast, sous vide egg bites, and Turkish coffee.

Ten minutes later, I'm less than two blocks from Cainan's apartment.

I haven't heard from him since yesterday, when we spent the majority of the day together before going our separate ways. Not that I should expect to hear from him …

He mentioned he was going out with some friends last night. He never got into specifics, and I tamped my intrigue into the ground as I told him I'd see him around.

I debate whether I should take an alternate route, irrationally convinced my thoughts are radiating off me like a nuclear cloud, when my phone distracts me with a text chime and I cross the intersection near his street.

CAINAN: ANY PLANS TODAY?

My heart whooshes in my ears, and a smile tugs at the corners of my lips.

ME: JUST HAD BRUNCH WITH A COLLEAGUE. WHAT'S UP?

CAINAN: THERE'S A VINTAGE BOOK FAIR IN SOHO. WAS THINKING OF HITTING IT UP. YOU INTERESTED?

My insides tangle with my somersaulting stomach.

I wasn't even this excited when Grant proposed …

ME: WHAT TIME?

CAINAN: TWO. I'LL SWING YOUR WAY. WHAT'S YOUR ADDRESS?

I text him the address to Maya's apartment and float home on a cloud, ignoring the voice in the back of my mind warning me not to play with fire, not to knot my heart around a man who can never be mine.

I want this—if only for today.

Maybe we can never be together, but I like the way I feel when we're together; a tranquil warmth melts me from the inside out.

It's much like going home.

Or being completely at peace and in the moment.

There's no noise when I'm with him. No dithering confusion.

I've never had that with anyone else.

And who knows if I ever will again.

34

CAINAN

"I'M FLYING HOME TOMORROW," she tells me as we head toward a little book market on Canal. "My sister, Alana, is about to have her baby."

I didn't intend to invite her along. Usually I hit these things alone, opting to browse in silence, a coffee in hand and the rest of the world leaving me the hell alone until it's time to check out.

But then I found myself texting her.

And when she wrote back right away, I wasn't turned off or annoyed as I would've been with anyone else.

"How long will you be there?" I ask.

"A few days."

My question is multi-pronged. I'd like to know for my own information—but also because I want to know how much of that time is going to be spent in the same city as Grant. She's made it clear she doesn't want to marry him, but people change their minds every day.

I can't count how many clients have backed out of divorces at the last minute, suddenly realizing they can't live without one another for some asinine, unforeseen reason.

The fear of being alone is powerful.

That said, I don't get the desperate-and-lonely vibes from Brie. She's present without being clingy. She listens without being over-the-top laser-focused. She doesn't try to impress me. Nor does she try to paint herself as perfect, the way some people do when they're trying to come across as the ideal match for someone they're into.

I shouldn't waste my time worrying.

She was Grant's first.

And she can never be mine.

But in this small moment, in these quiet afternoon hours with the city half-empty and the sunshine painting the tops of our heads as we stroll the city blocks ... she is mine.

If I can't touch her, if I can't want her, at least I have *this*.

"How much you want to bet Grant will show up at the hospital with flowers?" she asks with a chuckle.

I slide my hands in my front pockets, a feeble move to quell the ache of not being able to slip my arm around her lithe shoulders or rest my palm on the small of her back.

"Is he still trying to get back into your good graces?" I ask.

"That's the thing—he was never out of them. It's not like there's something he can do to magically make me fall in love with him," she says. "I wish he'd understand that instead of ... I don't know ... texting me about every little thing ten times a day. And he still calls me 'babe.' It's almost like he's trying to manipulate me into casually getting back together." She turns to me, placing her hand on my forearm as she walks sideways. "He asked if he could stay with me when he's back in town next week for work. Can you believe that?"

Yes. Yes I can.

"What'd you tell him?" My heart beats faster than it should.

"That I didn't think it was a good idea …" She faces forward, chuffing under her breath. "Come on. You and I both know that if I give this man an inch, he's going to expect a mile."

I exhale, more relieved than I deserve to be.

"Maybe you should stop taking his calls," I say before adding, "as much."

"Yeah. I've thought about that," I say. "But ghosting people isn't my style. It's so juvenile."

"And harassing them into getting back together isn't?"

Brie shoots me a look, though I don't know that she realizes it. I can only assume she's wondering where my loyalties lie and why I'm telling her to ignore my best friend whose heart she recently annihilated.

"Grant gets really fixated on things sometimes. Like a dog with a bone," I say.

"So … I should just yank it out of his mouth and chuck it over the fence?"

I snort. "Something like that, yeah."

We reach our destination—The SoHo Book Collector's Expo—and stop outside a table layered in vinyl-wrapped classics.

"I don't even know why he's into me," she says, tucking a dark strand behind one ear as she traces her fingertips over a copy of Anne of Green Gables. "He's always saying he's never met anyone like me, that he's crazy about me, loves my family, sees a future with me … but it never goes deeper than that, you know? It's superficial. He has to feel it too, right? It can't just be me. He's got to be projecting some fantasy onto me or something. That's the only explanation."

She moves onto the next table, but I stay behind.

Now that she says it, I realize that I've witnessed the same thing. He tells me how wonderful she is and how wild he is about her—but he never says why. And while he looked at her with stars for eyes the first time I saw them together, I've seen divorcing couples more in sync than the two of them.

But if I'm being fair ... love is one of the hardest things to put into words.

Sometimes it's nothing more than a feeling.

Maybe he just looked at her and he *knew*.

"Do I have something in my teeth?" Brie laughs and points to her mouth. I realize now that she'd been talking to me, though I didn't hear a word since I was lost in thought. When she smiles, I realize her front tooth has the tiniest chip in it.

Just like the dream.

"No. Sorry. What were you saying?" I ask.

"I said I think you're right. I need to yank the bone out of his mouth," she says. "When I see him this week, I'm going to tell him to stop contacting me. I think it'll be for the best."

There's a glimmer in her bright green irises. Hope or sunlight, I'm not sure.

Moving onto the next table, she fastens her attention to a small paperback before whipping around to show me.

"Look, it's our book," she says, head tilted and beaming ear to ear as she displays a first edition of *The Alchemist* in all its gold and purple eighties glory.

Our book.

Something that's ours and only ours.

One thing she'll never share with Grant.

Wide-eyed and rising on her toes, she says, "I want to buy it for you."

"You don't have to do that ..."

"Yeah, well I want to. So I am." Brie winks before tucking it beneath one arm and sliding down to the next stack of books. A few minutes later, she chooses two more books—an unauthorized biography on Jackie O. and a Paula Fox tome, and she tells me she's going to read them on the plane this week.

I peel my attention off the poor girl and grab a first edition of Franny and Zooey before following her to the check-out table.

It's barely mid-afternoon when we're done.

"What do you want to do next?" she asks. "Don't suppose I could interest you in a matinee of *Chicago*?"

"I hope you're joking," I tease, though the truth is I'd suffer through *All that Jazz* a hundred times if it meant being next to her a little while longer.

"Actually, I am." She sighs, shoulders turning slack as she subtly swings her canvas bag of books with each step. "I still need to buy my plane ticket for Phoenix, and more than likely I'll be catching a red eye ... which means I need to pack as soon as possible ..."

Brie tilts her attention my way, offering an apologetic squint.

"No worries," I say, hands sliding into my pockets, alive with the dissatisfaction of never knowing what her hair will feel like between my fingers.

I walk her home.

And I intentionally take us the long way.

When we get to her building, we linger outside near the front stoop.

"Are you always so quiet?" she asks.

"Would you rather me be an obnoxious loudmouth?" I tease.

Brie laughs under her breath. "I just feel like I do all the talking when we're together. I hope you don't think it's annoying or anything ..."

Annoying is the last thing I would ever call her.

But I don't tell her that.

I also don't tell her I'm going to miss her.

I don't tell her good luck with Grant—because I want to leave him out of this moment.

And I don't tell her that while no one's ever accused me of talking too much, the reason I'm particularly quiet around her ... is because my head is full of all the things I want to say to her—but can't.

"It's weird, actually. I'm usually pretty quiet around most people. And then when I get around you, I can't shut up for two seconds." She rolls her eyes and brushes a strand of hair off her forehead.

"You worry too much," I tell her.

Brie snorts. "You've clearly been talking to my sister, Carly."

My gaze narrows.

"She's always on my case about how I worry about everything and how I always play things safe and gravitate toward the familiar ..." Brie's words scatter into the autumn breeze that encircles us.

Does she feel it too?

The otherworldly familiarity that draws us together like an invisible thread?

"I had this dream." The sentence leaves my mouth

before I can stop it. "After my accident, I had this dream. There was this woman in it. She looked just like you, and—"

"—I'm so sorry." Brie digs into the bottom of her bag, and I realize now her phone is ringing. "It's my mom. It's probably about my sister. I'm so, *so* sorry to cut you off ... give me one sec."

She takes the call by a park bench several feet away, one finger pressed into her free ear as a firetruck blares a few blocks over.

My heart ricochets and my skin is hot.

The sidewalk slopes.

Or maybe it's just the world, tilting on its axis.

What if I tell her about the dream and she thinks I'm crazy? What if she looks at me the way Claire and Luke did? What if she chalks it up to the accident and brushes it off as a meaningless coincidence?

Mental gibberish.

"Okay, I really hate to do this, but my sister is officially in labor, and I *really* need to book that flight, so I'm going to head in," Brie says when she returns. Climbing the front steps, she turns back. "I want to hear all about that dream when I get back though."

She leaves me to bask in the remains of her soft voice, exuberant smile, and lively emerald eyes before disappearing inside her building.

I walk home with a single thought looping through my mind—if I tell her about the dream, it won't change the fact that we can never be together.

So maybe I'm better off keeping it to myself.

Why make things more complicated?

35

"OH, my goodness, Alana ... he's adorable!" I cradle my sister's newborn son, Bodhi Cassius, in my arms, soaking in how perfect he looks, from his pink skin to the tufts of blond hair on top of his head, to his button nose. "I don't know where all this blond hair came from."

Alana and her exhausted husband, Tucker, exchange weary-eyed yet proud grins.

Their first four came out with full heads of thick, dark hair, pointy noses, and triple chins.

But not this guy.

"The last ones always like to surprise us, don't they?" My mother winks at me from across the room.

My mother had no idea she was pregnant with twins until Kari came out and the doctor told her there was one more behind her ...

My chest tightens when I think of Kari missing this moment.

She was there for all of Carly's births. The first three of Alana's. But she never met Alana's fourth and she'll never meet little Bodhi.

Without waking the baby, I slide my phone from my pocket, snap a picture, and send it to a group of girlfriends. When I'm done, I also send it to Cainan, because even now, in this moment thousands of miles from New York, this moment that has absolutely nothing to do with him ... I can't help but wish he were here.

"Okay, stop hogging. My turn." Megan rubs her hands together before reaching toward us.

"Where's Dad?" I ask, handing him off.

"He ran to grab the pizza," Tucker says.

Ah, yes. *The* pizza. It's a White family tradition. Any time a sister has a baby, their first meal is always pizza from the little place in Scottsdale where Mom and Dad had their first date four decades ago. Once the manager casually mentioned to my father he was thinking of shuttering the doors so he could retire—which is when my dad promptly made a phone call and found a buyer on the spot.

"Knock, knock ..." A man stands in the doorway, obscured by a massive floral arrangement chock full of every kind of blue flower in existence. Hydrangea. Hyacinth. Forget-me-nots. Morning glories. Cornflowers ...

As soon as he lowers it, my mood sinks.

"Grant!" Mom rises from her chair and throws her arms around him, like she hasn't seen him in decades. "So glad you could make it!"

"The big guy called a little bit ago and gave me the news," he says. "I was in the area, so I thought I'd stop by for a bit."

The big guy.

So it was my *dad* who spilled the beans ...

My dad who also knew that I was here.

"Brie, hi." He pulls away from my mother, gaze fixed on me as if he's seeing me for the first time all over again. "Wasn't sure if you'd be here or not."

Right …

I stand and give him a hug because everyone's watching and I'm not about to make Alana's moment about me in any way, shape, or form.

"So good to see you, babe." Grant squeezes me tight, and for longer than necessary. "Looking amazing. As always."

Now I know that isn't true.

I literally hopped off the plane, found a crowded restroom on the other side of security, tied my greasy hair back, and freshened up before ordering an Uber and making a beeline for the hospital.

"Thanks for the flowers, Grant," Alana says from the bed. "So thoughtful of you."

"Here, take my chair." Megan stands, Bodhi still cradled in her arms, and offers Grant her chair before handing my nephew off to his mother.

Grant wastes no time claiming the spot next to where I was seated, and he lifts his brows as he waits for me to sit back down.

"You know, I'm actually going to grab something to drink from the cafeteria. Anyone want anything? Megan? Alana? Mom? Tuck?" I scan the room, waiting for orders that never come.

"I could use a coffee actually," Grant says. "Mind if I tag along?"

I offer a cordial nod and force some semblance of a smile, and he follows out the door and down the hall. We pass the nursery before we get to the elevator, and he stops for a moment to gaze inside.

"Can't wait to have one of our own someday," he says, though I'm not sure if he's speaking to himself or to me.

One of our own ...

I think of Cainan's words, about Grant being like a dog with a bone. And I think of my promise to yank that bone and toss it over the fence. I didn't want to do it here, on the maternal recovery floor of Phoenix General, but I'm going on about four hours of sleep and my self-control is waning.

"I could really use some caffeine ..." I point to the elevator.

He peels his gaze from the sleeping babes. "Right. Sorry."

We ride to the main level beside a pair of grandparents wearing "visitor" stickers that match ours, and Grant stands so close to me I can smell his cinnamon toothpaste. As soon as we disembark, I inhale a lungful of sterilized hospital air and walk two steps ahead of him.

"Babe. Wait up. What's the hurry?" Grant trots behind me, his dress shoes scuffing the floor with each step.

I stop in my tracks and turn to face him. "I can't do this."

He frowns.

"You're smothering me," I blurt.

A thirty-something pregnant woman in a hospital gown shuffles past, elbowing her husband as he gawks at our mini scene.

"You call me every day. You text me multiple times a day. You still call me babe," I say. "And then you showed up at the hospital."

"Your father invited me ..." his words are slow and careful.

"You and I both know why he invited you." A table full of nurses in pink scrubs, all of them lunching on colorful salads, peer our way. "I broke up with you last month. We're over. And nothing you can say or do is going to change that. Please leave me alone."

"Leave you alone?" he scoffs. "Is that what you really want?"

"Yes." It takes all the self-control I have not to scream it from the rooftops.

"This is about Cainan." He *laughs*. Not the reaction I was expecting. "Of course."

"Not sure I follow ..."

"You like him," Grant says, confidence infused in his tone.

"What are you talking about?"

"The other day when I asked what you were up to, you told me all about your day ... but you neglected to mention you spent it with my best friend," he says. "But he didn't. He told me he spent the day with you. He told me every single detail. And you know why? Because he's keeping tabs on you for me, just like I asked."

I try to respond, but my brain is stuck trying to wrap itself around this information.

All this time, my interactions with Cainan have felt natural, genuine, and unforced. But they've also been ... convenient. He's always there. He's always available. And when we spend time together, minutes turn into hours.

"He wouldn't do that," I finally say, though who am I trying to convince?

He knows Cainan better than anyone.

"Really? He's my *best friend*, Brie. You seriously think he'd be into *you*?" Grant chuffs. And with that, everything that has kept me walking on a cloud these past few weeks sends me into a free fall back to earth. "Sorry to break your heart, *babe*. Unfortunately I know exactly what that feels like."

With that, he leaves.

By the time he disappears from view, my phone vibrates in my pocket with a text.

CAINAN: CONGRATS!

I shove my phone away, grab a coffee, and make my way back up to my sister's suite, praying Grant's gone by the time I get there.

And he is, thank goodness.

But the blue flowers remain.

Along with freshly-planted seeds of doubt.

36

"EXPECTING AN IMPORTANT CALL?" Claire asks Thursday night at dinner.

"No." I glance beyond the salt and pepper grinders that separate us. "Why?"

"You keep checking your phone. Like every thirty seconds. Seriously." She reaches across the table in a feeble attempt to swipe it from me. "It's like you're not even here. Why'd you invite me out to dinner if you're just going make me sit here and watch you wait for some phone call that's obviously not coming. Unless it's the Secretary of State or Angelina Jolie, I'm going to have to ask you to holster your weapon, sir."

She's right—the call isn't coming.

It's Friday, and as far as I know, Brie's been back since Wednesday. Monday morning, she sent me a picture of her baby nephew. I responded almost immediately.

And then ... nothing.

I'm trying not to read into it, trying not to assume she had a change of heart and found herself back in the arms of the man she claimed she couldn't love if she tried. But I can't ignore the images of the two of them. Images that flood my vision every time I close my eyes at night, every time I check my phone for a new text.

I wouldn't be so paranoid if it weren't for the fact that Grant's been quiet this week as well.

Not normal.

None of this is fucking normal.

Then again, neither is obsessing like a lunatic over a woman you know damn well you can't have.

"*Cainan* ..." Claire groans. "Put. It. Away."

I slide my phone into my pocket, draw in a long breath, and browse the drink menu. But the options before me are all just a bunch of letters jumbled together. None of them make sense.

Nothing makes sense.

"Hey. Stop bouncing your knee. You're shaking the table." Claire flags down our server. "Can we get a couple of shots STAT? Vodka or something? I don't care. Just bring us whatever. We're not picky."

The waitress comes back in record time, two shot glasses filled to the brim with clear liquor.

Claire shoves them both toward me.

"I'm not drinking both of them," I say, shoving one back.

"Like hell you are. I can't. I'm pregnant."

I choke on my spit. "What?!"

"Surprise!" She grins wide, her fingers splayed into perfect jazz-hands.

"Then why'd you order a shot?"

"I'm sorry ... I think you said *congratulations, Claire?*"

"Jesus." Realizing the errors of my way, I shove myself

up from the table and wrap my little sister in a tight hug despite the fact that we've never been huggers. "Congrats, Claire. I'm happy for you."

"Thanks ..." she says as I let her go. "We actually just found out this morning. I'm not that far along. Six weeks or so. Total surprise."

I take my seat.

She looks like a terrified woman wearing the cheap mask of exuberance, but I keep that to myself, opting instead to inform her she's glowing already.

"Seriously though, why'd you order a second shot?" I ask.

"Because you looked like you needed it. Bottoms up ..."

She isn't wrong.

I shoot the first. I shoot the second. Within minutes, my skin crawls with heat and the room tilts.

"So what's going on?" she asks, elbows on the table as she settles in closer. "What's with all this nervous energy? I'm getting a vibe from you ..."

I roll my eyes. "You sound like Luke. Where is he anyway?"

"Meeting with some volunteers at his foundation's headquarters. And don't try to change the subject again. I'm the sober one here, and I'm fully prepared to interrogate the hell out of you if I have to." She smirks and pushes the drink menu in my direction. "Though we should probably order an appetizer. I want you spilling your guts, not puking in the alley."

I gather my thoughts, let the vodka course through my veins a few minutes more, and then I give her exactly what she wants—the unfiltered truth.

"Remember when you told me not to fall for my best friend's girl?" I ask.

Claire's jaw falls.

"Yeah, well. I didn't listen." Not that I could control any of it.

"Oh my God." She claps a hand over her mouth. "This is bad."

"I know."

"What are you going to do?"

"I don't know."

"Does Grant know?" she asks.

"Nope."

"Are you going to tell him?" Claire leans in, brows lifted.

"I don't even know if it's worth it. For all I know, she only sees me as a friend." I glance around the restaurant in search of our lavender-haired waitress who delivered the vodka shots and seemingly disappeared, never to be seen or heard from again.

My sister frowns. "Do you really believe that?"

"Not entirely."

"So you think there's something there? Something mutual?"

"We've been spending time together. And there's definitely a connection."

She sinks back, resting her chin on the top of her hand as she examines me the way I examine my clients when I feel like I'm not getting the full story.

But her scrutiny is for naught. This is it.

It's as simple as it is complicated.

As serendipitous as it is fucked up.

For the first time in our lives, Claire leaves me without a shred of advice. She tells me the situation is beyond saving, beyond fixing. She tells me I'm damned if I go for it, damned if I don't. She tells me no matter what decision I make, someone I care deeply about is going to be destroyed, the trajectory of their life forever changed.

"I wish I had a magic wand so I could fix this for you," Claire says, head tilted and eyes laced with sympathy. "I'll just say this ... you're my brother, I love you, and I want you to be happy. And whether that means sacrificing your happiness for your best friend's happiness or making a move for the woman who sets your soul on fire—I'm with you either way."

Yawning, she rises from her chair and gives me a hug.

"I'm heading home," she says an hour later, after three small plates and a shared tiramisu. "I'm exhausted. *You've* exhausted me with all of this soap opera nonsense."

"Or maybe you're just, I don't know, pregnant? And that's why you're so tired?"

"Nah. It's definitely your love life wearing me the eff out." She squeezes my shoulder, slings her bag over her arm, and shows herself out. I grab the tab and hit the bar for one last drink before heading home.

Sipping my last whiskey of the night—and against my better judgement—I text Brie one more time.

ME: YOU BACK IN TOWN YET? JUST SEEING WHAT YOU'RE UP TO THIS WEEKEND ...

The message shows as read almost immediately.

I wait for three blue dots that never come.

On the way home, I detour past her apartment like a goddamned stalker. The lights are on. Her silhouette moves from room to room, the curtains all pulled.

So close, yet a world away ...

... until I make a decision I may or may not come to regret.

Tonight, I'm going to say to Brie what I should've said a long time ago.

37

BRIE

THE BUZZER to my door rings as I prepare a cup of Sleepytime Tea. After spending a few days in Phoenix, it's taking me longer than I expected to settle back into my New York routine. The clock on the microwave shows a quarter past eleven.

It's got to be a mistake.

I'm not expecting anyone.

I toss the tea bag in the garbage, tiptoeing down the hall, when the buzzer goes off again.

And again.

Exhaling, I shuffle to the intercom system. "Can I help you?"

"Brie." I recognize Cainan's voice instantly. "We need to talk."

A half an hour ago, he sent me a text—which I ignored. As I did the other texts he sent this week ...

Despite the fact that ghosting isn't my style, I've found

myself paralyzed every time I try to think of a response. Maybe it's my pride getting in the way. All week, I've felt silly for getting caught up in whatever this was.

Or whatever this wasn't.

I let myself crush on a man I knew I could never have—all the while, he was playing me. At least, that's what Grant insists. And given what I know of Cainan, I have no reason to believe he would ever betray his best friend by hooking up with his ex.

He buzzes me again.

"If you're here to keep tabs on me, you can let Grant know I made it home safe." I'm being facetious, I know. But I can't help myself.

"Brie, buzz me up. Please. Let's talk." He slurs a couple of his words.

"I don't have anything to say to you."

"Fair enough," he says. "But you might want to listen to what I've got to say."

38

Cainan

"WHY HAVE YOU BEEN IGNORING ME?" Is probably not the best way to greet a woman I had to beg to buzz me up. But the words are out. There's no taking them back.

The floor is slanted, so I brace myself in her doorway.

"Good God. How much have you had to drink?" She hooks her hand into my arm and pulls me in, closing the door without letting me go. "You can barely stand."

Too much to exercise good judgement apparently.

Not enough to numb a damn thing.

"Sit down." She drags me to a velvet chair in the living room the color of electric raspberries. And then she wanders off to the kitchen, returning with a bottle of water. "Grant told me everything." Brie paces, hands on her hips. "I know you've been keeping tabs on me this whole time. I feel like such an idiot for thinking we actually had a connection ..."

Holy shit.

She felt it too.

It wasn't wishful thinking.

It wasn't just me.

"I haven't been *keeping tabs* on you," I say. "I would never. I ... Brie ... *I'm falling for you.* That's why I can't stay away. That's why I find every excuse to be around you, even if we're wandering around the city doing nothing at all. Even if I'm re-reading the same book for the millionth time because it's the only way I can feel closer to you without hating myself for it."

She's speechless, squinting or glaring at me—I can't tell.

"You chipped your front tooth when you were twelve. You have to get it fixed every few years ... Christmas is your favorite holiday ...Your hair gets frizzy in the summer ... Greece is at the top of your bucket list ... "

Brie blinks twice, head tilted, and then she frowns.

"Okay, Casanova, maybe you should lie down and sleep this off." She leads me to the sofa, slides off my leather shoes, and covers me with a knitted throw she grabs from who-knows-where.

A moment later, the lights go out, and everything fades to black.

In the middle of the night, I stir awake, eyes barely opening to catch a glimpse of her watching me from the bedroom doorway, her white t-shirt bathed in moonlight.

But for all I know, I'm dreaming.

39

I DIDN'T SLEEP last night. If I did, I don't remember it. I spent the majority of those midnight hours wracking my brain about all those things he spouted off about me, things I rambled off as I held his hand and tried my damnedest to keep him from fading away. I thought if he could just hear my voice, maybe he'd stay with me. So I talked for the sake of talking. I told him every little thing about me that I could possibly think of.

The fact that he remembered it is one thing.

The fact that he knew about my chipped tooth—is something else entirely.

I never told him about that.

I'm one-hundred percent certain.

It's a middle school memory I don't tend to bring up—and one I didn't so much as share with Grant during the tenure of our relationship.

There's no verifiable way Cainan could've known about it.

I wait until half past seven before making my way to the kitchen, desperate for coffee but not wanting to wake my guest from his liquor-induced slumber.

Only he isn't sleeping.

He's perched on the sofa, slipping into his shoes.

"Busted," I say.

Cainan peers up. "Excuse me?"

"You were just going to slip out of here and pretend last night never happened?"

His handsome face is painted in confusion, and he drags a hand through mussed hair.

"You don't remember last night, do you?" I ask.

"I'm sorry." He winces. "I don't."

"Convenient." I shrug. "Want to stay for a coffee? Maybe rehash things for a hot minute before you bolt?"

"I can't tell if you're being sarcastic. If you want me to go, just say so." He rises, his shirt wrinkled and his hair a mess, and yet somehow he still makes my breath hitch in my chest until I glance away.

"Stay." My back is toward him as I scoop coffee grounds into the shiny silver machine on Maya's counter.

"Brie ..." He clears his throat. "I want to sincerely apologize for anything I said or did last night that made you uncomfortable. I've never blacked out before ..."

"First time for everything."

The machine percolates, not unlike my thoughts or the cocktail of confusing emotions simmering beneath my skin.

After almost a week of being ignored, Cainan got hammered and showed up at my door.

That has to mean something ...

Unless he was just doing his due diligence as Grant Forsythe's best friend.

I pour two cups, remembering that he takes his black. And when I turn to hand him his coffee, I'm taken back to that day at Atlantis, when we sat down together for the first time and the world around us faded into background noise.

At least it did for me.

"Grant told me he asked you to keep tabs on me while I'm here," I say.

"He did."

Wow. Just like that, he isn't even going to try to deny it.

The wind is knocked from my lungs. My hand grips the mug until my palm burns.

"It all makes sense now," I say. "Why you've been so helpful. So readily available. So willing to sacrifice your weekends keeping me entertained. Shame on me for thinking we had a connection."

I take a sip and taste nothing but bitterness.

I don't drink my coffee black, but I'm too grounded in the moment to flit about the kitchen grabbing sugar and creamer like some effervescent cool girl who doesn't give a damn—because I do give a damn.

I liked him.

A lot.

And now I feel like a fool.

"We did have a connection," he says. "We do."

"How do you expect me to believe you when you just admitted Grant asked you to keep an eye on me?"

"Because he asked me," Cainan says. "But I never agreed to do it."

"So all that time we spent together, you did it because you *wanted* to?" Half of me wants to believe him. The other half has her heels in the ground.

His loyalty is to his lifelong best friend—not me.

For all I know, he's trying his damnedest to keep this whole thing going for Grant's sake.

He nods. "Yes."

"How did you know about my chipped tooth?" I ask while it's still fresh in my spinning mind.

He almost says something. And then he stops himself. "It's ... it's going to sound crazy."

I hook a hand on my hip, drinking my coffee. "Try me ..."

"I'm going to need you to have an open mind." He narrows his gaze at me, his tone colored in reluctance.

"Okay."

Sucking in a deep breath, he begins, "Remember when you asked me about the craziest thing I ever did?"

I narrow my gaze, nodding.

"After my accident, I dreamt of you. I don't know if that counts because I didn't do it on purpose. It just ... happened. But I did it. Technically speaking. *I dreamt of you, Brie.*" He watches me, maybe searching for a reaction. But I give him nothing. I need to see where he's going with this. "We were on this beach together. We had two kids. We were married. And when I woke up, I knew things about you. Little things. Things I couldn't explain. Your favorite authors, for instance. I knew them before you told me that day on the sidewalk."

I draw in a slow sip of coffee before exhaling and wrapping both hands around the mug. "When you were in your accident ... when we were waiting for the paramedics and you were clinging to your life ... I held your hand and talked to you. I told you a bunch of random things about me ... which is probably why you saw me in your dream and how you knew those things about me when you woke up. But that doesn't explain how you knew about my chipped tooth ... I didn't tell you that."

He doesn't blink. "I told you. It sounds crazy."

"It sounds crazy because it *is* crazy."

"Give me a pen and paper."

"Why?"

He motions his hand like he wants to draw something. "There was something else in my dream. Maybe you can make sense of it."

I tug open the junk drawer, retrieving a small legal pad and a blue gel pen for him.

Without wasting a second, he sketches a small drawing, rips the paper from the binding, and hands it to me.

"Oh my God." I take a step back.

"You need to go," I tell him.

"What does it mean?" His hazel eyes widen.

"*Now*." I point to the door. "Please. Go."

"Brie ... if you know what this means. You have to tell me ..."

I blink through tear-clouded vision and swallow the

lump in my throat, though I don't particularly feel like I owe him an explanation. "My sister's name was Karielle. My name is Brielle. A few months before she died, we were supposed to get matching 'elle' tattoos. I chickened out. She didn't."

My sister's final Facebook photo comes to mind—Kari grinning, her cheek resting against the inside of her hand, her wrist facing the camera and her tattoo displayed in perfect detail.

I'll never forget that image ... or the pangs of guilt I feel over never following through with my end of our agreement.

My stomach twists. I'm going to be sick.

"I can't believe you would do something like that," I speak through clenched teeth and fight the wave of tears that threaten to fall. "After everything I told you ..."

I think back to the night of his party, sharing with him my confession about wasting thousands of dollars on so-called psychics as an attempt to connect with my dead sister.

I was conned by each and every one of them.

And now I've been conned by him—the biggest con of them all.

"Leave." I can't look at him anymore.

"Brie, if—"

"*Get out.*" I don't recognize this shrill, pain-filled version of my voice, not at first.

By the time I do ... he's gone.

40

Cainan

I TRUDGE home with a hammering headache. In a mental fog. Numb. Replaying Brie's reaction to the tattoo again and again in my mind and growing more confused each time.

The tears in her eyes.

The pain in her voice.

"I can't believe you would do something like that ..." her words are fresh in my ears—and they make zero sense.

Does she think I knew about the tattoo somehow? That I'm attempting to manipulate her like some con man trying to scam his way into her heart?

I never should have told her about the dream. I never should have believed her when she said she'd have an open mind. My own sister couldn't even have an open mind when I told her about it.

By the time I'm home, I'm deflated and empty. I imagine this is what it feels like when you bet the house and lose your entire life savings. It was a calculated risk, sharing the dream with her and knowing damn well I was going to sound like a crazy person, but I was so sure it would pay off that I just went for it.

I kick my shoes off, draw the curtains, and collapse in a heap on the sofa. Pinching the bridge of my nose, I drag in a ragged breath.

I knew I couldn't be with her before, but at least I could've kept her in my life.

Now I can't have her at all.

I close my eyes and try to force myself back to sleep. I can't stand to be awake another minute with these thoughts.

Or my new reality.

41

Brie

"GUESS who's golfing with Dad right now?" Megan asks Saturday morning.

Moments after I sent Cainan packing, she rang my phone and told me she's coming into town next weekend to visit.

A divine intervention.

I didn't tell her what had happened. I didn't tell her about the tattoo or the chipped tooth. I'm still trying to wrap my head around it and make sense of it. Still wondering if I overreacted or if my inclinations that he was attempting to scam me were spot on.

"Sounds like I need to have another talk with both of them." I sip my coffee, which is now cold. I stick it in the microwave for thirty seconds. When it's done, I pour it down the drain. I don't want that cup anymore.

"Honestly, it's getting to be a little much. It's like Carly and Alana's husbands are chopped liver and Grant's the son he never had." She exhales. "And Mom invites him over for dinner at least once a week …"

I groan.

"Please. Make it stop," she begs.

"I had a talk with him last week at the hospital." To be fair, it was more of a verbal lashing than a talk. But after all the pestering, the man had it coming. And I thought it'd worked. I thought I'd gotten through to him … because I haven't heard from him since. "I guess I can talk to him again?"

"Also, I didn't want to tell you this … and I'm still a little weirded out by it … but I ran into him a few weeks ago at this nightclub downtown. We said hi. Whatever. Then he bought me a drink. And from the rest of the night on, he was hanging all over me."

"Hanging all over you?"

"Yeah. Putting his hand on the small of my back. Leaning close. Trying to flirt." She sounds like she's about to gag. "The whole thing left this really bad taste in my mouth. He was definitely trying to take things beyond … where they needed to be."

"Ugh. Megs. I'm so sorry. I'll talk to him again. And I'll talk to Mom. And Dad." I slide onto a counter stool and rest my cheek against my hand.

"There's more."

"There's more?" I sit straighter.

"I overheard Mom and Dad talking, and it sounds like Dad's about to transfer a bunch of his accounts to Grant's firm."

My blood turns to ice, and I almost drop the phone.

Is that all he wanted? All this time? My father's

accounts? Did he research me before our first date and figure out exactly who my father was? Anyone with half a brain cell in the Phoenix area has heard of him, has seen his billboards, has lived in one of his custom homes or apartments, or leased an office building.

My father has secured a place on the Forbes 500 every year for the past decade—it's public knowledge. And for someone like Grant, working in the financial sector, it's likely common knowledge, too.

"Brie? You still there?" Meg asks.

"Yeah. Yeah, I'm still here. Just thinking ..."

Everything makes sense now—how perfect Grant seemed. The way he treated me like a queen. Proposing to me so quickly, desperate to lock me down as soon as possible. The prenup.

Oh my God.

The prenup that Cainan drafted for him.

The letter mentioned clauses they'd discussed ... was Cainan in on this too?

Was this entire thing nothing more than a way to access my family's money? To swindle me any way they could? Did they run extensive background checks? Dig up every convincing detail they could find?

My throat constricts and my mouth is dry. A wave of emotions floods through me, but I force it away because if Meg hears one hitch in my voice, she'll demand to know what's going on, and I don't want to talk about any of this right now.

"Sweets, I'm going to grab a shower," I say. "Text me your flight details, okay? Can't wait to see you ..."

We end the call and I sit in stunned silence, staring at a humming refrigerator until the seven o'clock hour turns into something closer to nine.

Later this afternoon, when my dad and Grant should be done golfing, I'll compose myself. Make the call. And ensure damn well my father knows exactly the kind of person he's dealing with.

After this, I want nothing to do with Grant.

And nothing to do with Cainan.

42

Cainan

"*HEYYYY, ASSHOLE.*" Grant is hammered when I arrive at our penthouse suite Friday night. I drop my leather duffel and let the door float close. "About fucking time."

Every word is slurred and exaggerated. If I recall, his flight landed at one PM. It's now five. He's been drinking for hours. He tries to stand to greet me, only to slump back over on the overstuffed sofa. Giggling.

Giggling ...

It's going to be a long weekend.

But maybe it's for the best.

I haven't seen nor heard from Brie since last Saturday, when I drew the tattoo and I met a side of her I never knew existed as she told me to leave with tears in her eyes. I gave her a few days. Thought maybe she needed some space. Some time to calm down. I texted her Tuesday night, asking if we could talk.

She replied immediately with four axis-tilting words: DON'T CONTACT ME AGAIN.

"Grab a beer, asshole." Grant points to the fridge in the kitchen.

Beyond the window behind him, the Vegas lights glimmer and shine. The city is alive.

It's a feeling I haven't known in quite some time—aside from the time I spent with Brie, when everything felt Technicolor and animated in a way it never had before.

I hopped on my flight earlier today with every intention of breaking myself out of this, of convincing myself that whatever I thought we were destined to have was an unrealistic pipe dream that never would've worked out anyway.

But the instant the wheels touched down at McCarran International, I woke from my half-assed nap and discovered I was the same pathetic sap I was when I boarded the plane.

The hotel door swings open as I help myself to a beer from the overstocked fridge, and a handful of guys come in. I don't recognize two of them. I assume they're friends of his from Phoenix.

"What's up, man?" One of them gives our man of the hour a sloppy high five. He reeks of hard liquor when he passes me.

"Please tell me I didn't come all the way here for a goddamned sausage party," another one says.

"The girls are on their way," Collin Hilliard, a guy we've kept in touch with from our days at Montclair, squeezes behind me and grabs a can of Coors Light. "Good to see you, man. Heard about your accident. Sorry I couldn't come to your party, but hey, you're looking good. Feeling good?"

I twist the top of my beer and nod. "Yep. All good."

Lies. In every sense of the word. But it doesn't matter.

"What've you been up to?" he asks. "Still helping rich, miserable couples realize their dreams?"

"Every day. You?"

"Took over my dad's insurance agency a couple years ago. Becca and I just had our first kid a year ago," he says. "I'd show you pics, but I don't want the last thing we see before getting a lap dance to be my daughter's face."

Gross.

And agreed.

"No worries." I squeeze his shoulder and head toward the living room part of the suite, finding a chair by the window. Out of habit, I check my phone. Two texts from a couple of friends back in the city. Four new work emails. Nothing from Brie. Naturally.

The next knock at the door sends Grant to his feet, knocking over miniature glass bottles of vodka onto the expensive-looking rug in the process.

"It's the girls," Grant announces, like the horny frat boy he used to be.

Ten seconds later, the hotel suite reeks of a perfume cocktail and sounds like a coed slumber party.

"Thought we'd do a little pre-partying before we head out," Grant says to no one in particular. He grabs two girls by the wrist and leads them to the sofa, sandwiching himself between them and slipping his arms around their shoulders.

I don't know where he found these ladies.

The blonde to his right nuzzles up to him, nibbling at his ear and running her hand along the outside of his pants. The redhead on his other side bites her lip, anxiously awaiting her turn.

"Hi." Another blonde with hair down to her tits plops down beside me, though I'd hardly call it plopping since I imagine she weighs less than ninety pounds soaking wet. Her sapphire gaze is slightly unfocused, her eyes deep and hollowed. And she gives me a sultry grin as if she's about to make a meal out of me. "I'm Jazz. What's your name?"

I don't want to do this.

I don't want to be here.

"His name is Cainan, and he's not normally this fucking rude," Grant comes up for air.

"That's a cool name." She crosses her toothpick legs and lets her mini skirt ride up, advertising the fact that she isn't wearing panties. "Where are you from, Cainan?"

Apparently another fucking planet.

Up tempo music begins to blast over the Bluetooth speakers in the ceiling, loud without being obnoxious.

If only they'd drown out my thoughts.

Grant whispers something to his playthings, rises, and leads them to the bedroom, closing the door behind them.

"Can I read your palm?" Jazz reaches for my hand, but I jerk it away.

"No."

She pouts. "I'm a palm reader."

"I'm sure you are." I take a drink, avoiding her desperate gaze. "But no."

"Dude. What's your problem? Let her read your freaking palm. We're in Vegas. We can do weird shit here and no one gives a crap." Collin takes the sofa cushion on the other side of the blonde and extends his hand. "Here. Read me."

Her eyes light and she shifts her posture toward him before flattening his right palm and concentrating. "Okay, first, I need you to relax."

"Done," he says without hesitation.

"See this line here? It's your lifeline. It's long and unbroken. That tells me you're a dependable person. And this. This is your head line. It's on the shorter side. Are you an athlete? Do you run marathons?" she asks.

"Uh, I do actually ..." Collin glances at Jazz then back at his palm.

I roll my eyes. The dude clearly has a solid runner's build.

"You have a child," she says, not asking.

He nods.

"You're going to have two more," Jazz perks up. "Twin boys."

I finish my beer and grab another while she spews her bullshit generalities. When I return, Collin's expression is electric and he's running his fingers through his hair as if she told him he's going to win the lottery when he turns forty.

And hell, she probably did say that.

"Your turn!" Jazz rotates back to me, reaching for my hand. "I'm a fourth-generation palm reader. I have a client list a mile long. Celebrities. Foreign dignitaries. People fly from all over the world for twenty minutes of my time."

"And you're giving your services away for free *why*?" I uncap my beer.

She steals my right hand and flattens the palm over the top of her bony knee. "Because it's a Friday night. And I want to. Now, I need you to relax."

I exhale a hard breath.

"I'm serious. Relax and open your mind." She closes her eyes, sits straight, and inhales. "Okay, here we go."

Collin leans in, literally on the edge of his seat.

Jazz clears her throat, running a long fingernail down the center of my hand. "Okay, this is interesting ... your fate line ... this one right here ... it tells me how strongly your life will be controlled by your destiny. Now, your line is pretty deep. Deeper than most. Some people don't have one at all. But yours has this branch that connects to your lifeline. You have a predetermined destiny ... but there's a crossroads here. You're fighting it. You're denying it. You have to decide what you want and go for it. The universe will support you either way. But as it stands now, your life can go in one of two extremely different directions."

I jerk my hand away, done.

Tell me something I don't fucking know ...

43

"WHY DOES that girl keep staring at us?" Megan nods toward the back of the crowded bar Friday night. Four hours ago she hopped off her plane and cabbed it to my place, fully dressed and ready to paint the town.

After the week I've had, I'm not particularly in the mood to "party" but it's good to spend time with a familiar face—one I can trust.

Besides, she came all this way.

"Who's staring?" I scan the room.

Megan points. "That girl with the big blue eyes and the long wavy hair and the flowy marigold dress."

My gaze lands on the deep yellow across the room. How I missed it the first time, I don't know. But sure enough, the girl is shooting looks in our direction.

My direction.

Because that girl ... is Serena.

"I think she used to date Grant." I turn back to Megan. "Ignore her."

"Maybe you should tell her he's single?"

"What's the point?" I shrug and sip my lemon drop martini.

"I just don't like the way she's looking at you. I want her to stop." Ever the protective big sister, Megan glares back in Serena's direction.

"She's not worth it." I pat Megan's arm to redirect her attention. "Stop. Let it go."

"Oh my God. She's still looking over here." Megan scowls. "I'm going to say something."

"Don't ..."

Before I can utter another protest, she's on her way to the other side of the bar. Her back is to me and her hands move as she speaks—never a good sign. I turn away. I can't watch this. Sipping my drink, I peruse the bar menu before scrolling through my phone a minute or two. Checking back, I find them still going at it.

And then Serena whips out her phone. The screen lights the dark space around them, painting their faces in white-blue light. Megan leans in. And then for some crazy reason, Serena *hands my sister her phone.*

I'm half-tempted to go over there and investigate, but something tells me to stay put.

An endless minute goes by before Meg returns.

"That son of a bitch." She shakes her head and reaches for her drink.

"What? What just happened? I'm so confused ..."

"Well." She squares her shoulders. "I went over there and introduced myself as your sister. I told her that she needed to grow the hell up and leave you alone. I told her that you dumped Grant. That you were done with him.

And then I said he was all hers ... to which she responded: what made you think he never was?"

"Meg, how drunk are you? You're not making sense. I don't understand what you're telling me."

"Basically ... the whole time Grant was engaged to you, he was screwing her behind your back."

I have no words.

In fact, I can hardly bring myself to move a muscle.

I never loved him, not in any profound sort of way. But the sting of betrayal sends a searing heat to my core and a burn to my eyes.

"Hey." Meg reaches across the table, covering my hand with hers. "Don't cry over that asshole."

"I'm not." The tears fall anyway. "I just feel so stupid, that's all."

"He had you snowed. He had us all snowed. Just be grateful you went with your gut and got out of that before it was too late." She gives me a squeeze. "Want to get out of here? Let's go. We can loaf it up on the couch. Put on some Sex and the City. Maybe grab some microwave popcorn and cinnamon Mike and Ikes on the way home from that bodega on the corner?"

She's trying to cheer me up, and I love her for that, but this is one of those things I'm going to have to sit with for a sec.

I'll get over it.

I'm not worried about that.

I just need to let myself feel this molten wave of emotions so I know exactly how I never want to feel again: like a fool.

44

IT'S two solid hours before Grant emerges from the hotel suite bedroom, tucking his shirt down his pants and wearing a satisfied smile.

"Good to see you're taking this Brie thing in stride," I say when I bump into him by the fridge.

He grabs a beer, his satisfied smile fading. "What's that supposed to mean?"

"Seems like you're in better spirits, that's all."

"Yeah. Well. It's a lost cause." He pops the tab on his Coors, and I decide not to tell him his shirt buttons are crooked. He's probably too drunk to care. "She convinced her dad not to invest with me. He ripped up the contracts. Told me to get lost."

"So ... *that's* what makes it a lost cause?"

"Obviously." He takes two generous swallows.

"I thought you loved her?" All those phone calls, all the

self-pity, all the rambling he did about how perfect she was. "Or was it always about the money?"

Resting his back against the counter, he gives me a sideways smirk. "Don't be so fucking dense."

"Grant, you lied to me." My vision narrows and my jaw is taut. "You told me you met the woman of your dreams ... that she was everything you ever wanted ... that you loved her ... you said you wanted a house in the 'burbs and kids and a dog ..."

He hides his arrogant grin with his beer. "Yeah. I said those things."

Serena ...

The prenup ...

"You never loved her." I'm not asking.

He lifts a shoulder. "I mean ... I thought I could learn to love her. She was a nice girl. A bit vanilla in the bedroom but the sex was good enough. We could've had it fucking made, Cain. If she would've just—"

"—you mean *you* could've had it fucking made," I correct him. "She would've been shackled to an unfaithful prick who only married her because he wanted her family's money."

"Unfaithful prick?" He scoffs. "Little harsh there, don't you think? And why are you acting so protective of her? She was my girl. Not yours. Oh, wait. That's right. I remember. I asked you to keep an eye on her for me and you let her fucking fall for you."

"What are you talking about?"

"I saw the way you looked at her at my dad's funeral. Every time she thought I wasn't paying attention, she was staring your way. Then I busted you two outside, *alone*, at your party. And then *magically*, as soon as we get back to Phoenix, she dumps me and tells me she's moving to New York. I'm not a fucking moron."

"If you didn't trust me, why'd you ask me to keep tabs?"

"Maybe because a part of me did trust you. You're my best fucking friend, Cainan. Didn't want to think you'd stoop that low."

"*Stoop that low?*" If that isn't the pot calling the kettle black ...

"Or maybe you just wanted to get me back."

I fold my arms. "Get you back for what?"

"Mallory," he speaks the name of my ex from college, a girl I dated for three years before she had a pregnancy scare, admitted the baby wasn't mine, and found herself immediately single. In the end, she miscarried, losing the baby *and* the guy she supposedly "loved more than life."

"What are you saying ...?"

"Oh, come on. I know you know." He rolls his eyes.

"It was *you?*"

"It was a mistake. A one-time mistake. And I felt like shit about it after ... I thought she told you?"

My jaw clenches so hard it sends a throb to my temples. "Do you honestly think I'd forgive you for fucking my girlfriend of three years?"

"Well ... yeah. That's what brothers do." He chuffs.

"You're not my fucking brother." The words are a hoarse growl in my throat. "Not anymore.

I moved on from the Mallory incident a lifetime ago, but I never forgot how eager Grant was to help me pick up the pieces when I moved on. He personally saw to it that I was never empty-handed come the weekend and that I never went too long without a gorgeous piece of coed ass to numb the pain and forget the betrayal.

"You knew I didn't know," I say.

He shakes his head, nose wrinkled, looking every inch the part of a liar.

I see liars all the time in my office. People like him that think the rules don't apply to them. Who forget how to be a decent fucking human being. Who act like their wants and needs are above everyone else's.

"All you ever do is lie," I say. "But I can't even be mad at you right now. I can only be mad at myself for looking the other way all these years. For making excuses for you. For thinking our bullshit brotherhood trumped the fact that you're just a shitty asshole in an expensive suit."

All this time, I could have been pursuing Brie. Instead, I tormented myself, convincing myself that Grant's happiness mattered more than mine.

Now I know that had the tables been reversed, the bastard wouldn't have hesitated a single fucking second before making his move.

"You've changed, Cainan. You're not who you used to be," Grant turns up his nose. "Sometimes I feel like my best friend died in that accident ... because I don't know who the hell *you* are."

"Fuck you." I turn to leave, intending to grab my duffel, find another hotel room in a different hotel, and book the first flight back to Manhattan tomorrow.

Only before I take a second step, I catch a surprise left hook—and everything fades to black, nothing but a soft voice whispering in my ear.

Elay-fay-por-twah ...

Elay-fay-por-twah ...

Elay-fay-por-twah ...

I wake to two paramedics in blue uniforms hovering over me.

"Hey, there," one of them says. "You gave us quite the scare."

But the words play on a loop in my head.

Elay-fay-por-twah ...

Elay-fay-por-twah ...

Elay-fay-por-twah ...

There's no music.

No girls.

Not even Grant.

Elay-fay-por-twah ...

Elay-fay-por-twah ...

Elay-fay-por-twah ...

My head throbs with the intensity of a Mack truck.

Elay-fay-por-twah ...

Elay-fay-por-twah ...

Elay-fay-por-twah ...

I couldn't begin to make sense of that if I tried—it's not English.

Hell, for all I know it's a made-up language.

The paramedics sit me up.

"Easy does it," one says. "You're going to have one hell of a shiner. Nice little souvenir to take back with you. Not everything that happens in Vegas, stays in Vegas ..."

Someone hands me ice wrapped in a washcloth.

Elay-fay-por-twah ...

Elay-fay-por-twah ...

Elay-fay-por-twah ...

45

Brie

MEGAN'S on a plane back to home, and I'm folding the last of my towels Sunday night when a text comes through—from Cainan.

CAINAN: WE NEED TO TALK.

ME: LIKE I TOLD YOU LAST TIME ... DON'T CONTACT ME AGAIN.

I'm two seconds from blocking his number and being done with this when his name flashes across my screen.

He's calling me.

My thumb hovers over the red button, all the while my heart lurches into my throat. Half of me wants nothing to do with Grant or his connections in any way, shape, or form. The other half of me is drowning in a conflicting cocktail of 'what if' scenarios.

I tap the green icon and lift my phone to my ear. "Why are you calling me?"

"I just got home from Vegas," he says. "We need to talk."

"No thanks."

"Brie, please. Five minutes is all I need."

"Funny, you just spent a weekend with my ex and the first thing you do when you get back is check in on me ..." I fold the last towel and place it on top of the stack.

Cainan exhales hard into the receiver and we wallow in mutual silence for a beat.

"Listen," he finally says. "I'm not trying to harass you, and I didn't call to argue."

His tone is sincere. Believable. Then again, it always has been.

"I need to know if this phrase means anything to you ... *elay-fay-por-twah* ...."

I collapse onto the foot of the bed, eyes wet and completely at a loss for words.

"Brie?" he asks. "You still there?"

A thick tear slides down my cheek. I wipe it away with the back of my hand.

"Yeah." My throat is so tight it hurts to speak. "I'm still here."

"Can I come over?"

I swallow and attempt to steady my breath. "Yes."

46

"OH MY GOD." She gasps when she opens the door, hand clamped over her pretty mouth. And then she reaches for my eye. "*What happened to you?*"

"Grant. Grant happened."

She frowns. "Why?"

"Because I called him out on his bullshit and he didn't like what I had to say." I give her the shortened, condensed version for now. "Can I come in?"

Brie nods and steps out of the way, closing the door behind me.

"Did you know he was cheating on me?" she asks before I make it halfway to the living room. "With that Serena girl. The whole time we were engaged. Did you know?"

"Yes." I turn to face her, only to be met with the saddest green eyes I've ever seen.

She didn't deserve what Grant did to her. Not an ounce of it.

"Were you ever going to tell me?" Her arms fold across her chest and her glassy gaze is pointed.

"I wanted to, Brie. But it was never my place."

"Did you also know he was trying to convince my father to sign over his entire financial portfolio to Grant's firm?" she asks.

"I had an idea, yes. But I didn't know the extent of it," I say. "At least not until this weekend."

"You were drafting a prenup," she says. "I saw the letter you sent him where you mentioned some clauses ..."

"Unfortunately, I'm not able to share that with you. Attorney-client privilege."

"Of course ..." She sighs. "Must be nice to pick and choose when you want to be an upstanding individual."

"You're right."

Her eyes flick onto mine.

"I could have spoken up if I wanted to. About the cheating. About comments he'd made. I didn't. And I deeply regret the hurt it caused you to be on the receiving end of Grant's antics."

If I sound rehearsed, it's because I spent the entirety of the flight home practicing exactly what I wanted to say to her, like a trial lawyer rehearsing his closing remarks. I didn't know if she'd give me the time of day, but I sure as hell was going to try.

"*Antics*." She huffs. "You make it sound like he's some wayward juvenile delinquent and not a grown man playing God with other people's lives."

I take a seat in the velvet chair, rest my elbows on the tops of my thighs, and breathe into my hands.

"I was about six when Grant's family moved next door to us on Copper Street in Jersey City," I say. "First time we met, we got into this throwdown fight over whose bike was faster or some stupid thing kids argue about. I didn't like him. There was something about him. But the feeling was mutual. Anyway, a week later my parents got into one of their infamous blood-curdling screaming matches. I grabbed my baby sister, went up to my room, and locked the door like I always did when that happened. But as I was sitting there, trying to distract Claire with a handful of stale Cheerios, someone was throwing pebbles at my window. I went to investigate, only there was nobody down below. Just a faded patch of dirt and weeds. But then I looked across—realized it was Grant. His bedroom window lined up perfectly with mine. He'd been throwing Legos, trying to get my attention. When I finally opened the window and popped out the screen, he tossed me a Star Wars Walkie-Talkie. Asked if I was okay. That was the day he became my best friend."

She's quiet, gaze fixed on me as she worries the inside of her lip.

"I mean it when I say he was like a brother to me," I continue. "Growing up, we always had each other's backs. We were inseparable. Nothing—and I mean nothing—could come between us."

Brie takes a step closer. Silent. Reluctant. Attentive.

"He used to be a good person," I say. "But somewhere along the line, he became toxic. Self-serving. A bold-faced liar."

She takes a seat on the edge of the sofa, head in her hands.

"He lied to you, Brie. He deceived you in the worst kinds of ways," I continue. "But he lied to me too. I was too blinded by my decades-long loyalty to see it. We never want to think the people we care about are capable of using us."

She huffs, nodding. "What did he lie to you about?"

"Amongst other things ... his feelings for you," I say without pause.

Her dark brows knit. "I don't understand how that's a friendship deal breaker."

"Because from the moment I met you in my dream, I knew you were real. And I knew you were meant for me. I looked for you everywhere. I thought about you constantly," I say. "But then I found you. And you were his. And as much as it killed me inside, I had to respect that." I press my lips into a hard line, exhaling. "He'd go on and on about how much he loved you, how amazing you were. And all it did was solidify—for me—the fact that I could never have you. When I found out you were moving here, Grant asked me to keep an eye on you. He also asked me to pretend to date you so you wouldn't be able to date anyone else."

Her jaw hangs and her emerald eyes widen. "I guess I shouldn't be surprised given everything that's transpired recently."

"He offered me money, Brie." I don't hide the incredulousness in my voice. "I told him to fuck off, that I would never do that to you. I'd never do that to anyone, for that matter." Exhaling, I go on, "Anyway, you and I started spending time together. And out of loyalty to Grant—and despite the fact that I couldn't take my eyes off you for two seconds anytime you were around—I kept my hands to myself even when all I wanted to do was kiss you ... pull you into my arms as we strolled the sidewalks ... spend the fucking night with you. But I always said goodbye at the end of the day. Even if it killed me."

She tugs on her bottom lip, staring blankly ahead, quiet as a fucking mouse.

"Why'd you let me come over anyway?" I ask, realizing she's been eerily calm these last several minutes. "Last weekend you accused me of being Grant's henchman and told me never to talk to you again. Now you're hearing me out. What changed?"

Her sour-apple gaze rests on mine. I can't tell if she's about to get teary-eyed or if she's overwhelmed with sheer exhaustion.

"It was what you said on the phone earlier," she finally speaks.

"*Elay-fay-por-twah?*" I'm probably butchering it.

She blinks, eyes glassy. "Yeah. Where did you hear that?"

I draw in a long breath, praying to God she keeps an open mind this time. "When Grant knocked me out the other night, I passed out. When I started to come to, I heard this voice whispering in my ear. *Elay-fay-por-twah, elay-fay-por-twah* over and over. At least that's what it sounded like."

Maybe I misheard it. I was drunk and I blacked out the second Grant decked me. Because of my accident and previous head injury, the paramedics took me to the hospital to get checked out. If it wasn't for that, I'd have been home a day ago, but I had to spend hours in the imaging department, hours waiting for a doctor to read the results, and hours in observation before they'd clear me.

Fucking Grant ...

Without saying a word, Brie smooths her palms along her leggings, rises from the sofa, and retrieves a small notebook and pen from the kitchen. When she comes back, she scribbles a sentence into the paper and hands it to me.

"*Il est fait pour toi*," she reads it to me. "It means *he is made for you* in French."

I stare at the words. And then at her. My heart hammers with every passing second.

Brie's quivering pink lips can't decide if they want to smile or frown.

"I'm sorry," she says. "It's just … this is the strangest thing. My sister. The one who died. We studied abroad in Paris our senior year of high school. When we got back, any time we wanted to have a secret conversation, we'd speak in French because no one else in our family spoke the language. When we went off to college, we'd use it any time we saw a cute guy or whatever and wanted to point it out to each other. It was this silly little thing we did, I guess. But it was *our* thing."

"I swear to you, Brie. On my life. I don't speak French. There's no way I would've known that …" I watch her expression, worried this moment will explode in my face the way the last one did. "Just like the tattoo. I didn't know what it meant, just that it was in the dream. My sister, Claire—she can vouch for that. I used to scribble it all the time before I met you."

She lifts her hands, examining them before offering a humble half-smile. "I'm shaking."

"Are you cold?" I rise and grab a throw off the back of the couch.

Brie shakes her head. "I don't know what I am. In shock, maybe? All these years, I've been wanting a sign from Kari. Something. Anything. What if … what if …"

She doesn't finish.

I don't think she'll allow herself to.

"This entire thing is just as insane to me as it is to you," I say. "But I refuse to believe all of this happened for nothing—that it means nothing. It has to mean something. You see it too, right? You *feel* it too?"

Biting her lip, she offers a hesitant nod—all the confirmation I need.

I go to her, breathing in her vanilla-mint shampoo and the lavender fabric softener of her t-shirt, and finally … *finally*, I cup her square jaw and fix my starved gaze on her mouth.

The mouth that should have always belonged to me.

"When I'm with you," I keep my voice low, "I feel like I've known you a hundred lifetimes before. And I feel like I've been waiting a lifetime to do this …"

I slide my hands into her hair and claim her cashmere-soft, half-parted lips with a greedy kiss. Brie melts against me with a surrendering sigh, and I pull her close. I want to feel every inch of her against me. I need to feel the way we fit together like the final missing pieces of a puzzle I've been working on far too long.

"I'm crazy about you, Brielle White," I whisper, our mouths grazing as we come up for air. "And at the risk of sounding even crazier … I'm falling in love with you. And I have been since the moment I saw you."

I think of a line from The Alchemist: *She is a treasure greater than anything else I have won.* And in this moment, I am Santiago and she is my Fatima.

Only our journey isn't finished—it's just getting started.

And if there's one thing I've learned thus far, it's that love is messy, jagged, sticky, and at times, painful.

But it's always, *always* worth it.

47

Brie

FOR YEARS, I've waited for a sign from Kari.

Tonight, she finally came through.

At least I think she did. I want to believe she did. We can never be one-hundred percent sure with these kinds of things. Sometimes all we can do is listen to our heart of hearts and trust that it's never wrong.

There aren't numbers or mathematical equations that can explain any of this.

There are no formulas that exist to illuminate the inner workings of fate or destiny.

The concept of soulmates is only real to those who believe.

I don't need complicated statistical calculations to rationalize that every ounce of the fullness expanding through my body as Cainan's fingers lace through my hair ... is real.

Is happening ...

Is every bit as delicious and toe-curling as I dreamed it would be ...

I've wanted *this* since the night of his party, when we were standing on the sidewalk exchanging secrets, my lungs flooded with the crisp night air, my body hyperaware of his presence. I didn't let myself feel it though. Not fully. But it was there. That pull. That undercurrent of *something*.

His mouth is hot against mine, our bodies fused together as our tongues caress. I gather in his intoxicating woodsy scent and lift my arms around his broad shoulders, hungry for more.

I'm on fire for this man.

Desire thick in my veins.

His hands leave my hair, trail down my arms, and rest at my hips before he scoops me up. I wrap my legs around him, clinging with unapologetic greed.

My lips forage his as he carries me to the bedroom and lays me gently in the middle of the mattress, his fingers tugging at the waistband of my leggings as I pull my shirt over my head. His mouth burns against my stomach, which caves in delight as he peppers teasing kisses lower ... lower still ...

Sliding my panties down, he kisses trails along my inner thighs before settling at the apex. His tongue is hot along my seam as he tastes me. Every inch of me is fire and ice, melting against the covers, unable to stop writhing with impatience. But Cainan takes his time. He devours me. His fingers stroke me with gentle intention, and at times he stops to explore his hands along the rest of my body. His fingertips trail along every curve and valley as if he's mapping my body, trying to memorize it.

Something is missing, though ...

The faint tinge of eager unrest I normally feel when I'm

about to sleep with someone for the first time—isn't there. Instead, I'm washed in comfortable warmth, a familiar safety colored with the excitement of novelty.

Sitting up, I unfasten his jeans, tug his zipper, and take his hardness in my hands, pumping the length in my hands before swirling my tongue against the tip. He groans, head falling back and fingers tangling in my hair.

I swallow his girth until he fists my hair and tugs it down, forcing our eyes to meet.

"I can't take this anymore," he breathes. Before I have a chance to respond, he climbs over me, spreading my thighs, pinning me beneath him. "I want more of you, Brie ... I want all of you."

The heat of his engorged cock against my swollen clit is torturous.

I think of the first night we met—how I so badly wanted to be the girl who would let a sexy stranger touch her every crevasse and tease her into orgasm with his tongue all night before a round of marathon sex.

But I like this. I like the slow and sweet and worth-the-wait situation we've got going on here. We're not a couple of strangers filling themselves with meaningless sex. We're two souls who have finally found a way to be together after everything ...

"Then take me." I hook my hands behind his neck and close the distance between our mouths. My arousal is sweet on his lips, and his hips thrust against mine, though he's yet to push himself inside me. "I'm on the pill ..."

Without an ounce of hesitation, he reaches between us, grips his cock and guides it inside of me slowly, generous inch by generous inch.

My body tightens until he's all the way inside, and then I let go.

I melt below him, sinking with each insertion, though my soul is in the clouds every time our eyes lock.

I've never believed in soulmates. But after this? After him? After everything the universe put us through to be together?

How can I not?

He was made for me.

48

"WHAT ARE YOU DOING?" Brie stands in her doorway early Monday morning, body wrapped in a bedsheet and hair reminiscent of last night. "It's still dark out. My God. How early do you go into the office?"

"One sec." I lean against the kitchen counter, phone pressed to my ear as I wait for Paloma's voicemail greeting to finish. After the tone, I tell her to clear my day because I'm not coming in.

"Is everything all right?" She shuffles toward me, the sheet falling down around her breasts, though she's too out of it to notice. "You feeling all okay?"

Neither of us slept last night.

Too busy making up for lost time.

I'm exuberantly exhausted. Deliciously sore. And one-hundred-percent positive Brie feels the same.

"Can you call in today?" I ask.

Her brows furrow. "Yeah. I can. Why?"

"We're getting out of the city."

Her pretty face tilts to one side. "Where are we going?"

"Anywhere. We're just going to drive ..."

I haven't gotten behind the wheel of a car since my accident, but today has a different air to it, and I'm in the mood to get lost for a while.

Rounding the island, I make my way to Brie, scoop her into my arms, and carry her back to bed.

"I'm going to order a car. Probably won't be delivered for another couple of hours," I say, kissing the top of her head and working my way down her satin cheeks until I find her mouth in the dark. "Get some rest."

I'm almost to her door when she calls my name.

"Yeah?" I answer.

"Did you mean what you said last night." Her words are slow, sleepy, and she rubs her eyes. "When you said you were falling for me."

"When I said I was falling in love with you?"

Even in the dark and from the other side of the room, I catch her smiling. "Yeah."

"Yes, I meant it," I say. "Why?"

"*Je t'aime aussi*," she whispers. "I love you too."

49

BRIE

WE'VE BEEN DRIVING for hours now. I'm pretty sure we're somewhere in Connecticut, soaring along sleepy highways, one seaside town after another, all of them blending together with their picturesque main streets, changing leaves, and deep blue ocean backdrops accented with foamy whitecaps.

I could do this forever ... just drive ... with him.

Cainan takes my hand in his. The radio plays softly, some artist I've never heard of but one that sets the perfect mood for the kind of day that winds on and on and lets you get lost in your thoughts for a while.

"I've always wondered what it'd be like to live in a place like this," I say when we pass a beautiful Cape Cod style house with cedar siding and white flower boxes on every window. And then I laugh under my breath before adding, "Wonder if anyone here ever wonders what it'd be like to live in the desert."

Doubtful.

"Seriously though. Can you imagine being here in the summertime? Waking up and having breakfast on the patio or swinging in your porch swing as you read a book, the beach in the background? You could literally open your window at night and fall asleep to the sound of the ocean," I say.

"Is that what you want?" he asks.

I lift a shoulder. "Just thinking out loud."

Cainan lifts my hand to his mouth, depositing a kiss as if he's depositing a silent promise. Up ahead a green sign points the way to a public beach, and just before the turnoff is a little cliff above the sea with a metal guardrail and a handful of parking spots. He pulls off, kills the engine, and climbs out of the car.

A moment later, he gets the passenger door and extends his hand. Leading me to the trunk, he lifts me before leaning against the car and settling between my legs.

Cupping my face in his hand, he guides our mouths together.

"What's this?" I ask, smiling against his lip.

"Been driving for hours," he says with a sigh. "I just wanted to kiss you."

I kiss him again. Harder. And I slip my fingers through the silky hair at the nape of his neck, loving the way his musky scent mixes with the salt water air.

"We're going to have a little house by the sea someday," he tells me.

"Oh, yeah?" I lift a brow and chuckle. "You sound really sure about that. How do you know?"

"Trust me," he says. "I know these things."

50

Cainan

"HEY." I rap my knuckles against Paloma's desktop Tuesday afternoon. She's done a superior job of pretending like she hasn't noticed my black eye. Wish I could say the same for Deb in accounting and two of the junior partners in the east hall. "I'm taking the afternoon. You're welcome to as well."

"Wait ... what?" Her face is twisted, as if she's trying to comprehend a foreign language.

"My two o'clock cancelled. See if you can reschedule my three. If not, Renato will take her. I've got a few things I want to take care of outside the office."

"Oh ... okay." Her expression is laced in confusion but her tone is upbeat, happy to oblige.

I lock up my office and head out, stopping by a flower stand on the way to grab a bouquet of burgundy daisies wrapped in saffron tissue paper, and when I'm done, I text Brie and tell her to come over for dinner at six.

I can't remember the last time I cooked a proper meal in my kitchen, but I'm feeling ... domestic.

And I'm craving steak *au poivre* and a quiet night in with my girl—amongst other things.

I'm about to duck into the corner market and grab a few things when my phone vibrates in my pocket. I check the screen on the off-chance it's Brie—but it isn't.

My thumb hovers over the ignore button ... but since when have I been one to back down like a fucking coward? I don't know what he wants, but I'm happy to take this opportunity to tell him exactly where we stand.

"Yeah?" I answer.

"Hey." His tone is chipper. Mistake number one. If he thinks he can act like nothing happened, he's sorely mistaken. "I, uh, just wanted to apologize for last weekend. Things got a little heated. A little out of hand. We, uh, took things too far."

"We?" I chuff.

"Going to be in town for work later this week. Thought maybe we could grab drinks? Put this past us?"

Idiot.

"I'm going to have to pass, but I appreciate the apology."

"Oh, yeah? You have plans or something?" His voice is casual, as if he's playing dumb. But I know damn well he's fishing for information.

"Hanging out with Brie."

It's quiet on the other end. I'd be lying if I said I didn't enjoy the silence.

"So that's how it's going to be?" he asks.

"That's exactly how it's going to be."

I end the call and head into the grocery. By the time I'm checking out, Brie texts back to let me know she'll be there and she can't wait.

Strolling home, I'm sure I'm grinning like a lovestruck idiot, but I couldn't care less. Brie put this smile on my face, and God willing, it'll remain until my dying day.

51

One Year Later ...

BRIE

"WHEN DO you think he'll pop the question?" Carly asks. We're peeling potatoes for Thanksgiving dinner, elbow to elbow over our mother's kitchen sink.

My thighs are sore from christening our hotel room the second we landed last night—and then re-christening it this morning before heading over. The mere thought of having to be on our best behavior and having to practice restraint in front of my entire family for eight hours was enough to drive us both wild. At home, we're unencumbered and we can't keep our hands off one another for more than five second intervals. Today's going to be a challenge, but we can do this.

"Whenever." I shrug. "We're not in a rush. It'll happen when it's supposed to happen."

We glance into the next room, where my father and Cainan are deep in some discussion about foreign trade policies as it relates to building supplies. Cainan is doing his best feigning as much interest as possible, though I'm sure he's bored to tears. It's sweet that he's indulging my dad.

"Have you two talked about it at all?" She grabs the last potato.

"Not in detail, no. We both just know it'll happen someday. We're not worried about it." I scoop the peels from the sink and toss them in the garbage.

While we've only been dating a year now, Cainan and I feel like we've been together our whole lives—and we know we're going to be together the rest of our lives. Engagements, weddings, those are formalities.

We're choosing to focus on what matters: the relationship.

Besides, the last engagement left a bit of a bitter taste in my mouth. Fortunately, I've yet to run into Grant since everything went down. Cainan mentioned they spoke on the phone briefly after their altercation in Vegas, but he never heard from him after that. Though he still sent Georgette a card on Mother's Day—and the day she got it, she called and spoke to him for a solid hour about this, that, and everything else non-Grant-related.

I think she understands why the guys fell out.

And I think she truly sees Cainan as her second son.

I've yet to meet his parents. He doesn't like to talk about them. You have to pry details out of him like tweezers to a deep splinter. His sister's a little more forthcoming, though she's in the blissful throes of new motherhood, so I avoid dredging up anything from the past when we're all together.

I smile to myself when I think of Cainan with his baby niece, Hadleigh. The first time Claire put her in his arms, he claimed he wasn't good with babies. But he settled down and she settled in and the two became best pals from there on out. Now whenever we visit, he doesn't waste any time crawling on the floor with her and making ridiculous noises and silly faces to match.

To be honest, I was never one-hundred-percent sure I wanted kids ...

But seeing Cainan with Hadleigh sends a twinge to my ovaries like nothing before. And then there was that dream he had after his accident. He said we had two kids: a boy and a girl. I try not to let him go into detail whenever he brings it up.

I don't want to know what comes next.

There is beauty in not knowing.

Magic, too.

"Well, whatever you decide," Carly says, "just know that we all really like him."

"Appreciate it." I give her a wink, and I don't remind her that they all really liked Grant too.

Grant was my past.

Cainan is my future.

He was, is, and always will be the best man for me.

EPILOGUE

TEN YEARS LATER ...

Cainan

"I'M NOT READY TO LEAVE." Brie hugs her thighs against her chest, toes buried in the sand as we watch our daughter, Elle, and her kid brother, C.J., chase one another along the shore, giggling every time the ocean laps at their bare feet.

"Then we won't." I wrap my arm around her shoulders and pull her against me. Her bronzed skin is sunbaked, freckled, and warm, and the scent of her coconut sunblock carries on the salty ocean breeze that surrounds us. "I'll quit my job and we'll stay here. Forever. Every day will be just like this."

I've lived this before—this exact moment.

In my dream.

She turns to me, fighting the smirk that claims her full

lips, and then she pushes her cat-eyed sunglasses down her nose. "Don't tempt me."

"You're not happy in the city."

We've been here before. We've had this conversation before—only she doesn't know it.

While we've talked about the dream I had after my accident, it's never been in great detail—at her request.

From the beginning, she told me she wanted our life together to unfold organically, to be a surprise.

And for the most part, it has been.

I never could have anticipated moving to Phoenix for a few years shortly after we married. I also never could anticipate that she'd want to move back to the city—which we did shortly after C.J. came along. She said it felt like home, that it fit us better. And she felt more of a connection to Manhattan because it was where we fell in love and had all of our firsts.

First kiss.

First broken bed ...

First fight.

First (and only) wedding.

Brie slides her glasses up and turns to watch the children. "It gets claustrophobic sometimes. The kids come out here and there's so much space. They don't stop smiling for months. Then we head back to the city, cram ourselves in a narrow, three-bedroom brownstone, and live in that gray cinderblock world for nine more months. Things are so fast-paced in the city, you know? Life is literally passing us by. Out here, time moves slower. Or at least it feels that way."

"I told you the day I married you that your happiness is my happiness. If you want to move, we'll move."

She exhales. "I can't ask you to walk away from your

life's work. We tried that in Phoenix, remember? You were miserable."

"I can practice law here."

"Now you're just being optimistic." Her voice is soft, apologetic almost.

But she's right. With a population just above a thousand, I'd be lucky to land one new client every other week in Calypso Harbor. It's a blink-and-you-miss it village that an overwhelming majority of locals forget even exists. That said, if we sold the brownstone, we'd have enough to fund a new little venture, maybe something in e-commerce.

The opportunities are endless.

"We can figure it out." I tighten my hold on her.

"You make it sound so simple when it's anything but." That's Brie—the worrier. She's always been a numbers girl, gravitating toward the safety facts and figures give her, though I've helped her to loosen up a little over the years.

"Nothing's ever simple," I remind her. Our entire life together has been proof of that. "But we've always managed to figure it out. If this is what you want, we'll make it happen. One way or another."

I flip her wrist over and lift it to my lips, kissing the tiny tattoo that resides there—the one she got in honor of her twin sister shortly after we started dating. She was supposed to do it years ago and chickened out with a myriad of Brie-like explanations. I had to dial in my trial lawyer training from my law school days just to reason with her, and in the end, my persuasiveness did the trick. Shortly after that, I booked her an appointment with one of the best tattooists in Brooklyn and held her hand the entire time.

Elle and C.J. squeal with delight in the background, running from yet another gentle wave as it chases them up the shore, leaving a path of tiny footprints that get washed away in seconds.

Turning my attention to my lovely wife, I cup her cheek with my hand and claim her cherry-flavored mouth with a kiss—the mouth I could kiss a million times and never tire of.

But she doesn't kiss me back.

Instead she pulls away.

"Cainan ... there's something I've been meaning to tell you ..."

"Of course. You can tell me anything." My heart hammers, every second that passes more endless than the one before.

She bites her lower lip, looking away, and her shoulders rise and fall as she gathers a salted breath. And then she turns to me, green eyes dancing. "I'm pregnant."

My grandmother, Norma Jean, was sixteen when she dreamt she'd married a farmer, and in this dream, she found herself suspended from a crystal chandelier high above a room filled with farm animals of every kind.

Not quite ten years later, she was working at a bank in her hometown of Johnstown, Pennsylvania and engaged to a local man when she met a handsome young soldier from rural South Dakota. The country was in the midst of the second World War, and he'd been drafted and stationed near her home for training.

The star-crossed souls had an instant connection, and soon she found herself torn between two men—and two vastly different futures.

Norma Jean chose the soldier ...

... who just so happened to hail from a large farming family.

After the war ended, the two married in a civil cere-mony, loaded into a Chevy pickup with a top speed of fifty miles per hour, and drove for three days until they reached southeastern South Dakota. When the newlyweds arrived,

Norma Jean and the soldier were given a one-room house and some land from his family's homestead, and thus began her life as a farmer's wife.

Fifteen years later, on their crystal wedding anniversary, Norma Jean and her farmer husband had more livestock than ever before.

CHAPTER ONE

Astaire

It wasn't supposed to rain today.

I stand on the rubber entrance mat inside a bar called Ophelia's, soaked to the bone, water as cold as January dripping off my wool pea coat in rivulets, toes pinched numb in my pointed heels.

The sign for the ladies' room flickers in neon, and I waste no time trotting to the back of the narrow space, ducking through the swinging doors, and positioning myself in front of the first vacant mirror I find.

The instant I encounter my gaze in the reflection, I know I should have stayed home tonight.

What kind of person marks the one-year anniversary of their fiancé's death with a blind date?

A person who can't say no to anything or anyone —that's who.

Mrs. Angelino had good intentions, trying to set me up with her nephew, and I knew better, agreeing to go despite every atom in my body screaming for me to tell her the truth ... that I'm just not ready.

I hang my jacket on a nearby wall hook and return to my station.

"Weak." I slam my bag on the white porcelain sink and start digging inside for a hairbrush, a hair tie, anything to tame my damp baby-blonde waves. "Weak, weak, weak."

I locate a mini wet-brush and a rubber band so stretched it could snap without warning, and then I rake my hair back, twisting it into a low bun and securing it at the nape of my neck.

When I glance up again, I realize my mascara has settled beneath my lower lash line—not exactly the smoky eye look I was intending.

Yanking a paper towel from the nearby dispenser, I fold it into fourths before running it under warm water.

Behind me, a bathroom stall door swings open and a leggy blonde in an ecru sweater dress and black knee-high boots saunters out, bending over the sink a second later to wash her hands. Our gazes intersect as I attempt to remove the remnants of my Great Lash, and she offers a sympathetic half-smile.

"You okay?" The woman reaches for a paper towel, unhurried. Her ballet-pink nails are shiny and shellacked, her fingers long and slender. Everything about her is soft and elegant, a jarring contrast against my current condition.

"Wasn't expecting to get caught in the downpour. Supposed to be meeting someone in a few minutes. Kind of hoping he stands me up."

"Too late to cancel?"

"I don't know his number. A colleague at work set us up. It's her nephew. All I know is he's six feet tall with dark hair and his name is Garrett. She says he's *unbelievably handsome* but she's his aunt, so ..." I laugh through my nose at the absurdity of this entire situation, and it's then that I notice a section of hair still sticking out. Carefully I tug out the elastic and re-do my low bun, smoothing my palms over my half-dried mane. But there's nothing I can do about the fully-dried mascara under my eyes. "I can't meet a complete stranger looking like this."

The easy-breezy siren of a woman studies my face before placing her oversized handbag next to her sink.

"It just so happens I work at the Catherine DeAngelo makeup counter at the mall on weekends." Her voice is light, sing-songish "Which means I've got you, girl."

Within seconds, she pulls out a travel-sized pack of chamomile-infused makeup remover towelettes and offers them with a wink.

"You're a saint. Truly. Thank you *so* much." I tug one wipe from the case and clean myself up, only when I'm done, I look more exhausted than fresh-faced.

I swear the circles beneath my eyes are a shade darker than before—probably from all the rubbing and scrubbing— and my pale lashes are practically invisible.

I exhale, reminding myself that looks aren't everything, that there's a chance he'll find my drowned rat appearance ... endearing?

"Uh oh. I know that look. Hold on." Dipping a hand to the bottom of her bag, she feels around before producing a fistful of miniature lipsticks and mascaras. She checks the names on the bottom of the shiny gold tubes before handing me one. "This color would be perfect on you. Don't get scared by how bright it looks in the tube. It's completely different once it's on. Oh, and here's some mascara. These are brand new, by the way. In case you have a thing about germs."

"Oh, honey. I teach kindergarten. Germs don't scare me." I bat my hand before graciously accepting her gifts.

Uncapping the lipstick, I'm met with a bold bullet the color of psychedelic poppies, but I trust this woman so I slick it over my lips. The payoff is sheer, like a wash of fresh color on my pale pink mouth, instantly bringing my pallid complexion back to life. I swipe on two coats of mascara next. It isn't life-changing, but it offers a distraction from the dark circles, so I consider it a win.

"For the record, you look chic as hell—but you were beautiful before." She flings her bag over her lithe shoulder, one hand on her hip. "And any idiot who would care that you got caught in a rainstorm wouldn't be worth a second date anyway."

"I know ... it's just ... this is the first *first* date I've been on in ... a long time."

Five years to be exact.

I don't go into the whole dead fiancé thing because I find it tends to depress people—myself included, and I don't even know my new fairy godmother's name.

Unpacking all that heaviness onto a kindhearted stranger would be cruel.

"No, I get it. Dating is hard. It's even harder when you're out of practice." Placing a hand on my shoulder on her way out, she gives me a reassuring squeeze. "I'm Ophelia, by the way. My father owns this place. Tell Eduardo at the bar that your first drink is on me."

With that, she's gone.

I give myself one last glance in the mirror before pulling

my shoulders back, collecting my things, and heading out to the bar.

The Killers play from speakers in the ceiling and a group of middle-aged men with slicked hair and expensive suits order a round of tequila shots.

I don't bother scanning the room in search of Garrett, I head straight for Eduardo at the bar, cashing in my verbal coupon in exchange for a top-shelf gin and tonic, and then I help myself to a handful of pretzels because I haven't eaten since eleven o'clock today.

Ten minutes later, warmth rushes through me.

My breathing steadies, no longer hitching and uneven.

My shoulders thaw, allowing me to melt comfortably into my seat.

Two spots down, a handsy couple clink martini glasses.

The table of suits and ties are enjoying dark lagers now.

Three women, all dressed in their office casual best, commiserate over bright-colored drinks at a high-top to my left. To my right is an empty stool.

The clock above the door reads six twenty-seven. It would seem I am, in fact, being stood up.

Be careful what you wish for ...

"Can I get one more of these?" I lift my glass when Eduardo checks on me.

Tonight I'll drink to Trevor—to his memory, to what might have been.

A minute later, my old drink is replaced. I don't particularly like gin and tonics, but they were always Trevor's go-to. He was never into IPAs or craft beers or Jager-bombs-with-the-guys. And he hated anything remotely sweet. He appreciated the hell out of a nice, top-shelf classic—which was fitting because *he* was a nice, top-shelf classic.

My eyes begin to burn, but I force it away.

I told myself I wouldn't cry today.

Lord knows I've done more than enough of that over the past twelve months.

Taking a sip, my attention is hijacked by a frigid burst of air that sweeps through the bar and the floor-shaking shudder that follows when the door slams.

Glancing over my shoulder, I spot a dark-haired man, easily six feet tall. He retracts his rain-slicked umbrella and leans it against the wall before stalking toward the bar, and then he steals the last spot on the end—five places down from me, hanging his wool trench coat over the seat back before sitting.

Eduardo greets him, wiping the section in front of him with a clean towel, half hunched over and nodding in quick succession.

I wait until the Eduardo returns with the man's drink— which appears to be a triple shot of straight vodka over two perfect squares of ice in an old-fashioned tumbler—before appropriating a closer look at the mystery man.

Through the shadowy haze of Ophelia's, my unfocused gaze struggles to home in at first. And then I see him perfectly.

Chiseled cheekbones.

Impeccably-groomed obsidian hair.

Broad shoulders hardly contained in a navy cashmere sweater.

Jawline for days.

Could this be ...?

Is *that* Mrs. Angelino's nephew?

I take a generous mouthful of gin and tonic, contemplating how best to introduce myself. My palms tingle, and I rub them against the tops of my thighs, sucking in a shallow breath.

There's a chance this man isn't Garrett, and the more I think about it, he likely isn't. I've yet to catch him scanning the room in search of someone.

But still—if it is him, I'd hate for him to think he's being stood up. I would never do that to anyone, for any reason. My life's mantra can be boiled down to the whole *"do unto others ..."* saying.

Clearing my throat, I lean in his direction. "Excuse me?"

He doesn't hear me.

Waving my hand to capture his attention, I say it again, "Hi. Excuse me."

Still, nothing.

It's like he's in his own world—ten feet away.

The friendly, kindergarten-teacher smile teetering on my poppy-stained lips fades with the realization that I'm being ignored.

"Hi, excuse me ..." Third time's the charm. I wave once more, wiggling my fingers the way you'd politely flag down a restaurant server.

The man turns to his left, dark brows knit together and gaze tightened in my direction—and then he does the craziest thing: lifting his finger to his lips, he *shushes* me.

He. Shushes. Me.

Like a child.

Facing ahead, I take another drink, the glass trembling in my hand as a cocktail of thoughts swarm my head. The mirror behind the bar catches my reflection, and it isn't pretty, but this time it has nothing to do with the damp, wiry, dishwater-blonde bun or the bar bathroom makeover.

Basic human decency is the *one thing* I value most in this world, and this man has none of it.

The full weight of his piercing stare anchors me to my

seat, and every atom in my body is shouting for me to stay, to not march ten feet down the bar to give him a piece of my mind.

But today marks the anniversary of one of the worst days of my life, I was caught in a rainstorm and stood up, *and* I'm about two cocktails deep.

My self-control is non-existent.

Drink in hand, I slide off my seat and saunter toward the infuriatingly handsome asshole in the five-hundred-dollar sweater, but before I have a chance to utter a single word, he speaks first, "You seem incredibly insecure about something. Are you okay?"

"Excuse me?" I'm glaring, and I *never* glare. This isn't good. This man's about to bring out a side of me I never knew existed. And what the hell is he talking about? *Insecure?* "What kind of—"

"—what kind of asshole bothers a stranger for no reason?" he commandeers my question like he owns it. "Let me ask you this, when you saw me come in, saw me take a seat at the end of the bar away from everyone, what part of *that* gave you the impression that I wanted to be bothered?"

The man has a point—especially if he isn't Garrett.

But it still doesn't make him any less of a prick.

"I wasn't trying to bother you, I was—"

"*Really?*" His full lips tug into a taut smirk, his tone as sharp as it is incredulous. "Because I'm pretty sure when you were waving at me and smiling and saying '*Hi, excuse me*' in that cutesy little voice fifty thousand times ... you were trying to bother me."

"Are you always this cruel?"

"Are you always this desperate?" He doesn't miss a beat.

My grip tightens on my glass. I'd love nothing more than

to dump the remainder of this drink down his pretentious designer sweater.

Lucky for him that isn't my style.

Besides, it'd be a shame to waste all that top-shelf liquor on a bottom-shelf bastard.

"For your information, I was supposed to meet someone here tonight. Someone fitting your description," I say.

His jaw sets.

He takes a sip of his drink staring ahead, flashing a smirk that advertises a perfect dimple in the middle of his cheek. "Sure you were."

"What, you think this is something I do to meet men?" My voice is pitched higher than I intended.

"You said it." His brows rise as he centers his drink on a coaster.

"Don't flatter yourself. You're not my type."

He sniffs. "I'm *everyone's* type."

I'm ... speechless.

Is this jerk for real?!

Not only is this vexatious stranger cruel, heartless, and lacking in basic human decency, he's also the epitome of arrogant.

"You can leave now." He waves me off, but I'm stunned into silence as I try to gather my thoughts so I can leave him with one last zinger of a comeback.

"Everything okay over here?" Eduardo is hunched over the other side of the bar, his watchful stare passing between us. I swear he came out of nowhere—that or I was too distracted by this man's willful audacity to notice him approaching us.

The cocky Adonis shoots me a glance before turning his attention to the bartender.

"We're good, Eduardo," he says. "I was just giving our

friend here a lesson in etiquette, appropriacy, and basic decorum."

Once again, I have no words.

Rising from his bar stool, he finishes the remainder of his drink with a smooth swallow before shouldering into his wool trench, heading for the door, and disappearing into the cold, dark evening.

Rain drops pelt the windows, obscuring anything and everything on the other side of the glass.

Peeling my fruitless gaze from that direction, it settles on an umbrella leaning against the wall next to the door.

His umbrella.

The blackest black.

The color of his soul—or the empty space in his chest where his heart should be.

Fitting.

Without giving it another thought, I slap a twenty on the counter and slip into my coat.

A moment later, I'm grabbing the stupid thing and diving out into the rain, praying I catch him in time.

As incensed as I am, as infuriating as he is, sometimes the best thing to do is fight cruelty with kindness. It's something I learned early on in my life and something I instill in my students from the second they enter my classroom.

I spot him at the end of the block, waiting for the crosswalk to change.

Picking up my pace, I canter over cracked and pitted concrete, squeeze past umbrella-wielding locals—and make it to the end of the street just in time for the light to flick from neon white to warning-sign orange, forcing me to stop.

I wait where I am, my gaze trained on him in case he turns onto a side street.

The traffic signals begin to change, and within seconds, the crosswalk blinks to white.

I sprint across, ignoring the stinging cold rain drops pelting my skin, the frigid air biting through my clothes, and the painful clench in my jaw that keeps my teeth from rattling.

I'm a mere half of a block from him when he turns and disappears inside a local business.

But it isn't just any business …

… it's the Paulley-Hallbrook Funeral Home—a place I know well.

A moment later, I'm standing outside the very doors he walked into mere moments ago, frozen in every sense of the word.

The rain slows, gentle.

And then it stops.

Earthy petrichor fills my lungs as I witness the dark-haired, cruel-hearted mystery man as he's greeted by a lady in a charcoal pant suit.

She places a hand on his shoulder and gives him an apologetic wince before escorting him away.

I wanted to give him the umbrella to teach him a lesson in compassion.

The irony of that isn't lost on me.

CHAPTER TWO

Bennett

"Sorry I'm late. Got here as soon as I could," I lie.

I didn't rush here.

I took my time.

And I stopped down the street for a drink and to gather my thoughts first—a mistake in hindsight thanks to an audacious woman, but that's neither here nor there.

"Please, apology not necessary." The funeral director—a grandmother type who smells like dead flowers and discount perfume and gives too many hugs and arm squeezes—hangs my soaked trench on a wooden coat rack in her office. I left my umbrella at the bar. I won't be going back for it. "Why don't you have a seat there and we can get started."

I check my watch.

Take a seat.

Pray this doesn't take all night.

The woman, whose name tag reads CLAUDETTE PAULLEY, DIRECTOR, squeezes into her chair on the other side of the desk and retrieves a small booklet from a stack to her left. The cover showcases a glossy white casket surrounded by floral arrangements too perfect to be real.

"When we spoke on the phone earlier," she says, "you had mentioned cremation. Is that still—"

"—yes." I don't have time for her imprudent, time-wasting questions.

Once my mind is made up, there's never any changing it.

"All right then." She gives me a soft smile. Her bright pink lipstick bleeds into the lines around her mouth.

"Why don't we discuss the service." She glances up at me then down at her wringing hands. I must make her nervous. "And then I can show you some lovely urn options ..."

"There won't be a service." I shift in this impossibly

uncomfortable chair. "And you can choose the urn. *Surprise me.*"

Her lips form a wrinkled 'o' and she blinks before reanimating. "I see then."

"Larissa didn't have a lot of friends." At least none that I would presently allow within a hundred yards of this place. "And as far as family goes, we're rather private. A small memorial should suffice. An hour or two this Saturday if you can fit us in."

Claudette searches my face for what I assume are emotions, but her time would be better spent hammering out the final details of Larissa's memorial.

Reaching for a black, leather-bound planner, she flips it open to today's date before licking her index finger and flicking to Saturday.

"We could do ten to noon." She reaches for a logo-emblazoned pencil in a logo-emblazoned mug full of other logo-emblazoned pencils.

Classy.

"You don't have anything earlier?"

She squints. "Well, we could certainly move it up. The timing is typically more of a convenience thing. If we hold it too early, it could be difficult for some people to get here, especially if they're coming from out of town."

"I can assure you that won't be an issue." I check my watch again, not because I have somewhere else to be, but because this woman needs to get on with this shit show already.

She scratches a few words into her planner with messy, shaky handwriting. "Eight to ten it is. Now, as far as the obituary, I have a form you could fill out or I could go over everything with you personally."

"The form is fine."

Her yellow-oak chair creaks as she reaches to open a desk drawer, and then she fishes out a chipped plastic clipboard and a piece of paper before handing them over.

This place is all kinds of *fancy* and *formal.*

My couture-loving mother certainly spared no expense when she had them ship Larissa's lifeless corpse here.

The questions are endless and I don't know the answer to half of them.

The answers to the other half of them are extraneous and unnecessary.

I don't have time to write a fucking biography.

I scribble her birthdate into the first line—February 22.

They already have her death date.

Everything else is irrelevant.

CHAPTER THREE

Astaire

"Can I ask you something?" Back at Ophelia's, I slide my empty water glass toward Eduardo. I've been sitting here for over an hour now, waiting to sober up enough to go home. "It's kind of random ..."

That isn't true.

My question isn't random at all—I don't know why I said that.

"Sure." He shrugs, eyeing a couple as they stumble out the door.

"Who was that guy?" I point to the empty bar stool at

the end. "The one in here earlier?"

"The one you chased out of here?" He sniffs. I can't tell if he's annoyed, amused, or something else.

"He forgot his umbrella ...," I'm quick to defend my actions, "but yeah. Who was that?"

"Shane Bock." He wipes a speck of condensation from the bar top with his rag.

"Is he from around here?"

"He is." Eduardo lifts his hands. "But look, whatever you two had going on earlier, I don't want any part in that. Looked pretty intense."

"To say the least." I shake my head, our conversation still fresh in my spinning head. "I was supposed to meet someone here tonight and I thought that was the guy. Didn't even get a chance to ask him if he was Garrett before he started accusing me of hitting on him. Who does that?"

"Garrett, you said? Some guy was in here earlier by the name of Garrett. He was looking to meet up with someone, but he didn't wait that long. Think it was around six-ish? Didn't stay but ten minutes is all."

My stomach plunges.

It must have been when I was in the bathroom trying to salvage my date-night look.

"Dark hair? Tall?"

"Something like that," he confirms.

This day can screw itself. Truly.

I check the time on my phone. I could swear I've been here all night, but it's only been a couple of hours at the most.

To be safe, I decide to drink one more glass of water and wait one more hour—because that's what decent people do, and I'm a decent person.

I'm also decently curious.

"That Shane guy," I say to Eduardo when he comes by to check on me a while later.

A melancholic Muse song plays over the speakers, and outside a man lights a cigarette for a woman in a red dress. The place grows emptier by the minute.

"Ah. We back to that?" He rests his fist against the bar, feigning annoyance. Or maybe he truly is annoyed.

At this point, it doesn't matter.

Curiosity's steering the ship and there's no turning back.

"You said he's from around here?"

"Ever heard of Shane Bock Corporation?"

"Nope." I rest my elbow on the bar top and my chin on my hand, all ears.

"You're not from here, are you?"

I sip my water. "Moved here a couple of years ago. Took a job teaching kindergarten at Starwood."

"Adorable," he says, though I believe he's being sarcastic. "Two years here and you've never once seen a Shane Bock Bridge? Never driven past the Shane Bock Park? Hiked the Shane Bock trail?"

I rack my brain and can't think of a single instance when I've come across a Shane Bock anything. And what kind of man names all those things after himself? Unless it's a family name? Maybe his grandfather was a Shane, though I can't imagine that was a common name seventy-odd years ago.

"His family," Eduardo continues, "is practically Chicago royalty. You sure you've never heard of Shane Bock Corporation?"

I shake my head.

"They own that factory on the west side," he continues, pointing, "the one that makes plastic products. And they own those furniture stores that are all over the state. A national insurance agency, a major league baseball team ..."

I lift a palm. "All right. I get it. He's loaded and he diversifies. But is he always that ... extreme?"

I don't tell him about the funeral home on purpose—hoping Eduardo knows something and will share it voluntarily. I'll be damned if I tell him I followed him all the way down to the funeral home on the corner. Crazy is as crazy does, but I'm giving myself a pass for tonight.

Eduardo mulls my question, the corners of his thin mouth curling down as he lifts a single shoulder. "Honestly, he comes in here about once a week, and that's the most I've ever seen him talk to anyone. You should consider yourself lucky."

I laugh because he has to be joking ...

... only I'm met with a somber expression.

I'm seconds from responding when something catches the corner of my eye.

A silver logo.

On the umbrella's handle.

SCHOENBACH CORPORATION

Schoenbach ... *Shane Bock.*

"Anything else I can get you? Another water?" Eduardo changes the subject, his fingers rapping against the counter's edge.

Gathering a lungful of faded-perfume-and-whiskey-scented air, I shake my head, and the instant he's gone, I retrieve my phone from my bag. With electric fingers, I type the name "Schoenbach" into a search engine, combining it with words like "obituary" and "Paulley-Hallbrook Funeral Home" and "Worthington Heights, Illinois."

But I get nothing.

The man remains a mystery ... an infuriating, enigmatic

mystery man with a story begging to be unraveled so I can make sense of what happened tonight.

Two hours later, I'm lying in bed, phone in hand, searching in vain for something, a clue, a lead, anything, but all I manage to uncover is that his first name is Bennett and he runs the Schoenbach Corporation.

Everything else is a shrouded.

Even the biography on his company's website is two lines long: *Bennett Schoenbach is a lifelong resident of Worthington Heights. Succeeding his father and grandfather, Bennett assumed ownership of the Schoenbach Corporation in 2014.*

Growing up, I had a foster mom that used to tell me everyone had a story, that I shouldn't judge anyone without knowing it. As I got older, I learned that it's human nature to judge. In college, one professor theorized that it goes to our Neanderthal ancestry, when survival depended on sizing up the intentions and capabilities of those around us.

I reach for my remote and pull up the Turner Classic Movies channel, dialing the volume down until I can barely hear the comforting lilt of Rita Hayworth's voice in the background, lulling me to sleep.

Maybe I'm tired and overthinking, maybe I'm still trying to wrap my head around tonight's events, but I want to know his story.

I'm *going* to know his story.

One way or another.

I don't know how, but I will.

And I'm sure it'll explain *everything.*

CHAPTER FOUR

Bennett

"The Alcott expense report." I startle my assistant, Margaux, Friday morning. She damn near spills her coffee down her eyelet blouse, eyes wide as they lock onto me.

She wasn't expecting to see me today, which is a shame.

All these years working together and the woman doesn't know me at all. I'd have fired her early on, but her loyalty to my father during his tenure here has kept me from pulling the trigger.

My grandfather was always huge on loyalty. He believed it should be handsomely rewarded and never taken for granted. Besides, if she can handle him, she can handle me. And that counts for something.

"You said you'd send it last night," I refresh her memory, my finger rapping on the edge of her unorganized desk.

Last Christmas I gave her an extra week of paid vacation and when she was gone, I brought in a professional organizer to give her area a "makeover," thinking I was doing her (and the rest of us who have to walk past this hot mess on a daily basis) a service—only the spic-and-span tidiness lasted a mere six weeks before she had completely reverted to her old ways.

I tried.

"H ... hi, Mr. Schoenbach." She stutters when I make her nervous. My father had a soft-spot for her. Now I'm wondering if he had a hard-on for her too. She's completely incapable of doing this job. "I ... I was just finishing up ..."

I check my timepiece. It's a quarter 'til eight. Her coffee

is filled to the brim and her computer monitor is pitch black. Her orchid-colored lipstick is faded, like she's been engaging in recent idle chit-chat.

Liar.

She follows my gaze, her lips teetering as she searches for a response, but I walk away before she has the chance.

On the way to my office, I count four people whispering, six people staring, and one sad sap from accounting who dares to make conversation with me at this ungodly hour.

I'm sure they're all wondering why the hell I'm here on the heels of a family tragedy.

Unfortunately for them, it's none of their fucking business.

I shut my office door and take a seat at my desk, turning to face the cityscape outside my windows. The Chicago skyline is surprisingly in clear sight today, the sky behind it a surreal shade of vanilla-orange dreamsicle.

If I were a mawkish man, I'd be drowning in a puddle of tears over the fact that the sun rose this morning without Larissa.

But I'm practical.

And I'm well aware that life carries on with or without us.

We're nothing in the scheme of things.

And this is just another January sunrise.

Another Friday.

And I'm just another Schoenbach, ready to bury myself in meetings and paperwork until it's the appropriate hour in which a man can enjoy two fingers of Scotch, and then I'll show myself out—taking the back stairs so I don't have to make awkward, have-a-good-weekend small talk with the suits and skirts on my payroll.

I'm certain the majority of my staff despises me, never mind that I anonymously cover Yuri's daughter's private school tuition, privately donated a Toyota Camry to our most tenured maintenance man when his Pinto could no longer reliably get him to work. Never mind that I make donations in all of their names to the Hadley Heart Disease Foundation every January. Forget that I secretly paid off Margaux's mortgage the first year I took over, when her husband lost his job (and his battle with lung cancer six months later).

I'm self-aware enough to comprehend that working for me is no walk in the park, so I try to soften the blow when I can. Privately. Anonymously. Always.

I've no need for karma or accolades.

I'm seven answered emails into my morning when Margaux rings my desk phone.

"Yes?" I exhale into the receiver.

"Mr. Schoenbach? Your mother is here."

Lovely.

"Send her back." I hang up and finish composing my last response, managing to hit 'send' the instant Victoria Tuppance-Schoenbach strolls through the double doors.

I rise to greet her—not out of respect but because I'm not in the mood for the passive aggressive guff she'll give if I don't.

"Darling." She makes her way across the room, her thin red lips puckered into a faux pout, her arms outstretched. Leaning across my desk, she cups my face in her gloved hands and kisses the air beside my cheek. "Thank you so much for handling the preparations last night. I was in the area this morning. Thought I'd come here to check on you. How'd it go?"

After leaving the funeral home last night, I'd meant to

text her Saturday's details, but instead I texted Deidre-from-6A and had her come over for a nightcap—and to suck my cock.

"Fine, Mother. The memorial is Saturday morning. Eight to ten."

"Such a tragedy, isn't it?" She clucks her tongue, staring toward the scenic city abyss behind me. "Honestly, it was for the best."

"Excuse me?"

"Since the moment she came into our lives, she's caused nothing but trouble." She keeps her voice low despite the fact that this office is sound-proofed and a world away from anyone else who may or may not be nosy enough to listen in. "You know, I never liked that girl."

"You don't like anyone."

It's an incurable sickness.

Bred into the Tuppance DNA.

Passed down generation to generation like a genetic defect.

We don't tend to care much for anyone unless they're serving a direct and useful self-serving purpose.

"Fair to assume you won't be attending?" I lift a brow.

My mother gasps, a hand splayed across her heart. "Can you imagine what people would say if I didn't? My God, Bennett. You know how they talk around here. Would I rather be meeting the ladies for brunch at The Marigold that morning? Yes. Of course I would. But not going isn't an option."

A simple *yes, I'll be there* would have sufficed ...

"Your honesty is ... refreshing," I say.

"It's much too early for sarcasm, darling. Please. Enough."

"Have you spoken with Errol yet?" I change the subject.

Tugging at her pearls, she draws a resigned breath. "I have. He's aware of Larissa's untimely passing, and he plans to attend her memorial, but he won't be bringing his wife. We both know that's a good thing. Larissa and Beth never got along. Oil and water, those two."

It probably didn't help that my mother poisoned their relationship early on, pinning them against one another like some sick and twisted game solely for her own amusement.

All of their differences aside, Beth and Larissa never stood a chance where my mother was involved.

She's a destroyer, that woman.

She destroys all that is good in this world, whether she means to or not.

She destroyed our family, her marriage, my father …

It's as if she can't help but to meddle, to ensure everyone else is as miserable as she is.

"All right, well." She rises, straightening the hem of her boucle jacket. "I've got a million little things to do this morning and I'm sure you do as well, so I'll leave you be."

Thank God.

My email chimes with Margaux's expense report—fifteen hours late.

"And Bennett?" My mother stops at the door, turning back to me. "Call your brother. You and Errol haven't been on speaking terms for years, and I'd hate for things to be awkward Saturday morning."

"Will do," I lie.

Whoever said death brings families closer never met the Schoenbachs.

AVAILABLE NOW!

Wall Street Journal and #1 Amazon bestselling author Winter Renshaw is a bona fide daydream believer. She lives somewhere in the middle of the USA and can rarely be seen without her trusty Mead notebook and laptop. When she's not writing, she's living the American Dream with her husband, three kids, the laziest puggle this side of the Mississippi, and a busy pug pup that officially owes her three pairs of shoes, one lamp cord, and an office chair.

Winter also writes psychological suspense under the pseudonym of Minka Kent. Her debut novel, THE MEMORY WATCHER, was optioned by NBC Universal in January 2018 and her book, THE THINNEST AIR, was a #1 Amazon Kindle bestseller and a Washington Post best seller five weeks in a row.

Winter is represented by Jill Marsal of Marsal Lyon Literary Agency.

Join the private mailing list. <- HIGHLY RECOMMENDED!

Follow Winter on Instagram!

Like Winter on Facebook.

Join Winter's Facebook reader group/discussion
group/street team, CAMP WINTER.

www.ingramcontent.com/pod-product-compliance
Lightning Source LLC
Chambersburg PA
CBHW021339150726
47989CB00005B/2045